THE WIVES ASSOCIATION

INNER CIRCLE

EVELYN LOZADA

WITH COURTNEY PARKER

CASH MONEY CONTENT

CASH MONEY CONTENT

INNER CIRCLE

First Hardcover Edition

Book Layout: Peng Olaguera/ISPN

Cover Design: Michael Nagin

Photography: Stian Roenning

Make Up: Sheryl Lawrence / Artisans Agency

Styling: Ashley Lloret / Artisans Agency

For further information log onto www.CashMoneyContent.com

Library of Congress Control Number: 2011943462

ISBN: 978-1-936399-27-7 hc

ISBN: 978-1-936399-28-4 ebook

10 9 8 7 6 5 4 3 2 1

Printed in the United States

INNER CIRCLE

First Comes Love . . .

"*Where* the fuck are you?" Eve spoke her text message into her iPhone while she waited impatiently at the arrival curb of LAX airport for her boyfriend of six months, Los Angeles Leopards superstar wide receiver, Chase Landon. She rolled her eyes under her vintage Chanel sunglasses when she spotted what appeared to be two nosy bitches whispering to her left, trying to confirm who she really was.

"And what the fuck are you they looking at!" she whispered aloud when spotting the two women pointing and snickering in her direction. Even though Eve wasn't a celebrity, dating Chase made her just as vulnerable to the public attention that he experienced on a daily basis. Although the limelight could be exciting at times, there were moments when she dreaded the attention and just wanted to be left alone.

Within the six months they had been together, Eve had managed to come out to Los Angeles dozens of times from Miami. The cross-country trips were beginning to wear on her and had also been the topic of her and Chase's last argument. Chase almost never made it to Miami because of his hectic schedule, yet he insisted with each visit that Eve not return to her life in Miami.

"Are you crazy? I'm not giving up my condo or career for you.

I've worked too hard to get to where I am to just throw it all away. My mother sacrificed everything to send me to school. I promised her and I promised myself that I would always maintain my independence. Besides, what happens if this doesn't work? Then what? I'm stuck having to start all over again from scratch. No, I don't think so."

"What about a proposal? I love you, and I want you here with me every day in every way."

"A proposal for what?" Eve quizzed.

"Marriage," Chase replied.

"Please, you know you're not ready," Eve had said as she folded her clothes into her suitcase.

"Do you love me?" Chase questioned.

Eve turned toward him. Her heart pounded as she searched his face for any signs of doubt. "You're serious?" She almost hoped he wasn't.

From the beginning of their relationship, Eve had strong opinions and hard fast rules about a lot of things, but none harder than her position on never becoming emotionally involved with a professional athlete. In her line of work, she'd seen enough cases of athletes and their drama with women, finances, women, babies, women, and more women, to be a bit leery. With Chase being just twenty-four and her being twenty-five, in Eve's opinion, the lifestyle of a professional athlete was in no way conducive to marriage and family.

It was an opinion that was first introduced to her by her mother, Nadia Inez, even before choosing a profession that supported her mother's claims. Eve was the product of a one-night stand her mother had had with a professional athlete. After discovering that she was pregnant, Nadia received even worse news. The man she knew only as Hank was married. Nadia put up a brick wall whenever Eve asked about her father. All her mother would say was that she had had one momentary lapse of judgment that resulted in Eve's conception, but no matter how wonderful it had been, she would never date nor get involved with another professional athlete. In fact, that sentiment had become her mantra, so much so that by the time Eve was old enough to date, she avoided athletes like an STD.

Although Eve never intended to date a professional athlete, she'd been fascinated with football all her life, primarily because she always wondered if she could figure out who her father was by studying the game. With thirty-two teams and absolutely no information about her father besides a first name, identifying him was next to impossible. Eve didn't even know whether her father was black or white, and because her Puerto Rican features were so strong, she knew it could go either way.

Try as she might to avoid them, athletes of all sorts pursued her in droves. In college and throughout her early twenties, Eve turned down football players, soccer players, basketball stars, and everything in between before meeting Chase. Eve's desire was to represent athletes, not date them, which was why she started working as a paralegal with one of the largest sports and entertainment law firms in Miami.

Eve knew that her sultry Latin curves, naturally sun-kissed blond-and-brown hair, and bombshell Sophia Loren looks would make it hard for the men in her office to take her seriously, yet she didn't let that deter her from accomplishing her goals. Her looks not only got her on the best cases with the most high-profile clients but also afforded her countless nights out wining and dining. A-list clients insisted that Eve be present at all of their events, even if it meant paying for her to travel around the world. She was the tempting carrot at the end of the stick that all the top attorneys dangled in an effort to sign, seal, and deliver a deal.

Most women in the firm would've taken offense at being considered the office eye-candy, but Eve didn't care. She was on the fast track to becoming an agent, and if using her looks advanced her in that direction, so be it. She was the only paralegal at the firm with an expense account, company car, and endless bonuses for just being pretty. *Fuck 'em,* she thought, because she was getting hers. And as long as she didn't have to compromise her body or standards for those luxuries, she couldn't care less about what people thought of her.

It didn't matter if you were a girl or a guy, straight or gay, people in Miami prided themselves on their looks and their game as their means of getting in or out of any and all situations. Miami had it all: the fake-it-'til-you-make-it types, the actual real-deal Holyfields, the wannabe, gonnabe, gottabe somebodies, and finally the don't-ask-don't-tell-but-their-shit-was-real types.

Eve also knew that a lot of women from Miami had reputations of being either gold diggers or opportunists. So when her boss, powerhouse entertainment attorney and firm partner, Andrew Rothberg, introduced her to his star client, Chase Landon, she greeted him cordially but immediately shut down his romantic advances toward her. She'd worked too hard at not mixing business with pleasure and wasn't sure she wanted to change that now.

Chase was persistent, though. For one year straight, he wooed Eve with calla lilies he sent to the office with a card that repeatedly asked her out to dinner. The last month, however, was the clincher. Chase was so determined for Eve to say yes that he started sending flowers every day. Finally, Andrew insisted that she accept, because there was simply not enough desk space to support the absurd number of bouquets that were coming in.

It only took one yes to ignite a full-fledged relationship between the two. Eve was smitten with Chase halfway through their first date, which made it hard for her to make him abide by her six-month no-sex rule. Yet not only did he abide by her rules, Chase was so committed to Eve from the start that he had often joked about making her his wife, a fact that after her last visit to Los Angeles, she knew he actually meant.

Eve repeatedly ran her fingers through her hair and tugged at her ponytail. Her frustration waiting for Chase brought back the same anxious anticipation of the night he first proposed. As she scanned the line of passing cars, she shook her head recalling their conversation.

"Of course I love you, Chase. But I don't believe in living with someone I'm not married to. I wasn't raised like that. And I know you—your impulsiveness and persistence is what brought us together, but I'm not going to just quit my job and move here to be with you."

"If you're worried about the money, I'll pay you your salary."

"This has nothing to do with money, Chase. This is about our life together. Listen to you. I mean, is this even a proposal of marriage, or is it a proposal to shack up? You know how I feel about that. Anything can happen, and then I'd be the one who's stuck."

"You know I wouldn't play you like that, Eve."

"I know, but this feels rushed. Besides, I don't want you presenting me with a proposal you truly haven't thought out. L.A. is your home, not mine. And I don't want to move here only to move into your house. I'd want my own home. Something that's ours together, you know? Besides, what would my mother say? She doesn't even like the idea of us dating, let alone the thought of marriage. A proposal would kill her."

"So is that a no?" Chase smiled.

"No, it's not a no." Eve pulled him close, leaning her head on his chest. "Let's just call it a 'not right now,' okay?" She gently bit his bottom lip. "Babe, you know how I feel. I told you all about growing up not knowing my father."

"I'd never do anything to hurt you, Eve. You've gotta believe me."

"I do believe you. That's what scares me."

"Don't be scared, babe. It's okay to let yourself fall in love. Catching is what I do." He laughed. "I got you, Evie."

Eve glanced at her watch. Because Chase was notoriously late, she'd lied and told him that her plane was landing thirty minutes earlier than it really was. It wasn't as if she worried about Chase being with another woman. He knew better than to cheat on her and get caught, yet his love for attention from the media and his fans often left him distracted, which, in turn, always made him late. Eve shifted her Louis Vuitton bag again and reached for her cell phone. She saw that Amber had already called twice. She checked her voice mail.

"Hey, Evie! Just wondering if you made it in and double checking to make sure we're still on for shopping tomorrow. It's going to be great having you here for two whole weeks! Call me when you get this. Smooches!"

Eve cut her eyes when she noticed that the two nosy bitches had now turned into two sneaky bitches, pretending to take pictures of each other when it was clearly Eve that they were trying to capture in their shots.

"Oh no, you didn't," Eve said loud enough for the women to hear. She pushed her glasses down far enough so the bitches could see her eyes, then gave them a hard stare.

"Snap another picture and I'mma snap your fuckin' necks," she mumbled, causing the women to walk away.

"To delete this message press seven, to save it press nine," her voice mail recording stated, reminding Eve that she was still on the phone. Eve deleted the message with a smile. She couldn't wait to hang out with Amber and catch up on the latest gossip. She was glad that her childhood best friend was married to an athlete but hated the fact that Chase wasn't a fan of Amber's husband Sean. Chase claimed it had something to do with a beef he and Sean had over a chick during their years at USC, but Eve suspected otherwise. Although she pressed the issue a few times with the three of them, the only agreement she could reach was that whenever they were all together, they promised to be cordial.

Just as she began to dial Amber's number, she heard the commotion.

"Chase, that's Chase Landon's truck! Since signing that new eighty-million dollar contract, pictures of him have tripled. Chase!

. . . Over here!" a slew of paparazzi shouted, interrupting Eve's reverie.

She shifted her purse to her other arm just as Chase's Range Rover pulled up to the curb. Because Chase was the Los Angeles Leopards' most popular player, Eve knew flashing lights from the paparazzi were to be expected. She also knew that because of the paparazzi, she needed to be red-carpet ready when she got off the plane. Only once had Eve made the naïve mistake of arriving in sweats and tennis shoes sans makeup, costing her a month of unflattering blog reports and photos with captions like, "WHAT WAS SHE THINKING?" After that experience, she vowed that the paparazzi would never catch her slipping again.

Chase Landon emerged from the driver's side with his eyes set on Eve. She sized him up as he slowly approached her. He looked good dressed in dark jeans and a cream Ralph Lauren sweater. Eve loved the way he wore his clothes. At six foot four, two-hundred-twenty-five pounds, he was the epitome of athletic perfection. Chase was an agent's dream client, with camera-friendly looks that could position him in both *GQ* as a model and Air Jordan as a spokesperson. For added measure, he had a perfect set of teeth, compliments of three sets of braces that showcased an award-winning smile that he now flashed for Eve and the growing crowd of onlookers.

"You know I'm sucking in all of your beauty, don't you, baby? I see you rocking those new Louis Vuitton shoes I sent you, too. You do 'em justice."

Eve tried hard to contain herself as she blushed, handing him her bags. "You're late," she snapped hoping he didn't hear her stomach growling, the true cause for her frustration.

"Never late, love. I'm always on time." He kissed her on the cheek, smiled big for the cameras, then ushered her to the passenger-side door.

"Oh my God! That's Chase Landon! I told you that was his girl-friend."

"Chase, can we have your autograph?" one of the women squealed.

"Yes, and can you make mine out to Kandi with a K instead of a C and an I instead of a Y," the other lady added.

"Oh my God, Chase, I love you . . ." the first woman screamed.

Eve slid into the passenger side, leaned her head against the soft leather seat, and closed her eyes. She knew it would be a minute. Chase Landon liked nothing better than attention. In fact, he welcomed it. If there was a backdoor entrance, he took the front; if the invitation said casual, he wore a tuxedo; and if the team needed someone to make a celebrity appearance, he was the first to volunteer. For those reasons and more, the fans and the media loved him, and he loved them right back!

Through the side-view mirror Eve watched as Chase signed T-shirts, caps, purses, and anything else that was handed to him. Cameras and cell phones flashed intermittently as the crowd began to grow. Suddenly there was a bright flicker of red and blue lights followed by three quick horn blasts. It was the traffic security on a motorcycle accompanied by two other officers on bicycles.

A voice came over the loudspeaker. "Clear the area!"

The crowd slowly began to disperse as Chase made his way over to the officer. Eve heard a quick exchange, then light banter, followed by laughter.

"If you follow me, Mr. Landon, I'll get you out of here," the officer advised, pulling alongside the truck.

"Thank you, kind sir, I'd appreciate that."

Eve watched as Chase placed her bags into the trunk of his truck, then slammed it shut.

"Y'all know that's about to be my wife, right? The future Mrs. Eve Vashay Inez-Landon. How's that for a story?" he smiled, then he hopped into the truck and placed his hand gently on Eve's thigh.

Eve removed her shades, cocked her head sideways, and smiled as she looked at Chase. "Really? You just gonna put me on blast like that?"

"What?" he smiled back, feigning innocence.

"Don't *what* me. You know what."

"Oh, you mean that? Aw, come on, baby. I was trying to leave, but you know I can't disappoint my fans."

"Oh, please! You know you love that shit. For you, attention is like flour, and you roll around in it like a piece of chicken!"

"So what are you trying to say?"

"What I've always said. *You*, Chase Everett Landon, are a media whore."

"Okay, there you go with that again. Well, if I'm a media whore, you know what that makes you!"

"What?" She couldn't imagine where he was going with this.

"Well, let's see. You're supportive, you buy me nice things, and you protect me from hurt, harm, and danger. I'd say that makes you a pimp!"

"A pimp?" Eve laughed as she gave him a playful smack on the back of the head.

"See," he chuckled, "you just pimp-slapped me!"

The officer pulled into oncoming traffic, sounding his siren and flashing his lights as Chase prepared to follow. Just as Chase drove off, he pumped his brakes, making sure the paparazzi and fans got a glimpse of his brake lights glowing around a license plate that read "CHASE ME," a signature phrase he lived on and off the field. Eve knew exactly what he was doing as she checked her side-view mirror, watching the reactions from the crowd. As usual, the fans loved it, and as the future Mrs. Eve Vashay Inez-Landon, she knew in her heart that she'd grow to love it too.

"I've missed you." Chase reached for Eve's hand.

Eve leaned over and kissed his cheek. "I've missed you, too. You get my message?"

"What? You know it. I played it over and over again. Matter of fact, I was listening to it in the car on the way over." Chase played Eve's message again.

"HEY, BABE, I WANTED TO SAY I'M SORRY. I'VE BEEN THINKING A LOT ABOUT WHAT YOU SAID, AND YOU WERE RIGHT. I DO HAVE TO TRUST IN LOVE MORE. I JUST WANT YOU TO KNOW THAT I'M REALLY READY TO TRY. I CAN'T WAIT TO SEE YOU TOMORROW. LOVE YOU."

"Okay, okay." Eve buried her face in her hands.

"No, I'ma milk this for everything it's worth. Not only did you apologize, but if I'm not mistaken, didn't you also say you were wrong and I was right?" Chase laughed. "Here, let's listen to that part again . . ."

"You better not." Eve slapped his hand. "I hate when we fight."

"Me too. But I've got to be honest: I've really been looking forward to making up."

Eve shook her head as Chase softly squeezed her hand.

The sun began to set on the 405 Freeway when Eve noticed that Chase was not taking the normal route to his house in Cheviot Hills.

"Babe, where are we going?"

"It's a surprise."

"I'm really not up for hanging out tonight, Chase. I was hoping we could just relax. It was such a long flight . . ."

"Shhhh . . ."

Eve tried to relax but couldn't stop fidgeting in her seat. The last thing she felt like doing was entertaining, especially Chase's teammates' phony wives, girlfriends, and baby mamas. But it didn't take long before they pulled into what appeared to be a new development still undergoing construction. When the truck stopped, Eve looked at a dusty, vacant lot and scrunched her face as she tried to imagine why Chase was bringing her here.

Chase got out of the car, then walked over to Eve's side and helped her out. It was a breezy Southern California evening, and she felt a bit chilly. A gust of sea air swirled over the Playa Vista hills. The view of sailboats floating across the orange-dusk-colored marina was breathtaking—literally.

"Chase, what are we doing here, baby? I'm cold."

"I know, just give me a minute." He took off his jacket and placed it around Eve's shoulders. "I need to say something to you."

Eve noticed the concern in Chase's eyes. "Baby, are you all right?"

"I wanted to apologize. I need to tell you how sorry I am for . . ."

Eve's head throbbed with worry about what he was going to say. His words became muffled as her thoughts began to ring in her mind. *He cheated! Son of a bitch,* she thought to herself. She knew better than to date an athlete. And even worse was she'd finally let her guard down, opened herself up, and allowed herself to fall in love with him. She began to tear up. "Stop . . . Oh my God," she cried. "I can't breathe."

"Eve, baby, what's wrong?" He grabbed her hands.

"Don't touch me!" She pushed him away, wiping the tears from her eyes. "Please tell me you didn't bring me here to tell me you've done something stupid."

"Something stupid? . . . Oh, naw, babe." He laughed. "Nothing like that."

"Then what is it?" she asked. "You sound so serious."

"This *is* serious, Eve." He took her hands again. "I wanted to apologize for how I handled things the last time you were here. I wanted you to know that I heard you. And I promised myself that the next time I brought you out to L.A. and picked you up from the airport that I was going to bring you home. Not to my house, but to *our* home . . . so here we are."

Eve shook her head. "Chase, what are you talking about?" She looked around at the dusty construction site again.

"I bought this lot. Six-and-a-half acres of land. I didn't want to do anything major without you."

"What?" Eve asked, her tears returning.

"I was driving around, and this place just hit me. It felt like home. Our home."

Speechless, Eve looked into his eyes. She knew he wanted this and that he believed in her, and, more important, that he believed in the possibility of them. It was finally clear to her that his vision was full of the thought of their lives together.

"I love it, Chase!" Tearfully, she hugged him.

"We're home, Eve."

The wind whipped around them, interrupting their moment. Chase reached into his pocket, pulling out an eight carat, classic-cut solitaire diamond ring. "I hope you didn't think the land was it. You know how I do."

"Oh my God, Chase . . ." Eve was captivated by the flawless pale pink diamond. Goose bumps covered her arms as she took in everything that was transpiring. "I'm no rabbit, but I'm definitely feeling the carats in this ring," she responded playfully in an attempt to mask her slight fear.

"I love you, Eve. Forgive me for not asking you to marry me properly the last time. Allow me now to get it right now." Chase got down on one knee. "Eve Vashay Inez, would you do me the honor of becoming my wife?"

Eve's eyes sparkled as brightly as the ring on her finger. Her body shivered as a wave of emotions rippled through her mind. *Although I've met his mother and sisters, how will they feel about accepting me into their family, and did they even know about the proposal? What will this all mean to my career now that I'm going to be his wife? Does this mean he wants to have children right away? The mere thought of motherhood scared her to no end. Speaking of mothers, what will my own mother say? Will she even show up at the wedding?* Eve's heart and head pounded as she tried to slow down the thoughts that raced through her mind. She searched Chase's eyes for any signs of doubt but found none. Immediately, she knew that all that really mattered was what she felt for him in the now as opposed to any fears she'd have in future. Although hesitation remained in her mind, there was no hesitation in her heart.

"Yes, Chase. I'll marry you."

The warmth of his lips against hers made Eve forget about the chilling breeze. Just the thought of her life and name changing to complement his excited her. At that moment, every doubt she'd previously had about their love and future together disappeared with her answer of "yes."

"*That's* what I needed to hear." Still with her hand in his, Chase led her back to his truck. Before closing the door, he kissed her forehead and whispered, "You're not still scared, are you?"

"No," she responded confidently. As she wiped away her tears, she whispered to him, "Thank you."

"For what?" he replied.

"You promised to catch me, remember?"

"I remember," he said with a smile.

"Thank you for keeping your promise."

Eve parted her mouth, allowing Chase's tongue to tango with her own. Their lips applauded the dance, sealing the deal and their decision to marry. Eve's eyes were fixed on Chase as he closed the passenger door and got into the truck. She knew she was making the right decision. As they drove down the hill, Eve gazed at the lights of the city. The hesitation she felt about moving to Los Angeles had suddenly subsided. She trusted Chase to be everything he'd promised her he'd be. Her only wonder was if she could be to him what he'd promised to be to her.

1

After "I Do"—Five Years Later!

Eve moaned softly as Chase gently massaged her shoulders. Today was their fifth-year anniversary, yet it had been weeks since the last time they'd made love and Chase was eager to get something started. She'd promised him that if he helped her out by giving her a massage, she'd return the favor by giving it to him exactly the way he wanted it.

Her traveling back and forth from one coast to the other twice a week for work had her entire body in knots. Chase made it clear when they got married that if she wanted to keep her job, she'd have to promise never to miss one of his games and to be home at least four nights a week. Keeping that promise had proven to be even more challenging than Eve thought. Maintaining a balance, while juggling her career and home life with only five hours of sleep a day had taken a serious toll on her, especially with Chase's huge sexual appetite. Part of the reason he required her to be home four nights a week was to satisfy him. Because of their agreement, she could never let on that half the time she was actually either too sore from traveling or too tired from work to enjoy having sex with him.

Although her shoulders were starting to feel a little better, she knew she couldn't pull off a sex session with Chase; she was still in far too much pain. The strain from traveling and carrying her bags back and forth left her shoulders and back in great distress, yet she knew better than to make excuses. Eve rolled over on her back, pulling Chase's shirtless body on top of hers. They exchanged kisses for a moment until she interrupted their foreplay.

"I have something for you."

"I know," he said, trying to pull down her panties.

"Not that," she protested. "I meant a gift."

"It's been two weeks. Trust me, you're gift enough."

Eve moved his hand away from her crotch. "I'ma hook you up, I promise." She reached over to the cream-colored marble nightstand and pulled a small box from the drawer.

Chase rolled his eyes as he accepted the gift. Eve knew she had to do something to change his mood because his expression had gone from pleased to pissed in less than sixty seconds. She straddled him, fighting the spasms that flitted up and down her spine. Her fingers caressed his chest as she seductively tried to lighten the mood.

"Do me a favor."

"What?" he said with a pout.

Eve felt the temperature of his body warm. Slowly she allowed her hips and center to move like a wave against him.

"Say thank you," she teased.

"What am I thanking you for?" His breathing became heavy.

"Open your gift."

Eve watched as Chase slowly unwrapped his present. She'd made sure the gift was wrapped with just enough complication that ripping it open wasn't an option. As Chase tussled with the ribbon, Eve escaped from her panties and placed the fullness of his love inside her. She smiled as she watched him struggle to concentrate.

"Keep going," she taunted as she gently moved her body back and forth, enjoying the thickness of his love inside her.

Eve laughed as Chase ignored her instructions and ripped the package open, revealing the custom-made diamond encrusted watch she'd bought him. "You like it?" she moaned as she felt her body yielding to the pleasure of their lovemaking.

He tossed the watch to the side and grabbed her hips, forcing a more vigorous movement. "*This* is what I like," he said, smiling as he moved his hands from her hips to her breasts. "This is what I need."

Eve kept up with the rhythm of movements Chase directed. Her body became his playground, and like a child, he left no inch untouched. Her moans were both of pleasure and pain as Chase aggressively switched up their positions.

The very thing she loved about being married to an athlete in terms of heightened stamina was the one thing she was beginning to dread. Chase worked out for a living, keeping him in greater shape than the average person who worked a regular job. Yet despite how tired she was on any given occasion, keeping Chase happy sexually was a duty she couldn't dare take for granted.

Eve had already had her fair share of incidents involving groupies who were always willing, ready, and able to do anything she wasn't. If Chase liked it orally, Eve took a class. When Chase had a fetish for strippers, Eve had a pole built in the bedroom and took a class. When Chase wanted to experiment with role-playing, Eve bought out a costume store and created her own little trick-or-treat closet to ensure his happiness. She even had a plastic surgeon on speed dial just in case Chase wanted her full Cs to become double Ds.

"Daaaaaaamn!" Chase yelled after he reached his climax. "Baby, you're the best."

Eve remained silent and nodded her head. Not only was Chase well endowed, the tightening of her back left her far too sore to speak.

"You all right?" he questioned as he pulled her close.

Eve sat up and used her hands as rollers down her back. Her sigh was the only response that reminded him of her pain.

"Awww, babe, I'm sorry. I completely forgot about your back. Your shit is so bomb that when you give it to me like you do, I guess I just explode. I've been missing it, you know."

"I know, baby. I'll be all right. I wanted to give you what you wanted. It's our anniversary."

"I've got something for you too, you know?" He smiled, shifting the sheets back in place.

"Really?"

"It's a surprise, but trust me, you're gonna like it."

"Hopefully more than you liked the watch I just gave you," she complained. "Baby, you didn't even look at it."

Eve watched as Chase retrieved the watch from the nightstand.

"Aw, it's cool. I like it," he said, placing it back down, then stuffing his hands between her legs. "I just like this more."

"You're impossible," she laughed.

"So what's next, breakfast?"

"You expect me to cook?" she asked sarcastically.

"Well, after giving you all this good loving, a brotha sho' is hungry."

Eve rolled out of their custom-made California king-sized bed, leaving Chase to rest and reminisce about both the gifts she'd just given him. She knew he had an afternoon practice, which left her just enough time to prepare his favorite breakfast: an egg-white and spinach omelet, blueberry medley protein shake, plus a Chai soy latte to go. Although Chase insisted on hiring a chef for them during the season, Eve took her role as his wife very seriously. She was adamant about being very hands-on in her own house, especially on special occasions.

Eve also had a strict no-attractive-female-staff-allowed policy that she wasn't about to break. And for the female staff that was permitted to work in the house and on the grounds, Eve made sure that the prerequisite for each staffer would have to consist of a marriage with at least twenty years and two children attached. She knew the chances of any mature woman throwing away her marriage and forsaking her children's feelings for a fling with her husband were virtually zero. Besides, Eve knew that Chase wouldn't be at all interested in screwing someone that resembled or even slightly reminded him of his mother.

She also made sure she was an excellent employer, paying attention to everything—birthdays, holidays, anniversaries, religious interests, and so on—and making certain that no occasion went unnoticed. She not only gave expensive gifts but made sure that each gift was both thoughtful and extremely personal to ensure her staff's loyalty.

On top of that, Eve also made sure that every paycheck to her staff bore her signature and not Chase's. She even went as far as to amend their prenup to include a clause that stated in the event of a divorce, she could decide who, if anyone, could continue to be employed at the Landon estate. There was even a provision added allowing her first pick of any staff member to come and work for her at full salary for up to five years, to be paid for by Chase, in the event that she wasn't permitted to keep the house.

Eve had heard the tales of players getting involved with their staff long before she'd met or married Chase. The firm she worked with was a full-service firm, catering to everything and everyone in sports entertainment. From divorce to domestic violence, contract negotiations to criminal court appearances, Eve was prepared for anything. She was smart, always anticipating the worst, even while being prepared to demand the best.

When word got around about how strict Eve's hiring process was, many of the other wives thought she was being a bit ridiculous. But she didn't care; she knew she was protecting herself from any "incident" that might occur, just like what had happened to her best friend Amber at her house, involving their family's personal chef.

Although Eve warned Amber of the risks of hiring female help, Amber insisted on hiring a beautiful, young chef by the name of Sa'Myra whom Amber met after she was hired to cater their mutual friend Paula's birthday party a few months back. Sa'Myra's dishes were exquisite, but while the taste of Sa'Myra's rosemary jerked chicken still made Eve's mouth water, she knew that anyone who looked and cooked with such perfection was not to be trusted.

"*Are you fucking kidding me, Amber?*"

"*Come on, Eve. I mean really. Sa'Myra is all about her work. She's been here three weeks already and not once has she even looked in Sean's direction. Olivia adores her, Sean and I are eating healthy and losing weight, and we have more time to spend with each other. Our sex life has never been better, and frankly, her rosemary jerk chicken dinners have us all looking forward to Fridays. We haven't been this happy as a family in a long time.*" *Amber selected a pair of sandals from her closet and slipped them on while Eve touched up her makeup.*

"*I hear you, girl, but I still wouldn't trust any bitch that looks better than me parading around my husband,*" *Eve recalled saying while she dusted the shine from her face with her makeup brush while sitting in Amber's bathroom.*

"*Wait! Are you saying Sa'Myra looks better than me?*"

"*Umm, yeah! Have you looked at her? Don't get me wrong. You're cute, and when you actually take the time to do the work, you give the average woman a run for her money, but let's keep it one hundred: You don't always do that. Take the outfit you picked out today,*" *Eve said, raising an eyebrow.* "*With a broad like Sa'Myra in the house, jeans, a tee, and your hair in a ponytail won't cut it.*"

"*Well, not everyone feels the need to look like they just ripped up the runway, Eve. Some of us can't afford to spend our entire day shopping, getting pampered at the spa, or grooming all the damn time. We have houses to run."*

"Bitch, please. I work! And I say this with love: You're the queen of all those things. Don't front! You've got a nanny, trainer, housekeeper, house manager, driver, assistant, ass kisser and wiper. Need I go on?"

The ladies laughed as Amber threw a shirt at Eve.

"I'm just saying, Sa'Myra is not just some non-muthafuckin' factor kinda chick. She's freaking Halle Berry pretty, so be careful. A woman like that usually has a plan. And I'd make for damn sure that the only thing she's jerking in this house is the chicken."

Eve closed the door to her refrigerator. Thinking about that conversation brought back major concerns. She wished she'd been wrong about Sa'Myra, yet time soon gave confirmation to her suspicions. Less than three months after she'd been hired to cater their daughter Olivia's seventh birthday party, Sa'Myra turned her attention to Amber's husband. As soon as Sean's basketball off-season ended and preseason resumed, Sa'Myra made her move.

The low blow came when after months of serving Amber's family with food, she quit her job as their personal chef and served Sean with paternity papers requesting prenatal care and payment for their unborn child.

"Babe!" Chase shouted from the garage interrupting Eve's train of thought.

"I'm in the kitchen," she bellowed back. "I'm making you breakfast."

Within minutes Eve had prepared the omelets and Chase's favorite protein shake, and she was cutting fresh fruit by the time he'd reached the kitchen.

"What were you doing? You were supposed to be resting," Eve asked.

"Nah, I was making sure your gift was ready."

Eve beamed with excitement. Chase took every opportunity he could to spoil Eve with the absolute best. Their first five years of marriage read like a fairy tale, complete with houses, cars, jewels, shopping sprees, exquisite trips: the whole nine yards. Eve had a particular fetish for shoes and cars, and although she had a museum-quality collection of each, more was definitely merrier.

The only thing missing in her fairy-tale life was a fairy godmother, or in Eve's case, a mother at all!

Eve's mom objected to everything associated with their marriage, to the extent of not even showing up for the wedding. Eve tried everything, including paying off her mom's house in Miami and purchasing a store in the posh neighborhood of Coral Gables in order for her mother to live out her dream of owning a boutique. Eve even kept her job, working part time with Andrew's most VIP Los Angeles clients, hoping her mom would recognize that she still had her independence. But even though they spoke on occasion, it wasn't the same.

"For you, my lovely wife . . ." Chase smiled slyly with his hands behind his back.

"What have you done?" Eve asked, eyeing him suspiciously.

Chase held out a small Tiffany box. "Happy anniversary, babe."

Eve tried hard to mask her disappointment. She loved Tiffany's, but she wasn't a huge fan of jewelry, and Chase knew it.

"Well, what are you waiting for?" he cross-examined her. "Open it!"

Eve sighed, remembering she hadn't given any hints about what she wanted this year. Usually she'd leave Chase clues around the house or in his practice bag suggesting things she wanted, but this time she was hoping he'd surprise her.

She took a deep breath as she opened the small blue box. To her surprise, there wasn't a ring or earrings inside; instead, there was only a signature blue pouch that didn't look like it held any kind of jewelry.

Eve opened the pouch and pulled out a key chain. On the chain was a small device with a Bentley symbol.

"It's outside," Chase smiled.

Eve darted toward the front door, flinging it open. To her surprise, Chase had purchased her dream car: a tomato-red Bentley Continental GT-Diamond edition. Eve couldn't believe her eyes.

"Chase . . . I don't know what to say."

"I do. The pink slip is in your name," he joked.

"What are you trying to say?" She smiled nudging him sarcastically.

"Don't even try it. I hear you all the time schooling your girls about making sure they get stuff in their names, just in case something happens and their relationships don't work out. I also know how we players are. But I want you to know that not only do I got you, but I trust you, and I want you to trust me. I wanted you from the very first moment I saw you. And when you agreed to marry me, I promised myself I'd never do anything to hurt you. What's mine is yours, babe."

"What about the prenup?" she teased.

"You give me five more years like the last five, you know the deal. The prenup disappears. Hell, I'll get rid of it tomorrow if you'd finally agree to get pregnant."

"Chase," she pouted, "we've talked about this. I just made junior agent last year. I don't think I'm ready to give that up just yet, nor am I ready to become a mom. You know it's not about the money. It never has been. I love you, but I also love me. And I just need to know that my dreams matter."

"I know, and trust me, babe, they do," he said, wrapping his arms around her. "And that's why I love you. It's also why you're dropping me off at practice today, in your new ride."

"Only on one condition," she teased.

"You're kidding, right?"

"No," she said, slipping open her robe. "I'll give you a ride in my new car, *if* you promise to let me ride you one more time."

Chase lifted her into his arms and kissed her passionately. "It could get a little bumpy. You sure your back can handle it?"

Eve bit his ear in anticipation. Marriage was about sacrifice, and after what he'd just done for her, she was willing to sacrifice everything to make him half as happy as he'd just made her. "Start your engine, daddy. I'm ready."

2

You Ain't About This Life!

Jackie nodded in approval of the ruby-red sateen blouse and navy blue pencil skirt with matching navy pumps, her KTEL station wardrobe stylist had just picked out. She shook her finger and her head as she motioned to her staff not to speak to her because she was on the phone. She gave a polite wink to her segment producer, acknowledging his signal to her needing to wrap up her call. As she took her seat, a team of hair, makeup, and manicurists immediately went to work on transforming Jackie's natural beauty into an on-air masterpiece.

"I heard what you said, Eve, but I don't know how convincing you think I can be when I don't exactly buy this whole Wives' Association bullshit myself. Hell, unless you can convince me otherwise, this shit looks like another one of my Saturdays spent with another group of stay-at-home, unemployed, designer-wearing, Chanel bag-carrying, weaves-always-right and bodies-always-tight, superficial-ass bunch of athletes' wives."

"Well, damn, Jackie, why don't you tell me how you *really* feel?" Eve laughed.

"You know what I'm talking about. Hell, you've been around five years now, and you and I both know damn well that forming another organization just means we've got to spend time getting to know some excited-ass rookie wife. Hell, I work, and when I'm not working, I'm trying to put in as much time as possible with my girls and their little fast, spoiled asses. I swear to God, if one of them makes me a grandmother before I'm forty . . . whew, chile!"

"Jackie, now you know, you know me better than that. Besides, I work too! And The Wives Association isn't just some social group who bakes fucking cookies as fundraisers for our husbands. This is about us protecting ourselves as wives. Jackie, you've been in this game the longest. Your support would mean a lot to me. But I'm doing this regardless."

Jackie rolled her eyes as she snatched her hand back from manicurist until she finished her call. "Now, don't go getting yourself all worked up. I didn't say I wouldn't help you. I simply said I wasn't completely convinced."

"Oh . . ." Eve paused. "Well, I'm glad you're going to help me. Thank you, Jackie."

"Yeah, yeah . . . Send me an e-mail with the details and I'll see what I can do. But, bitch, you owe me," Jackie stated matter-of-factly. "And I ain't talking about some simple-ass gift either. In terms of hierarchy with this association, I need you remember this *very* big favor you're asking me for . . . got it?"

"Got it!" Eve agreed.

"Now, I've gotta go. I'm on the air in half an hour."

"Perfect, I'll see you at the house tomorrow evening around six o'clock for our first gathering with the other women."

"Mmmmm-hmmm. Six o'clock, tomorrow! Now, get off my phone!" Jackie heard Eve laughing prior to hanging up the telephone. Although she had major reservations in the beginning about Eve, since becoming a part of the Leopards' family after marrying Chase, she and Eve had become really good friends, in a love-you-hate-you kinda way.

"Mrs. O'Conner, here are your commentary notes for today's

segments with singing sensation Rihanna. Sean says he'll be down in a moment to walk you through the segment points. Is there anything else I can do for you?" Erin, the KTEL production assistant, asked politely.

Jackie took a long pause before answering. "Nooooo!" Although she liked Erin a lot, she detested the fact that KTEL didn't hire nearly as many black assistants as they did white ones and made it her personal business to change that. She knew the importance of providing as many opportunities to young women that looked like her as possible and was always looking not only to provide those opportunities but also to create them. "Where's La Shawn?"

"She's working with Mr. Felton today, and I got assigned to you," Erin smiled.

"I see. Well, thank you. That'll be all!" Jackie replied.

Jackie O'Connor was in a league of her own. As a celebrity entertainment journalist, she had received recognition throughout the industry and had won numerous awards for her groundbreaking stories. Not to mention how she sometimes single-handedly got exclusive stories from celebrities that even Oprah, in her heyday, couldn't get. Jackie had a style that set her apart from other journalists, and that style had eventually catapulted her career to celebrity status.

Being married to the Leopards' lineman Ray O'Connor had only broadened her appeal by giving her a personal connection to the world's most prestigious professional athletes. Quite simply, Jackie's celebrity stories had an added air of interest because they were being reported by someone who not only talked the talk but had also walked the walk.

Since joining the cast at KTEL, Jackie had watched the show's viewers and ratings increase. It was no secret that that success could be directly attributed to her celebrity entertainment segment. She turned viewers into fans, making them fall head over heels in love with her. The fact that she was an Inglewood, California native was icing on the cake.

Viewers loved knowing that Jackie was living out her own rags-to-riches story, creating a name for herself like other local home-grown celebrities such as Tyra Banks, Shaunie O'Neal, and Paul Pierce, just to name a few. And Jackie was more than happy to make them all proud. As long as they were willing to watch, she'd definitely make sure they always tuned in to something spectacular.

"Mario," Jackie called out, "find out who put La Shawn on Eric Felton's team and tell them that I demand to have her back on mine. No offense to Erin, but I'd prefer my PA's like I prefer my coffee . . . black with no cream. Got it?"

Mario laughed as he whispered into his station radio to locate La Shawn.

"You know you're a mess, Mrs. Jackie. But I respect what you're doing. It's about time somebody with clout looked out for us."

"Hell, we're the only ethnicity that doesn't make it a priority to hire our own. And if I have anything to say or do about it, little brown girls will always be working with women that look and think just like me."

"Amen, Miss Thang," Karen, her manicurist, praised. "I'm so sick of trying to make my Puerto Rican ass pass for Asian just to get a job. These stereotypes ain't nothing nice, I promise you."

"You are a fool for that, girl," Jackie laughed. "I don't give a damn what you are. If you're a minority and a woman, I'm all for keeping you employed. Hard as I had to work in order for someone to give my Inglewood-bred ass a chance, I'm making for damn sure it's gonna be easy for the next sista coming along."

"We as women have to have each other's back," Karen affirmed.

Jackie twirled around in her chair and rose to her feet. She thought about her countless conversations with Eve and how passionate she'd been about starting The Wives Association for just that reason. Although distorted at times, Eve had a point in wanting to bond together to protect their families, fortunes, and overall futures as wives. Jackie smiled to herself taking in fully Karen's comment and applying it to her own life, especially as it related to Eve and The Wives Association. "Girl, you ain't never lied. And sticking together will no longer be just what I do. It's going to become part of who I am."

Jackie picked up the commentary for the day's show and made her way out the door. She liked knowing that although life was good, the best was truly yet to come.

3

Inner Circle

"*I've* been telling you bitches that it was just a matter of time before something like this happened. But did anyone listen to me? No! Call me crazy, but I know that two-faced, backstabbing bitch of a president, Paula Andrews, set this whole thing up." Eve bypassed her Cosmo and poured herself a shot of Ty Ku Soju instead. Although technically considered the minibar in the grand room of her house, covering almost 150 square feet of the room, Eve's bar was fully stocked with a plethora of top-shelf wines, champagnes, and liquors.

"Now, now, Eve, don't even go there! Paula wouldn't do that; she's one of us. She's president of the Lady Leopards, for God's sake," Jackie protested.

"So you think her introducing her girl Sa'Myra to Amber was a *coincidence*?" Eve quizzed. "Come the fuck on, don't be so naïve. I did my research."

"Here she goes, fucking 007," Jai joked.

"Call it what you like, but I knew that shit stunk the moment Paula tried to pawn that bitch off on me first. Why the hell would someone lobby that fucking hard for her girl unless there was an ulterior motive in play? She was looking to set one of us up. When she got wind of how I roll when it comes to my staff, she pulled back and set her sights on someone a lot more lenient." Eve darted a sympathetic glance in Amber's direction.

Amber rose to her feet and walked to the wall-sized window in Eve's master study. Eve could only imagine her thoughts as tears rolled down Amber's cheeks. For nearly four years Eve had been pressing the ladies to start a private association that specifically pledged an order of protection from such a thing. The ladies in the group would be privy to private information about each other's families, such as travel plans, staff information, the in- and off-season schedules of their husbands, old and new players on each of their husband's teams, as well as players' spouses, girlfriends, baby mamas, and possible jump-offs. Upon agreement to actually start, Eve's association would ensure that everyone in their inner circle was protected.

By becoming founding members, Amber, Jackie, Callie, Jai, and Eve would agree to use their talents, resources, personal and professional connections, and whatever else was needed to make sure that no one could get near their husbands for the purpose of cheating. If cheating did occur, all information gathered would be held in safekeeping as a means of leverage for the relationship. The association would also provide financial protection for any lady that felt her marriage was in jeopardy of coming to an end. With each member's commitment to contributing a tenth of their monthly net income, the association would have enough in savings to hire the best divorce attorney money could buy. It would also require that each woman helped the others in establishing businesses where each of them would sit on the board and act as principle investors for one another. Their pact would be so strong that nothing could break or stop them.

Eve walked over to Amber and placed her hand on her shoulder. "It's not too late, you know."

"Eve, you don't understand. He cheated on me and clearly slept with this woman without protection. He actually told me he *liked* her," she whispered.

"What?"

"Nothing," Amber quickly retracted.

Eve grabbed Amber by the arm and pulled her into her bathroom, closing the door behind them. "Please tell me Sean didn't catch feelings for that trick?"

Amber's tears persisted. "I don't know what to call it. All I know is that when I confronted him, the joke was on me. He said he was glad he finally got caught because he was tired of pretending that things with me were okay. He said the only reason he married me was because I got pregnant and his father told him that if he didn't, he'd look like the typical black athlete stereotype. He said that marrying me was a good look and that it would get him points with the team. Apparently, the owner gives some kind of private incentives to players who show stability with a family. Better PR."

"Did he threaten you?"

"Worse. He reminded me of our prenup."

Eve fumed with anger. "That muthafucka'!" She bit the tip of a freshly manicure nail. "What are you looking at if you leave?"

"Seven thousand five hundred a month at best, plus a condo, and I get to keep a car."

"Amber, I don't know what to say." Eve paced to and fro. "Do you have some stash?"

"I've got about sixty grand and some jewelry. Sean has me on a tight budget in terms of liquid assets. I get eight thousand a month in an allowance, and I have access to only one of his credit cards. In college, Sean was a finance major, and he's notoriously smart when it comes to his money. His dad is the deputy COO for the Chamber of Commerce in San Francisco . . . In other words, I'm screwed."

"What about your online store?" Eve was desperate for a solution. "With the other wives always shopping and supporting your site, you've got to be pulling in at least five figures a month, right?"

"I do all right, but honestly, Eve, how much support do you think I'm going get if I leave him? Sean said he'd make my life a living hell if

I didn't get on board with this. He said that I needed to just enjoy my life as his wife with all the perks that come with it . . . or else."

"Or else what?"

"I'll never know." Amber wiped the tears from her face, took Eve's duster that was lying on her vanity counter, and blotted the brush gently around her watery eyes.

"So that's it. You just become Stevie Freaking Wonder to his cheating ass? It's like you're giving him fucking permission to screw around on you."

"What would you do? If I leave him, Eve, I have nothing. I'm nothing without Sean. And what about Olivia? She loves her daddy. I can't imagine raising her as a single mother."

"Women do it all the time," Eve reminded her.

"But I don't want to be one of those women, Eve."

"So, you're just going to take his shit?"

"Unfortunately, every woman isn't like you, Eve. Some of us didn't come into our relationships with a law background or a ready-made attorney looking out for us. Some of us actually came into our relationships buying into the fucking fantasy that true love really existed."

The ladies were interrupted as Jackie walked into the bathroom.

"How long do you two intend to keep us out there? We came over here to give Amber some moral support and figure out how the hell we're going to help. Now you asked me to bring my ass over here to help you convince the other ladies to finally form this association, and I'm here. But we can't do that if you two are locked up in this bathroom," Jackie said matter-of-factly.

Eve gave Jackie a sharp glance. "This shit is worse than we thought. We're organizing the association tonight," Eve said, heading into the study.

Jackie followed closely behind while Amber hesitated. "What good is that going to do me now? The damage is done, and I'm just going to have to accept it." .

"You don't have to accept shit! Listen, he may have you by the balls right now, but give me three months after the establishment of our new association, and I'll personally see to it that the choice to stay or leave will be strictly up to you. Once we establish our bylaws and get the association in play, which shouldn't take me more than a month, prenup or not, our men will know that we are a group of women you *don't* want to mess with."

"You make all of this sound so easy, Eve. What makes you think forming an association is going to protect us from these kinds of things? I mean, forgive me for being a skeptic, but none of this sounds realistic. Men—especially men in positions of power—cheat! How is our sticking together with some 'little club' going to change that?" Jai Rodriquez, wife of baseball sensation Tony Rodriquez, protested. Although Eve and Jai had been friends for the past four years, Jai wasn't the type of woman to play into a hand of drama. From what she consistently conveyed to each of the ladies was a flawless marriage that couldn't be interrupted. If there were holes to her story, she made for damn sure she kept them covered.

"Well, I'm open to a solution," Callie said while fidgeting with her four carat pave canary yellow diamond ring. "Drew is constantly putting me through the fucking wringer with some little whore. It's ridiculous. Six months ago it was a Hooter's girl he met while negotiating his new U.S. contract. Last month it was some little Ty Ku server chick from the team's events, and now I think he's screwing some hair model he met while shooting a commercial," she whined.

"A hair model?" exclaimed Jackie. "You mean to tell me that your muthafuckin' husband got that 'Tresses for men' endorsement deal? Ray told me they went in a different direction, but a soccer player?"

"Drew has worldwide exposure. He's on some David Beckham-type level. You know Ray's ass can't compete with that!" Jai laughed.

"I'm glad to see you two think this funny, but this isn't about an endorsement," Eve reminded them.

"Callie, why didn't you say anything?" Amber sat beside her in the toast-colored leather chair. "I didn't realize you were going through something too."

"What am I supposed to say? I'm in L.A., fresh off the freaking boat. All my family is in Brazil. I have three boys, ages two, five, and seven, who barely speak English. And to make matters worse, I may be pregnant again. I was hoping that when we moved to Los Angeles, things would be different. But I just met you ladies, and already I'm starting to wonder," Callie lamented, pulling her dark brown, butt-length hair into a cinnamon roll-like bun.

"I don't know what gave you that idea in the first place! Hell, girl, it's always the same. A new team always translates to a new city with a whole lot of new pussy!" Jackie sassed. "I've endured three trades during Ray's career, and, girl, I know what you're going through. I've got two girls myself and a job on TV. You'd think as a celebrity entertainment analyst I'd be up on my game, but it never ceases to amaze me how Ray pulls the shit he does. This last stunt he pulled with our nanny showed up in my news files. It's a good thing my executive producer is cool and allowed me to bury the story before it hit the wire. Cost me a hundred grand to pay that bitch off, but I'd do anything to save face for my girls right now. They've been through enough."

Jackie took a swig of her beer. "I swear, no matter what I do, it's never enough. I can pluck him, suck him, and fuck him, but the minute some new pussy crosses his path, Ray's got his dick out ready to divide and conquer. I swear, the thing that bothers me more than the cheating is the fact that that muthafucka' is so fucking careless with his dick that he could actually bring some nasty-ass disease home to me. That's why I make his ass wear a condom."

"And he actually *wears* one?" Callie quizzed.

"Hell, yeah! If he wants to get anywhere near *my* pussy he'll do whatever the fuck I tell him to."

"This is exactly what I'm talking about," Eve jumped in. "And Jackie's right. We're crazy to think that our men may or may not be cheating. Quite frankly, I couldn't give two shits about trying to stop them from cheating anyhow. The cheating isn't my issue. My issue is when they do something wrong and get caught and *we're* stuck with these fucked-up ultimatums." Eve took a sip from her drink. "If Amber leaves Sean now, she gets nothing."

"What?" Jai quizzed.

"Yeah, that son of a bitch has her stuck with no fucking leverage. You think it's an accident that my agreement with Chase looks the way it looks? No! It took me months, while we were engaged, to find just the thing I needed to ensure myself a good deal should we break up. My mother hated the idea of my marrying an athlete, so when I did decide to go ahead with it, it wasn't without some major insurance. Now, don't get me wrong. I love my husband, and I want nothing more than to stay married to Chase and have the happily-ever-after life we all dream of having, but just in case he decides to go to the left on me, I'm covered."

"How do you get leverage once you're already married?" Callie asked. "Hell, I'm just like Amber. My prenup is ironclad to the benefit of Drew. I don't work. Raising our kids is my job, and Drew knows that. Our kids are the only thing saving me. Fortunately, there's a preset child support amount established for each child should we ever split, and that's only because Drew loves them so much he'd want them to have the best possible life."

"Well, if I'm hearing correctly, sounds like we've all got issues that could benefit from an association. Just know that if you're in, this is going to get real personal, ladies. The information I'll need to get on each of your husbands will determine your level of leverage. You'll need to really think about it before we start this process. If you're not down, I understand. Because once we start, there is no turning back. I'll give each of you a list of things I'll need from you regarding your men. Then, we'll sit down with each other to determine the next steps. We'll have to agree that the information gathered never leaves this circle. That, by far, is first and foremost the most important thing about our association. We make up the 'inner circle,' and that circle cannot and should not ever be broken."

"Am I the only one who feels like we're in high school?" Jai laughed.

"That depends on your issue," Eve declared.

"Tony and I don't have an issue. My husband doesn't cheat," Jai stated proudly. "I know the stigma when you marry a professional athlete is that all of them cheat, do drugs, gamble, or something, but that's just not the case with us. Tony is faithful to me. He's a good man; always has been, and always will be. Now, I'm not saying that to rub it in anyone's face regarding their circumstances. I'm here, and I'll help. I didn't marry into this lifestyle. I come from money, Cuban money, so you see, I was already accustomed to it. My family is very, very wealthy. Eve, anything you need, you just let me know, and I'll cover it. But, ladies, my leverage is love, and Tony is proof that good men do exist."

"Respect!" Eve replied to Jai. "Thank you for that. And you're right: There are some good men out there. It's just hard to remember that when the one you love does something incredibly stupid, then has the nerve to make you feel like shit for it."

"Well, I'm sick of feeling like shit," Amber said, her frustration evident. "I can't believe Sean did this to me. I thought we were happy. I don't want to leave him; I just want to get back what we had. We have a daughter, and quite frankly, I like being a basketball wife. I'm nothing without that title. It may sound pathetic, but that's where I'm at. Eve can tell you, we grew up poor. I worked my butt off to get a scholarship to USC. When I met Sean, I knew exactly what I was getting myself into and have sacrificed everything to be with him. I don't care what it takes, I'm in. Just let me know what you need."

"Me too," Jai agreed.

"I'm in too, but I swear, Ray's ass better not ever make me need whatever this so-called leverage is," Jackie said, shaking her head.

"That muthafucka' knows it's damn sure cheaper to keep my ass. Besides, I take my vows seriously. I'm a for real, "til death do us part' kinda bitch, you feel me? The way I see it, the only way he leaves me is in a body bag."

Eve looked at each lady in the room, confirming their participation in the association with direct eye contact. She knew that she couldn't promise perfection in any of their marriages, no matter what information she gathered against their men. She could, however, promise protection by means of a bond of friendship that would unite them on a higher level. As she proposed a toast, she vowed that from that day forward she would forever have each lady's back, and, as an added bonus, she'd have their fronts and their sides too. The only true question that raced through her head was whether they'd always have hers.

4

Did You Know?

After working two straight twelve-hour days, Eve made her way into the kitchen feeling a little overwhelmed by the previous night's events. It had been three days since the ladies agreed to start The Wives Association, and the confessions of infidelity still weighed heavy on her mind. Although she and Chase hadn't had any real issues regarding infidelity, when situations like the one with Amber arose, it always made her second-guess his loyalty.

Chase was sound asleep when she got home, and her suspicions ran wild. Chase was brilliant in how he handled Eve, but Eve was hip to his methods. Although he willingly gave her the codes to both of his cell phones, what he failed to realize was that she not only knew about the secret cell phone he kept locked in the glove compartment of his Toyota Prius, a car he knew she'd never drive, but that she had the code to that phone as well as all the passwords to his Twitter, Facebook, and even his BBM accounts. Even though she hadn't monitored those accounts in a while, at the moment, she felt it was certainly about time she did. She knew Chase and Sean weren't all that close, but once upon a time they were, and for some reason, Eve suspected that Chase knew about Sean's affair.

She popped a cinnamon raisin bagel into the toaster and loaded a caramel macchiato into the coffeemaker. Grabbing a yogurt from the fridge, she made her way into the adjacent breakfast nook, iPad in hand. This was one of her favorite spots, and she took a seat directly in front of the French doors, one of four exits to the rear of the house.

Eve relaxed, pulling her feet into the chair Indian-style and enjoying the moment as she slowly ate. She dialed Amber's number, but it went straight to voice mail. *Odd*, she thought, especially since Amber was a phone stalker making sure she answered all calls at any and all times. When she had finished her yogurt and popped the last of the bagel into her mouth, Eve sat for nearly half an hour sipping her coffee and enjoying the view, still caught up in what Amber must be feeling. She let out a heavy sigh, recalling the countless conversations she'd had with her mother about these exact kinds of situations.

"Do you realize what you're getting yourself into? You are not exempt from the hurt this guy will bring."

"Not all athletes cheat, Mama! Not every athlete is my father, and not every woman is you."

"So you're better than me? ¿Planteo que les dará a ustedes todo y piensas que eres mejor que yo? No!"

"Mama, I don't think I'm better than you. Just different! I love Chase. And he loves me. He's not my father. I just want you to respect that." Eve watched as her mother unlocked the doors to her newly located South Beach store Pashions.

Instead of joy, Nadia's face displayed intense protection and disapproval. Even though Eve had done everything else her mother had asked her to do in terms of being self-sufficient and financially independent, Nadia still couldn't get over the fact that she'd actually gone through with marrying Chase. It didn't matter that for the past two years Eve had actually been happy and able to fulfill her mother's ultimate dream of owning and operating her own store.

"All I'm asking is that you give him a chance, please?"

"¡Nunca! Sé que va a hacer daño. La madre sabe. Sé,"
Nadia snapped. *"He will hurt you. It's not a matter of if; it's a
matter of when. But you're my daughter, and I love you. I'll be
here for you, but I do not agree with your choice, and that's that.
The only respect I'll give you is the respect of staying silent."*

Eve stirred the remains of her coffee, thinking Nadia had truly
kept her promise. Two years later, and with five successful years of
marriage, Nadia still hadn't offered Eve one piece of advice, criticism,
or anything else, for that matter. It was hard for Eve because it was at
times like this that she desperately wanted to talk to her mother.

"Whatcha thinking about?" Chase's question startled her.

"Amber, my mother . . . I guess everything." Eve rose to accept his
kiss as Chase leaned forward.

"I hope you're not getting any crazy ideas."

"What do you mean?" Eve placed her saucer and mug in the
dishwasher.

"I know how you women think: one man cheats, all of us cheat."
Chase reached over her shoulder grabbing the bag of bagels from the
counter. "I'm not Sean and have no desire to fuck around on you."

"I never said you did."

"But are you thinking it?"

"No!" Eve lied. She took the bagel from his hand and placed it in
the toaster. "You want coffee?"

"Nah, I'm good. I'll make my shake," he said, heading to the
blender.

"I'll make it for you," she said, immediately peeling a banana and
tossing spinach into the blender. "I wonder though . . ."

"Here we go."

"Babe, I'm wondering . . . did you know?" Eve tossed the ice and
vanilla Silk into the blender.

"Did I know what? Did I know that Sean was banging his chef?

No! Did I know he was an asshole? Hell, yeah. But what's that got to do with me?"

"So you knew he was cheating?" Eve poured the protein shake into Chase's favorite shake bottle and placed it and the creamed bagel in front of him.

"I just said I didn't know he was banging ole' girl. I know it's in a man to cheat, but it's also in a real man to be faithful. Don't bring me into this shit, Ev, I mean it."

Eve relented. She could tell Chase was getting more and more frustrated by the minute, and going in on him would only create strife in their marriage. She stroked the top of his head gently with her hand, then kissed his forehead. "I'm sorry, babe, I didn't mean to sound accusatory. You've never given me a reason to doubt you. I guess I'm just tripping. Amber is my best friend, and Sean's really putting her in a bad place, you know? I just wished there was something I could do to help. She's got Olivia to think about, and if she leaves him right now, they get nothing. How is she gonna take care of that baby?"

"First of all, Olivia is seven, and Sean may be a lot of things, but a deadbeat dad isn't one of them."

"Wow, that's a lot coming from you." Eve kissed him again only this time on the lips. "You think it'll be okay if I invited Amber and Olivia to stay here for a couple of days, just until she's able to sort some stuff out?" Doubts about having a vulnerable woman live under the same roof with her and her husband were immediately dismissed when Eve remembered that the vulnerable woman was her best friend.

"I think we should stay out of it, babe, seriously." Chase placed his hand on her thigh. "Give them an opportunity to work it out. Besides, isn't Sean's big birthday party next week? Knowing your friend, she's not going to let Sean's affair ruin the event she's been planning for months."

"For someone who doesn't care much for Amber, you've sure paid attention to her party planning. Does this mean you're going with me?" Her playful suspicion turned into sheer excitement.

"As if I had a choice ..." Chase patted Eve's ass before rising from the table. "I'm going to practice. You headed into the office today?" He placed his saucer into the sink and grabbed the duffle bag that was lying in the corner of the kitchen.

"No, I'm supposed to have lunch with Amber and Callie. Geeeez, I don't know what it is about that woman, but for some reason, I can't stand her." Eve went right behind Chase moving the dish he'd placed in the sink into the dishwasher.

"She seems all right to me, and besides, all those free box seats to Drew's soccer games are like Christmas, baby. You know soccer is my second love. Don't ruin that. I mean, finally you have a friendship that's actually beneficial to me." He grabbed his keys and headed for the door.

"You're too much!" Eve followed closely behind him. "Have a good practice."

"Love you." Chase kissed her on the cheek.

"Love you too," Eve said, closing the door as Chase made it to his car. She thought about his words regarding Callie and realized that perhaps she hadn't really given the woman a fair chance. Up until last night, she'd always pegged Callie as the "Little Miss Perfect" type. Perfect house, perfect husband, perfect kids ... she couldn't stand it. As sad as it was, she was almost relieved to discover that Callie was having issues in her marriage. Even though she wasn't ready to be a mom, Eve had a rule when it came to the female friends in her inner circle: By no means could their situation look or be better than her own. As queen bee of The Wives Association, she absolutely *had* to be the Alpha, with all the other bitches serving as Betas to the organization she'd created.

Eve had lounged too long, and it was almost eleven o'clock. If she was going to make it to lunch with Callie and Amber at the marina by noon, she would have to leave soon. She rinsed the remaining dishes in the sink and placed them in the dishwasher for Dana.

Back upstairs, Eve turned on the shower while she selected something to wear. Her walk-in closet was enormous, nearly the size of a small bedroom. At first glance, it appeared to be an empty room with oak walls. A closer look, however, revealed twelve recessed panels that, when pressed, opened to expose her extensive wardrobe, shoe, jewelry, purses, and accessory collections. It was an awe-inspiring testimony to her shopping skills.

Eve showered and took extra time to smooth her hair into a perfect ponytail. She applied her E by Evelyn Lozada makeup and finished with a generous coat of burnt-orange lip gloss. It was a perfect match to the oversized, off-the-shoulder slouch top she was wearing over her stretch jeggings. Gold butterfly earrings hung to her shoulders and on her right wrist she stacked eight coordinating Honesty bracelets. The only jewelry on her left hand was the huge platinum wedding ring Chase had given her when he proposed. A matching Louboutin bag and six-inch pumps rounded out the outfit. She looked in the mirror and liked what she saw.

Although it was a casual lunch, Eve knew the restaurant would be crawling with name brands, designer bags, red-bottomed shoes, and lots of bling. Fine with her: she loved to dress to impress.

She tried calling Amber, but once again it went straight to voice mail. Since Amber was the one to initiate the lunch, Eve was even more puzzled when she still wasn't picking up. Eve looked at her phone before placing it into her purse. Why wasn't she answering?

Eve slid into her Bentley and started the engine. She loved the way it purred. She scrolled through the music selection and decided on Drake's new CD with special attention to his song "Headlines." She had decided to cruise, but once on the 405 Freeway, she couldn't help herself. She turned up the music, applied pressure to the gas pedal, and headed south toward the 90-East. She loved her car, her husband, and her life, which were all reflections of prayers that God had truly answered!

It was a relatively light traffic day for a Thursday afternoon in Los Angeles, and Eve enjoyed a carefree drive to Marina Del Rey, arriving at the Cheesecake Factory in record time. She looked around the parking lot for Amber's car but didn't see it. She tried her on her cell again.

"Amber, I'm here at the Cheesecake Factory. Where are you? I've been blowing up your phone all day, and I'm getting worried . . . Call me."

Eve pulled her car into a nearby space opting not to valet. Any other time she'd welcome the attention of the paparazzi that was posted right outside the front door, yet with everything going on with Amber, she thought it best to keep as low of a profile as she could. She had Jackie keeping her eyes and ears open for any breaking news, with Jackie promising to try to calm the waters if the story of Sean's secret love child got out. She was also making sure she'd be the one to get and give the exclusive in order to maintain The Wives Association's positive perspective. When it was all said and done, Eve already had a plan, and if things went her way, Amber would certainly come out on top.

5

Girl, You Okay?

As Eve approached the front doors she spotted Amber seated on the outside patio. She made her way to the table, wondering why Amber wasn't answering her phone.

"Amber?" Eve called out to her, obviously breaking her daze.

Eve gave her friend a quick once-over, wondering why her oversized Gucci sunglasses rested on the table instead of masking her blotchy makeup-less face and bloodshot eyes. Amber's otherwise naturally tamed curls were wild and scattered loosely about. Surprisingly, Amber had managed a relatively cute ensemble pairing an oversized black tee with a pair of cute-fitted leopard-printed skinny jeans. "I've been calling you. Girl, you okay?" Eve leaned down to give Amber a hug when she noticed Amber's raggedy flip-flops. That was the bullshit she was talking about.

"Sean took away my iPhone. He shut down my credit card access too. Left me a note along with this Visa, saying a five-thousand-dollar-a-month limit is what my life would look like if I decided to leave him."

"Fuck him. He's just trying to scare you. Where's Olivia?"

"He dropped her off at school this morning on his way to his workout."

"Are you comfortable with that?"

"Sean would never do anything to Olivia. She's his whole life. Frankly, I think she's the only reason we're still married. That's why I've been so determined to have another child. His family believes in building a legacy. I told you, if I hadn't gotten pregnant in college, I don't know if Sean would've married me. His mother wasn't a fan. She felt her son could do better. When we told them I was pregnant, she had the audacity to imply that I'd gotten pregnant *on purpose.* 'Gold-digging groupie bitch' was the mild sentiment."

Eve tried to mask her concern. Secretly, she'd always wondered how Amber could allow herself to get pregnant without being married too but promised herself she'd never ask. As her best friend, it wasn't her place to judge, at least not her life choices. Her wardrobe choices were another subject though.

"You'd think after eight years of marriage your mother-in-law would be in a different place with you by now." As she sat down, Eve glanced at the table. Empty wrappers confirmed her suspicions. Amber was practically addicted to Smarties candies and was notorious for leaving the clear wrappers laying everywhere. It was obvious she was depressed, because at least twenty wrappers covered her side of the table.

"Well, she isn't. She hates me!" Amber said, popping a handful of Smarties into her mouth.

"You should just start smoking instead of this candy bullshit. It's so annoying."

"It's my thing, and besides, you know I hate cigarettes and smoke of any kind. Why do these bother you so much? I never understood that, even when we were kids. It's only candy. What's the big deal?"

"I don't know. I think I just hate the fact that it's a candy without substance. I could see if it was chocolate or some shit. And look at all those fucking wrappers. You leave them everywhere. That's the annoying part. Eat a cookie, some ice cream, or take a fucking shot like a real bitch, but Smarties . . . I'm just saying," Eve jabbed.

"A drink sounds perfect right about now, but not without you! The last thing I need to be is drunk, depressed, without a phone or money, and alone. Besides, with a five-thousand-dollar limit on my only credit card, I can't afford to fucking drink," Amber snapped back.

Eve beckoned the waiter to the table. "A bottle of Ty Ku Liqueur, please."

Amber looked at her, raising a curious eyebrow. "A whole *bottle*?"

"Hell, yeah. You're in a fucked-up position, and sorry to say, but you look like shit. From where I'm sitting, drunk is the only place you need to be right now."

Eve loved that she managed to put a small smile on Amber's face. She hated the fact that Amber was going through such a mess. Eve wanted nothing more than to write her a check and have her come and stay with her and Chase, but she knew that couldn't happen because she had to respect her own husband's wishes.

"I just want you to know, anything you need, Amber, I'm here."

"I know, and thank you. You'd think I was the one who cheated the way Sean is making me feel. It's so messed up how you dedicate your whole life to a man, and he puts you in a position that makes you feel helpless. And what's worse is that instead of trying to determine if I still want to be with him, all I can think about is whether he still wants to be with me."

"No one said being an athlete's wife was going to be easy. You know my mom's philosophy on it. Weren't you dating someone else at USC? You know, the mystery guy you were messing with when you and Sean were on that so-called 'break'?"

"I don't know what you're talking about," Amber responded shortly.

"Sure you do! The guy you claimed knocked your fuckin' socks off in bed. Remember the fine glass of chocolate you said you drank dry?" Eve laughed. "Hell, if I can recall, you said he fucked you every which way for hours on end, and since he was the only other man you'd been with besides Sean, you let him. Girl, you may need to look his ass up.

What did he do again? As long as he isn't an athlete you may be in business. Hell, right about now, maybe we should pray mystery man studied law."

The waiter returned with the bottle of Ty Ku and menus.

"I'm starving; let's eat," Amber insisted, quickly changing the subject.

"Good idea. Why don't we start with spinach and artichoke dip for the table, plus I need a Caprese salad. Should we order something for Callie? Where is she, by the way? Wasn't the whole point of this lunch to help her ass as well? The least she could do is be on fucking time."

"Give her a break! She has three kids and a husband that's cheating. I'm dealing with the same shit with only one kid, and I barely made it . . ."

Eve watched as Amber ran her hands through her long, thick, naturally curly hair. Her dark mocha skin was the feature Eve loved the most about her, a true gift she'd inherited from her Cuban and black father. Although her Latin roots weren't as strong as Eve's, Amber's appearance and personality definitely displayed a variety of cultures.

Eve glanced at her watch. "All I know is she's late."

As if on cue, Eve spotted Callie Peteers sashaying through the door. Cheating husband and all, Callie managed to make miserable look fabulous. She wore a bright orange floor-length Maxi dress with her long brown hair pulled back into a neat ponytail. Her skin looked as if she had stepped straight out of her esthetician's chair by way of the Mac counter. Her flawless olive complexion gave Eve the impression that the sun was her best friend and that everything society said about women from Brazil was true. Callie had an ass that put J. Lo's to shame, and her teeny-tiny waist damn sure didn't seem like it belonged to a mother of three.

"Finally!" Eve said, making Amber aware of Callie's arrival. "I gotta hand it to her, she makes depressed look good. You should really take some pointers from your friend. The bitch is fierce!"

Eve made eye contact with Callie, and in return, Callie gave Eve a wave of acknowledgment. Callie's exclusive Hanae Mori perfume greeted them first while her air kisses followed.

"Ladies, I'm so sorry I'm late. My meeting with Drew Jr.'s Little League soccer coach ran over and the nanny was late getting to the house. Have you ordered?"

"Just appetizers," Amber answered. "We were just getting started on our cocktails. Care for a glass?" Amber lifted the bottle of Ty Ku.

"No, none for me, thank you. It's way too early for alcohol, at least for me. For some reason, I can't drink until after 7 P.M. Besides, I have a doctor's appointment next Tuesday to determine if I'm expecting, remember?" Callie patted her perfectly flat abs.

"You sound excited . . ." Eve said, confused.

Callie placed her purple Prada hobo in the nearby chair, then took her seat next to Eve. "I am excited about the possibility of another child, especially if it's girl. I'm not excited about the circumstances with Drew and the state of my marriage right now, though." Callie's huge doe eyes sparkled as she draped her pashmina on the back of her chair. "I really do believe that children are a gift from God. If He allows me to conceive, I feel the least I can do is be grateful for the gift of life that He's given me."

"Girl, you're good. If my man was cheating on me with some Pop-Tart hair model while I was at home raising his kids, the last thing he'd get from me is another baby. Hell, he wouldn't be getting any pussy to begin with, and he damn sure wouldn't have the opportunity to leave me stuck with four damn kids and an ironclad prenup. If I was pregnant, the only appointment I'd be making would be an anonymous appointment to the clinic . . ." Eve downed her shot of Ty Ku and poured herself another.

"I could never abort my child. My children are my life, and I love them with all my heart. I wish I could say that I don't care about my husband, but I do. I love Drew. I just hate what he does sometimes."

"I hear you, girl. I was just telling Eve that I hate what's happening between me and Sean. He's the one that did the dirt, but I'm the one that feels like I made the mess."

"I don't want to overstep here, ladies, but I don't get how two beautiful, smart, and vibrant women can sit here and allow these assholes to make you second-guess yourselves. You two sound like some new, green bitches. Here you both are with kids you're raising by these men, and you're allowing them to make you feel powerless. I know you signed prenups, but damn, everything in life and love is negotiable," Eve said.

"I'm sorry, Callie, I kind of told Eve about your situation with Drew." Amber narrowed her eyes and frowned at Eve. "Unfortunately, Eve has very strong opinions about certain things, and sometimes she can be a bit abrasive in her comments."

Eve answered, unfazed, "Hey, I call 'em like I see 'em!"

"Are you ladies ready to order?" the waiter asked, placing their appetizers down on the table. They quickly ordered their entrées before diving into the appetizers. After a few very drawn out minutes, Eve broke the silence.

"Hey, I'm sorry if I hurt your feelings. Honestly, that wasn't my intention. I just don't understand how you could know about a woman who's screwing around with your man and you haven't beat that ho down yet."

"Believe me, if I felt like that would make a difference, I would," Callie said, toying with her food. "You don't know how bad I want to take these pictures and shove them down their throats. Then we'll see who's embarrassed!"

"Pictures? What pictures?" Eve's curiosity was aroused.

"Wait! You have *pictures* of him and the model? Doing *what*?" Amber asked at the same time.

"Things he should only be doing with me, and some things that even as his wife I would never do!"

"Where did you get these pictures?" Eve took a bite of her salad, poured herself another drink, and then filled Callie's glass. She didn't give a damn about Callie's 7 P.M. rule; it was clear that she needed a drink—bad. She handed the bottle to Amber.

"I hired a private investigator." Callie looked surprised, as if the answer should be obvious.

"Girlfriend, you have dirty pictures of your man and some Tresses model trick, and you're putting up with this bullshit?" Eve couldn't contain her disbelief.

"I know, and every time I try, I just can't seem to confront him. I look at those pictures, and I see *her* . . . " Callie clinched her fists. "I get so angry I don't know what to do. We have kids; I have my boys to think about. My family is everything to me."

"Where are the pictures?" Eve asked.

Eve watched as Callie retrieved a thick manila envelope from her bag. "Right there. You see her?" She pointed to the picture on top of the stack.

"You can barely see her through all that damn hair," Amber replied, pouring herself another drink.

Eve turned the photo around to another angle. "Oh, her? I think I just saw her on a late-night talk show." Eve looked thoughtful as if trying to recall. "Isn't her name Karla or something?"

"Her name is Carmen. Carmen Garza. She's in the United States because she is the new face and spokesmodel for Tresses Hair Care," Callie answered.

Eve snapped her fingers in recognition. "Okay, now I can place her. That's the one!"

"Yeah, we all know what Tresses hair care is," Amber added. "I've seen the commercials. She's the one with the hair down to her ass, right? And I hear it's real!"

"Yes, that's her." Callie's shoulders rose as she sighed. She dabbed her eyes with her napkin in a futile attempt to fight back tears and resumed eating.

"So let me get this straight. You know this chick, you've seen her face-to-face, and you've done *nothing*?" Eve still couldn't believe that someone could be so naïve and stupid.

"So what would *you* do?" Callie asked with a trace of defiance in her voice.

"Again, like I said earlier, that ho would've been beat down by now. Then after I beat her ass, I'd have a heart-to-heart with Drew. Fuck that whole fear of being deported or losing your family bullshit. His ass would know that *I* know he's cheating." Eve had to catch her breath before continuing. "Now, I don't want to tell you how to handle your business, but I'd jump that jump-off and dare her to *ever* see Drew again. Then I'd give her a copy of one of those pictures and tell her that if you even *think* she's still fucking with your man again, the next time she sees that picture it'll be on the desk of every executive at Tresses!"

Callie laughed, taking a deep breath. "I've gotta ask, what is a jump-off?"

"Jump-off, you know, ho, trick, chick on the side! And to jump a jump-off simply means, you jump her ass and beat the crap out of her! The catch is to do it subtly, though."

"Drew would kill me if he found out that I did anything like that!"

"Boo, please, you beat that ass right and Drew will never know what the hell happened, and to be honest, she wouldn't either. I guarantee you that after my visit with little Miss Thang, their fling would be over." Eve laughed to herself. She picked up another one of the photos from the table and shook her head. "While you're at it, I'd cut off the bitch's hair. That would teach her to fuck around with your man."

"Eve, you're a mess!" Amber laughed. "Hell, while you're plotting, you need to throw some of that evil advice my way. Fuck cutting off Sa'Myra hair. The bitch barely has any. Since she's a chef maybe I can poison her or something."

"No, you'd have to cut off her fingers. Or better yet, brand that bitch with a searing pan." Eve laughed even harder. "Give her your own scarlet letter. An *A* for adulterer and Amber."

"Could you imagine?" Amber slapped Eve's hand.

The two giggled in unison.

"You're kidding, right?" Callie stopped laughing. "I don't know if I could confront her like that. I'm not exactly the fighting type." She looked genuinely frightened.

"Boo-boo, she knows you're married. She's totaling disrespecting you, and if she's the fucking-your-husband type, you need to be the beat-a-bitch-down type! All I'm saying is that you need to flip the script!" Eve waved her hand, signaling for the waiter to bring them another bottle. "And Amber, all jokes aside, Sa'Myra needs her ass kicked too."

"Girl, I know. And trust me, I want to. But she's pregnant, Eve. I can't fight a pregnant woman. What if I hurt the baby?"

"I can't . . ." Eve said, not bothering to look up. "These women are fucking your men, and you have the nerve to give a damn about anything concerning them? . . . Really!"

"Hey! There's Angela Bassett!" Amber exclaimed, glad for an opportunity to change the subject. The conversation was getting way too deep.

They all watched as Angela disappeared into the restaurant.

"And look who just pulled in," Amber continued. "Callie, isn't that Jared?"

Jared Parker was a teammate of Drew's on the Stallions. Amber and Sean had just met Jared and his wife at one of Callie and Drew's dinner parties.

"Yes, that's him." Callie raised her hand ready to wave to him, but stiffened suddenly. A grave look crept over her face. "That's him, but that's *not* his wife!" She almost spat the words.

Callie was right, and Amber grimaced as she watched the valet hold the door and steady the leggy blonde as she exited Jared's Porsche. She was gorgeous, clad only in a black catsuit, rhinestone belt, and red pumps. As they made their way to the entrance of the restaurant, Jared's hand rested casually on her behind as if it was a customary gesture.

"That bastard!" Callie tossed her head and crossed her arms. "Why do these men bother to get married if all they are going to do is cheat? Hell, you'd think he'd be worried to be seen in public with her." She took a long swig from her water, then slapped the table sharply.

"I have a good mind to go over there and, as you say, give him a piece of my mind."

"No, boo-boo, you need to save the few pieces you have for your own situation. Besides, men like that always have an excuse or two up their asses justifying the bitch as something business-related," Eve said, pouring herself a drink. She sipped her drink as she looked back and forth, waiting for a response from either Callie or Amber, but neither of them spoke. Getting the waiter's attention, she gestured for the check.

"Listen, ladies, I'd love to stay for lunch, but frankly, I've lost my appetite," she sighed, plucking her napkin from her lap and tossing it onto the table. "I want to be supportive, but all this cheating and whining and feeling-sorry-for-yourself shit isn't sitting well with me. Amber, you know I love you. Anything you need, you know I've got you. If you choose to stay with Sean, I'll rock with it. If you want to leave his ass, I'll roll with that too.

"Callie, you have my advice. Take it or leave it. Either way, you'll get no judgment from me. But this shit is exactly why I need to go ahead and establish our association's bylaws so that you two will be protected no matter what you decide to do." Eve laid three one-hundred-dollar bills on the table, reached for her scarf and purse, and rose from the booth.

"Eve, you don't have to leave. Let's just finish lunch," Amber insisted.

Eve rolled her eyes and sighed. "I can't." She reached into her purse and pulled out a BlackBerry. "Here. It's my spare phone. I call it my Bat line. Keep it until you get your phone back. I'ma call you on it a little later, okay?"

"Thanks for lunch," Callie said.

"No problem. By the way, Callie, my leaving isn't personal. We all have our own way of handling things, that's all. Mine may be a bit intense; hell, even irrational, but that's just me. I'm sure in time you'll find your own way of dealing." She extended her hand and Callie accepted.

"Thank you for your honesty."

"I'm just trying to keep it one hundred."

Callie laughed with a look of confusion.

"Trying to keep it real; be honest . . . one hundred!" Eve laughed.

"I'll try to remember that one," Callie smiled.

Eve headed for the exit, looking back toward her friends as she approached the door. She realized the only difference between her and them was that she was on the opposite side of the marriage coin. Heads was happy while tails took a turbulent turn. As the wife of an athlete, she knew at any given moment her own coin could take a turn for the worse and she could find herself on the tails side. Right now, her friends needed her support, so what she couldn't offer in advice, she'd make sure she offered in actions.

Her newfound mission was to hammer out the association's bylaws, providing protection for her friends for times like these.

For Eve, life and love were always about facts and factors. The fact of the matter was that the men her friends loved had destroyed their trust.

Eve smiled as she turned in the direction of her car. She wouldn't rest until she was able to help Amber and Callie out. Perhaps it was her only-child syndrome or the fact that she had yet to have children of her own, but regardless of what it was, Eve felt the need to control someone other than herself. Her friends were the factors in her life, and since their husbands had made it a point to affect their lives, Sean and Drew had now become non-muthafuckin' factors that would ultimately be dealt with.

6

¡Mi Casa, Su Casa!

Eve chewed on her bottom lip in anxious anticipation for Andrew Rothberg to wrap up his current call. Although the two of them had missed each other repeatedly whenever she'd been in Miami, she knew that in order to make lunch with her mother in Coral Gables from Rothberg Enterprises' downtown office, she'd need to leave soon.

Glancing at her watch she struggled to contain her expression. She'd learned a long time ago that if Andrew asked you to wait, you waited with little to no complaints. For almost a decade, Andrew had personally mentored Eve, grooming her in his own likeness as an agent. Despite the rumors of the two of them having slept together, thus awarding Eve the perks and advantages she'd received throughout the years, nothing could have been further from the truth. Andrew had always remained a true gentleman where Eve was concerned, with his only goal being one that benefitted his company. He'd often informed Eve of the scarcity of female sports agents and that if she were to take advantage of everything he was willing to teach her, then she'd find herself not only a very wealthy but a successful and rare commodity in sports and entertainment. Like a sponge, Eve absorbed everything Andrew offered and taught her. She shadowed his every move for years, imitating his actions to a T. If he was the first one in and the last one to leave, so was she, prompting her to know exactly what he liked and how he liked it, a quality that made her invaluable quickly.

Andrew circled his finger in the air as an indication that he was wrapping up his call. Eve smiled politely, hoping that the beads of sweat that began to heat the back of her neck didn't make their way to her brow. As she waited she thought about how much she actually missed Miami. Los Angeles had proven to be good to Eve, yet, there was nothing like being home. Although L.A. was where she and Chase lived, even after five years, she personally hadn't been able to become firmly rooted there enough to call it home. After all, Miami had been the place of many firsts for Eve. It was where she first learned to walk, attended her first day of school, and even lost her first tooth. It was also when she first fell in love, first had sex, and had her first heartbreak.

Nadia had immigrated from Puerto Rico and settled in Miami when she was only seventeen. Prior to giving birth to Eve three years later, Nadia had made the trip home to Puerto Rico at least twice a year. Although the details surrounding what had happened to cause her to stop visiting her family had always been shaky where Eve was concerned, Nadia vowed that once Eve was born, she would never return to Puerto Rico again.

At twenty-nine, Eve had never met any of her mother's family. Although she knew about her mother's seven siblings and grandmother and grandfather, outside of pictures, a few calls, and a couple of Christmas and birthday cards, Eve had never spent time with any of them. She would often beg her mother to allow her to go to Puerto Rico during the summers, but her mother would always reject her requests, stating that everything she needed was in Miami. When Eve was a teenager, she'd saved her money with hopes to surprise her mother by arranging to have her sister Sylvia come for a visit. However, when Nadia got wind of what Eve had planned, she beat her with a dustpan from the room she was cleaning until Eve promised to

Almost as if on cue, Eve rose from the plush chocolate-colored leather chair she was sitting in and gave Andrew a good-bye hug. "Dinner when you come to L.A. next week?" she quizzed as she gathered her things and made her way to the door.

"Most definitely!" he replied, making his way around his desk and back into his oversized cherry-leather studded chair. "Have Kimberly put it on my calendar on your way out. Good seeing you, darlin'."

Eve closed the door to Andrew's office behind her, stopped at Kimberly's desk in an effort to coordinate her schedule to accommodate Andrew's visit to Los Angeles, then darted to the elevators and out the door to the town car awaiting her with hopes to make it across town in time to make lunch with her mother. With six months having passed since their last visit together, she knew being late to meet her mother was not an option.

Eve secured her seat belt and tried to relax her mind. She focused her thoughts back to Andrew's advice about cutting her mother some slack. Although Nadia had refused to come to her wedding, refused to meet Chase's family, and refused to come or even set foot in their house in L.A., Nadia was still her mother, the only blood relative she knew and had. And even though the rules of the game weren't fair, the situation was what it was, and if Eve knew her mother, how it was, was exactly how it would stay.

Eve leaned her head against the air-conditioned cool leather booth back as she waited for her mother to complete her order. She rolled her eyes at her mother's constant ability to drag out even the simplest of tasks. Every time she took her mother to lunch it was always to the Houston's across the street from Nadia's store. No matter how many changes they made to the menu, Nadia always ordered the same thing: salmon with a side of asparagus, lightly seasoned, with a large iced-green tea, yet Nadia insisted on having the waitress recite the selection of specials anyway.

Eve laughed out loud as the waitress took her mother's usual order as well as her Ahi Tuna salad request.

"Why are you laughing?" Nadia asked as she placed her napkin on her lap.

"You do this every time, Ma. You make the waitress go through all of that, only to order the same thing. Why do you even bother?" Eve joked.

"You never know when I may hear something that prompts me to change."

"The day you change is probably the day the world comes to an end." Eve took a long swig from her plum martini.

"I'll have you know, the last time I came here, I ordered the swordfish," Nadia stated proudly.

"Let me guess. Before they filled the order, you had the server cancel it and bring you the salmon, right?" Eve stated matter-of-factly.

"Stop acting like you know me," Nadia laughed out loud. "The fact remains, I ordered something new. Baby steps, *mija* . . ."

"I hear you, Ma." Eve joined in her mother's laughter. "How's the store doing?"

"Well, you should stop by and pick out some things for yourself instead of having me send you boxes of new clothes every month."

"What are you complaining about? You know me and the other wives are some of your best customers. You're racking up five to ten grand a month on me alone. Not to mention the eBay store you've got set up on all things I wear once then return to you."

"You're not the only savvy businesswoman, you know."

"I'm not knocking your hustle, Ma," Eve laughed out loud. "I want you to do well. Actually, I'm really proud of you." Eve placed her hand on top of her mother's.

"I'm doing all right. Can't complain. At least not about work anyway." Nadia took a sip of her iced-green tea.

"Well, you look great, Ma. You seeing anyone?" Eve cringed as soon as the question departed from her mouth. "I didn't mean to pry."

Nadia pursed her lips and dusted her neatly cut honey-colored bangs with her fingers. "It's okay. Yes, actually, I am seeing someone. Three months now."

There was an awkward silence between them. Eve waited for an invitation to further explore the conversation, especially since Nadia had made painfully clear during her last visit to not ask about her love life since any and all comments regarding Eve and Chase's relationship was off-limits.

"You seem happy, is all. I'm glad you found someone."

"No, I'm glad the right man found *me*," Nadia corrected.

Eve took a deep breath trying hard to fight the urge to say what was really on her mind. She tasted a small trickle of blood in her mouth as she chewed the inside of her cheek so hard that it broke the skin.

"What is that supposed to mean? So now, Chase is not a good guy?" Eve snapped.

"Who said anything about Chase?" Nadia snapped back. "You asked me about me."

"And yet you always manage to throw jabs at my marriage. What the hell kind of comment is that, Ma? No, a good man found you . . ."

Nadia chuckled. "Every time, *mija*. Every time you find offense with my words. I don't need to throw jabs at you. You've already made your choice. I couldn't stop you then, and I'm not trying to influence you now."

"It's always my fault, huh, Ma?"

"I don't know what you're talking about, Ev. I haven't said anything about you. If you're feeling a certain way, than that's on you. But don't go ruining my happy moment because you apparently have issues."

"Chase and I are fine. We just celebrated five fabulous years of marriage together," Eve boasted.

"Great," Nadia said dryly.

"Unbelievable!" Eve shouted, causing stares from a few curious onlookers.

Nadia looked around and smiled politely at the handful of guests looking their way. "What is your problem?" she managed to say between clenched teeth.

Embarrassed by her outburst, Eve lowered her head. "Why won't you come to L.A. and visit me, Ma? I've been married five years. I've been happy for five years. You were wrong." Eve wiped the tears that had taken up residence in the corners of her eyes. "Chase is a good man. Why can't you just give us a chance?"

"You don't listen—"

"I've heard every negative thing you've ever said about Chase," Eve interrupted her mother.

"Proof! You see, *this* is what I mean, Eve. You don't listen . . . You just hear. You only hear what you want to hear rather than listening to what I've really said. This isn't about Chase. This isn't even about me coming to Los Angeles. This is about you and your need to control everything and everybody. But not me. No! L.A. is your home, and Miami is mine. The difference is this—mi casa is su casa, not vice versa. Understood?"

Silence returned as the waitress placed their meals down in front of them. After confirming everything was correct with their orders, the server walked away, leaving them under the thick cloud of discomfort their conversation had just created.

"I just miss you, Ma." Eve whispered as she struggled to swallow the knot of pride that had formed in her throat.

"I miss you too, *mija*. But I'm not ready for L.A., and unfortunately for you, coming to L.A. is my choice to make." Nadia took her fork and scooped a huge portion of Eve's Ahi Tuna salad from her plate. She opened her mouth wide, stuffing the contents inside it.

Eve watched in amazement as her mother chewed the large bite of food slowly. She'd never seen Nadia be so daring with food before in her life. Eve realized this was her mother's way of lightening the mood she'd so dramatically created and for that Eve was grateful.

"Not bad," Nadia confessed.

Eve burst into laughter as she welcomed her mother to another helping of her salad. Waving her white flag of defeat, she knew there was no winning the visit to L.A. battle. She realized now that in order to win the war with her mother, she'd have to choose her battles a bit more wisely. And instead of jumping into a full-on fight, forcing her will and her way onto her mom, she'd take her mother's advice of taking "baby steps." She whispered the answer to herself, knowing that was truly the only way to win the war.

7

The Association

"*So* you're finally getting your association," Amber said as she sat across from Eve at the kitchen table, reading through the documents.

Following the ladies' agreement to establish the association, Eve had spent two weeks drafting bylaws, rules, and regulations based on everyone's input. On her recent visit to Miami for business, Andrew Rothberg had offered the services of the firm to oversee the legal preparation and filing of the documents, and Eve and Amber were working feverishly in order to forward the first draft for review. They had spent the entire morning making additions and changes.

"*Our* association," Eve corrected. "This is not just about me." She continued writing, stopping periodically to cross items out and highlight others.

"Okay, *our* association. But still I don't get it. You and Chase have the perfect marriage. Why is this so important to you?"

"Well, I can thank my mother for planting that seed of doubt. And let's be real. There are no perfect marriages, and only fools thinks there are. There are good marriages, and I'm thankful that that's what I have, but the association is what's called insurance. It's what you have for your car, your house, and your valuables, but we never think about protecting our lifestyles. Our husbands have their prenups as their insurance so that if we ever want out of the marriage, we leave under their terms. Think of the association as our postnup." Eve smiled, amused by her own wit.

"There's a lot of stuff here," Amber said, continuing to read. "But it looks like you've covered everything."

"There's a lot here because there's a lot at stake. We're protecting our livelihoods and our children's futures. Olivia will thank you for this someday." Eve sipped her latte and continued. "Take a look at page fifteen and make sure we covered everything that was discussed about creating a board to direct any business ventures."

Amber ran her finger down the page, making notes where necessary. She reached in her purse and pulled out a handful of Smarties. Ignoring Eve's dramatic eye roll, she plopped them on the table, opened one, and poured the entire contents into her mouth. "Maybe we can word this a little better," she said. "It's not clear how we determine profit sharing." She handed the page to Eve.

Eve read slowly, then made a note in the margin. "I'm kind of sketchy on how that should work. I'll have one of the guys at the firm outline that for us." She inserted the page back into its place.

"How does this sound?" Eve asked, reading from her notes. "Rule #1: you must be the wife of a professional athlete. Baby mamas, long-term girlfriends, and common-law wives are not applicable. Rule #2: you must be willing to provide any and all personal information requested by the association (such as players, schedules, financial statements, credit scores, business ventures, etc.). Rule #3: you must be willing and able to provide the agreed upon financial support to the association. If you are unable to pay your share into the association, the difference will be paid from an emergency fund that we will establish, and you will be required to reimburse the fund within a given period of time. Rule #4: you must have access to credible resources that are available and useful in support of the association's objectives."

"Exactly what does that mean?" Amber asked.

"It means you can't just come to the association with your hand out. You have to bring something to the table. The association is not going to be some sort of charitable organization catering to every whining wife that finds herself in a shitty situation. We want women who have something to offer us. They need resources that we can use like attorneys, therapists, and doctors. We'll need private investigators that we can trust. Hell, we'll even need a friend in the police department! I'm getting excited just thinking about it!"

"That's some heavy shit. Where do we find wives with those qualifications?"

"See, that's the problem," Eve said. "Everyone thinks that the wives of professional athletes are just a bunch of lucky bitches that found a way to marry a baller. The reality is that that description only represents a small percentage. If you did a background check on a lot of us, you'd find women with degrees, professional jobs, and entrepreneurs with businesses of their own. Those are the wives we want to attract, and in answer to your question, we don't find them, they find us. We make this shit so attractive that we'll be turning bitches away."

"And how are we going to make it attractive?"

"By making it successful. When we start posting success stories about the support from The Wives Association, they'll be lining up like we were giving away free weaves!"

"Damn, Evie, this could be big!" Amber said. Eve's excitement was becoming contagious.

"Damn straight! The NFL, NBA, and all those other organizations won't have shit on TWA. The Wives Association is going to put women's lib back on the map! Only this time, instead of burning bras, we'll be burning prenups and any negative press releases related to our marriages."

"I'm starting to really feel you on this, Eve. Is there a rule #5?"

"Yep," Eve said. "Rule #5 is probably the most important rule of all. You will be required to sign an agreement that forbids sharing any information regarding the activities of the association with any persons outside of the association. It'll be damn near like a team's playbook. You don't want another team to get their hands on it, because once they know your plays, they can beat you at your own game. Confidentiality, loyalty, trust, dedication, they're all words that must be synonymous with the association. We're going to be documenting some serious shit on a lot of important people. That information will be the foundation of The Wives Association, and we will use it when and *only* when one of our own is threatened. But we have to protect that information as if it were one of our children, because in the wrong hands, at the wrong time, it could be lethal."

"I know. I can just imagine how bad it would be if word got out about Sean and Sa'Myra," Amber said, unwrapping another Smartie.

"My point exactly," Eve smiled.

Amber chuckled. "So definitely no fiancées, no ex-wives, and no baby mamas, huh?"

"Hell, no. It's sad to say but even fiancées don't make the cut. Unfortunately, if they haven't earned the title, they can't participate in the process. Ex-wives have already lost or lucked out, and baby mamas are one of the main reasons why we need The Wives Association in the first place. With any luck we can protect our husbands from any trick out there hoping to get a DNA payday. I'm not trying to share Chase with anyone, and I definitely ain't trying to have none of them damn blended-ass families either. The fact that Chase has no children outside of our marriage is a fucking miracle, and one that I'm most grateful for. My only prayer is that he remains patient with me until I'm ready to give him some of his own."

"I hear you, girl, but knowing Chase, you're enough for him," Amber added.

"For now . . ." Eve mumbled.

"So once we've got all the kinks worked out, how do you become a member?" Amber asked with hopes to lighten the mood.

"In the beginning I would say that you have to be vouched for by a member of the inner circle. We'll thoroughly check each candidate out to make sure they're legit, because I'll be damned if we go through all this trouble to establish an association, only to have to protect the association from itself!"

"But that's what we're working on. This is our protection of the association, right?" Amber quizzed.

"Right! But every time we bring in a new wife, we run the risk of someday letting someone in who will seriously test the loyalty of the group. My thought is we keep it nice and tight. Exclusive! Kind of like having a black card. You're invited in, and if you break a rule or find yourself in certain circumstances, your ass is out!"

"And what do we do when that happens?" Amber asked.

"Well, I say we beat that bitch's ass, but I haven't been able to figure out how to write that into the rules."

"Once you figure it out, I want to be on the beat down committee," Amber laughed as they high-fived.

"So right now we limit it to the inner circle," Eve said, becoming serious again. "And we nail down this charter to make sure there are no loopholes, no ambiguities, and no oversights. In order for the association to work, it has to be an airtight contractual agreement. We all have to understand how it works and be willing and able to abide by every rule with no exceptions. When we sign on the dotted line we'll be pledging an allegiance."

"And if you break that allegiance, you're out," Amber declared.

"Exactly! You fuck up and break the rules and you leave with nothing."

"That's a pretty serious consequence," Amber said, playing devil's advocate.

"I know, and we're counting on everyone in the circle feeling the same way. We want every member to be afraid to screw up. It's just more insurance."

Eve and Amber continued to work on the documents for another hour before they were satisfied that they had a decent draft for the firm to review. Then they both stretched. It had been a tedious process, and they were mentally exhausted.

"I have to hand it to you, Evie, if this works, do you know how many wives of professional athletes will want a piece of this insurance policy?"

"It's what I've been trying to tell you guys all along," Eve said, biting the end of her pen. "I just hate that you had to go through what you went through in order to get this thing off the ground."

"I guess I'm taking one for the team, huh?" Amber sighed.

Choosing not to comment, Eve smile sympathetically and put down her pen. "How are things?"

"Honestly, I feel like a prisoner. Sean has been walking around as if nothing's happened. And quite frankly, I haven't known what to say. It's odd. Here I am in the middle of a crisis and planning his big thirtieth birthday party."

"I was going to ask you about that. So you're still going through with it?"

"I invited his parents, his teammates, cousins, out-of-town family, the works. No one knows what's going on between us, and to cancel the party at this late date would only raise suspicions that we've got personal problems. Until I figure out exactly what I'm going to do, going through with the party seems like the only option."

"I don't know, Am. I don't think Sean deserves to be celebrated right now. I mean, hell, you're barely tolerating his ass, and he gets a party? But it's your call, not mine. It's like I said before, I'll support you in whatever you decide to do. How can I help?"

"Everything's done except for the food. I still haven't been able to hire a new chef or even a caterer, for that matter. Sa'Myra really screwed me up. For the last two weeks, we've relied on everything takeout. Boston Market has become my home away from home. That bitch has me afraid even to ask for help."

Eve laughed. "Girl, you know you're crazy! I'll ask Sandy for a referral, and I'll conduct the background check for you. In the meantime, call Creative Caterers and ask for Sir Paul. Tell him I recommended you, and he'll hook you up. Sir Paul is a happily married gay man who wouldn't think twice about even looking in Sean's direction. He's expensive as hell but worth every cent."

"Ev, you're a lifesaver. Speaking of food, I'm starving. You mind if we order a pizza?" Amber asked, looking at the clock on the microwave. "Sean said he'd drop Olivia off here pretty soon, and we usually have pizza on Saturdays. I hope you don't mind."

"Sure," Eve said. "Why don't we just do the whole family thing that comes with wings, salad, and soda? With Chase away in Denver this weekend, we'll call tonight a girl's night. Do you and Olivia want to stay over?"

"I'll check with Sean to see if he's okay with that. When it comes to Olivia, he's very protective. And it's been weird. Ever since he was served with the paternity papers from Sa'Myra, he doesn't let Olivia out of his sight. I swear it's as if he's gotten all protective of her. I can't explain it."

"When does he take the test?" Eve asked.

"Hopefully, sometime next week. The doctor says the fetus has to be at least twelve to sixteen weeks old before paternity can be established in the womb."

"It's good to know you guys are at least able to talk about this," Eve stated while looking for the takeout menu for Stefano's Pizza at the Howard Hughes Center.

"It's like I said, he's acting as if nothing's happened."

"Does he feel any remorse though? Has he even apologized?" Eve picked up her landline and dialed the number to Stefano's.

"I wouldn't call what he gave me an apology. And what's worse is I actually think he's excited about this baby. You know, Sean's always wanted more kids. I just wished I was the one actually giving them to him."

"Are you fucking kidding me right now?" Eve hung up the phone. "Give me those papers. I need to add another clause." Eve took the stack of documents from Amber and handed her the phone instead. "Here, you order the pizza."

Amber laughed and asked, "What are you going to do?"

"Try justifying the association paying for a mandatory abortion for any trick that gets pregnant by one of our husbands, or at least establish an emergency payoff fund for these ballsy bitches."

"You really think a woman would go for that?" Amber said, pressing redial.

"From where I'm standing, anything's possible and for damn sure worth a try."

8

Plot of Protection

Carmen Garza slowly cruised the 5 Freeway in her newly gifted Maserati, making the last few miles along the wind-kissed coast to her condo in the finely manicured suburban-filled Laguna Beach area. It had been a long day of fittings and selecting the wardrobe for her upcoming Tresses campaign, and she was exhausted. Landing the job as spokesmodel for Tresses was the big break she had been waiting for, but it would not be without its challenges. After today, it had become obvious that the schedule would be grueling, leaving very little room for anything that even remotely resembled a personal life. It was a good thing she'd met Drew.

Pierre, her manager, warned her beforehand that the contract would require long days, extensive traveling, and numerous personal appearances, and this was just day one. Still, it was the opportunity of a lifetime, and she was determined to make the most of it. As the former Miss Teen Argentina, she had gotten a taste of the business with a few commercials and a few soap-opera spots, but with a bit of luck and the right connections, her Tresses contract would be her opportunity to break into the entertainment industry seriously.

Carmen heard the phone ring and glanced at the caller ID. It read "ANONYMOUS," and she smiled as she answered the call.

"Hello!" She waited for the familiar voice.

"Hey, baby, where are you?" Drew's Brazilian accent was thick.

"Almost home," she responded slyly.

"So how did it go today?"

"It was fabulous! We spent all day selecting my wardrobe for the next two weeks, including the pieces for the first photo shoot. As exciting as it was, I still couldn't help but think of you," Carmen flirted.

"Nice. Sounds like you had a pretty busy day."

"Yeah, it was cool. I can't wait to start shooting."

"I'm happy for you, but you know I'm going to miss you once you start the tour," Drew whined.

"I'll miss you too," Carmen said. "Am I going to see you tonight?"

"No, I'm sorry, baby. I thought I was going to be able to get away, but my wife had a thing, and I'm home with our boys. You understand, don't you?"

"Sure," Carmen lied. "Guess it's for the best. I'm exhausted," she yawned quietly.

"Well, get some rest. I'll make it up to you tomorrow."

"Promise?" she teased.

"You got it."

Carmen sighed as she disconnected the call. True, she was exhausted, but she had been looking forward to an evening of romantic lovemaking with Drew. Besides the Tresses campaign, Drew had been the best thing that had happened to her since she arrived in L.A. nine months prior. Although she never aspired to be anyone's mistress, after two weeks with Drew, she couldn't resist him. Not only was he irresistible, but Drew made being a mistress something most women would only dream about. Disappointment, however, came with the territory. It was the one downside to being involved with a married man, especially one with celebrity status. Of course, the upside included several perks, including gifts and endless connections, all of which kept Carmen interested and content with their now eight-month relationship.

She glanced at the five carat diamond bracelet Drew had given her last week. The thought of him made her moist. She wasn't sure if it was his dick that gave her so much pleasure or the expensive gifts he always left behind after fucking her. Either way, she vowed to go along for the ride for as long as he was willing to travel.

Almost drunk with exhaustion, Carmen momentarily veered off the freeway. She turned up the music and rolled down the window, hoping the noise and cold air would help keep her awake.

Finally home, she pulled her Maserati into the garage and lowered the door. Suddenly the hairs on the back of her neck stood up as she checked her rearview mirror, sensing the presence of someone. She failed to see the black-clad figure that darted under the door just before it closed.

Carmen entered the condo, turned on the light, and quickly punched in the alarm code. She tossed her bag onto the kitchen counter and slipped off her shoes. The clock on her microwave read six o'clock. Exactly fourteen hours had passed since she'd last read it earlier that morning. The six-inch stilettos she just escaped from had registered every minute, and she wiggled her toes, trying to bring life back into them as she made her way down the hallway to the foyer. Pausing a moment, Carmen retrieved the mail from the front table where her housekeeper had left it before leaving for the day. As she made her way back into the kitchen, she poured herself a glass of Merlot and sat down to review the small stack of envelopes.

There were three bills which she set aside for her assistant, a postcard reminder from her dentist, and a letter from her little sister back in Argentina.

"Probably asking for more money," Carmen whispered as she tossed the letter onto the coffee table. She sipped her drink and pushed the button to retrieve her voice mail.

"You have no messages," the machine announced.

Carmen was surprised that Pierre hadn't called. Pierre Jourdan had been her manager, agent, and best friend, as well as the driving force behind her career for the past ten years. He had discovered her at the age of fifteen shopping in a mall in Buenos Aires, and after what amounted to begging and pleading, had finally convinced her mother to enter her into the Miss Teen Argentina pageant. Carmen won, and Pierre had immediately taken over the reins of her life. Any success she had attained could be traced directly back to Pierre's efforts. It was Pierre who had the foresight to convince Carmen not to cut her hair six years ago, and it was her waist-length mane that had ultimately sealed the Tresses deal.

A quick scroll through the missed calls revealed that Pierre had indeed called three times. She smiled, knowing that he hated leaving messages. Carmen considered calling him back but with further thought decided against it. It would take her at least an hour to cover the events of the day with all of the detail that she knew Pierre would require. Today was one of the first meetings he'd missed, yet she didn't mind, because she knew his sights were set on even bigger things for both of them.

Carmen rose from the table, planning to bathe before tackling that conversation. She looked around her quiet condo, realizing just how much she hated being alone in such a big space. And since she knew Drew wouldn't be coming over to rock her world, she was eager to bathe in order for her to get her rocks off in a conversation with Pierre about all the money they would make with this new campaign.

Turning out the light, Carmen headed down her plush carpeted hallway toward her bedroom. In the bathroom, she lit a candle, turned on the shower, and grabbed her loose-fitting cotton lounger that hung behind the bathroom door. She peeled off the spandex leggings and oversized top, then removed her black lace panties and matching bra. Her nakedness was soothing. Gathering her hair into a ponytail, she braided it tightly and pinned it into a bun on the top of her head. Climbing into the shower, she closed her eyes and stretched, allowing the water to massage her stiff muscles.

Carmen didn't hear the door open as the black-clad figure

entered the house from the garage, and she never saw the figure make its way past the kitchen and down the hallway to her bedroom.

It happened so suddenly that she had little time to react. The first blow sent her head crashing into the shower wall with such force that she nearly passed out. Before she had time to recover, she felt herself being pulled backward by her hair as she gasped for air. Carmen tried hard to resist as her arms flailed wildly, but it didn't work. Instead, her resistance just made her more vulnerable as her feet slipped, causing her to fall face forward into the water. Managing to turn over onto her knees, Carmen caught a glimpse of a figure completely dressed in black and wearing a ski mask. She punched upward, surprised when the blow landed on what appeared to be her attacker's chin. Then she felt a kick to her side, and when she reached down to protect herself, she felt the heel of a boot stomping her wrist. The pain was unbearable. She grabbed her attacker's leg, making the attacker lose balance and tumble backward.

Carmen seized the opportunity to stand and run, but her attacker was quick, tripping her and sending her sprawling face-first into the wall. She landed in the hallway and could feel what she knew was her own blood splattering onto her cream carpet. She screamed out, not knowing if anyone could hear her. She felt her acrylic nails give way as she gripped the carpet in an effort to crawl away. She was too late, though. Her attacker was on her back, digging a knee into her shoulder blades, causing her to scream even louder. She searched for any identifiable sign from her attacker but couldn't find one—the room and her attacker's onyx-colored attire were way too dark. She opened her mouth with hopes of biting her attacker, but her face was forced into the floor negating any attempts at self-defense.

Carmen braced herself, sensing that rape was imminent, but instead of penetration, she felt her attacker wind her braid around a fist, pull her head backward, then slam it into the floor. Dazed, Carmen struggled to keep her focus. Her heart raced as she imagined her own death.

"Please . . . don't kill me," she managed to whisper. "You can take whatever you want, just please, spare my life."

Her attacker remained silent until Carmen heard a loud buzzing sound nearing her ear. Suddenly she felt a sharp pain at the base of her neck.

"Stop! What are you doing . . ." she screamed while trying to toss her head from side to side. "Heeeeeeeeeeeeeelp!" she screamed even louder, but the attacker pulled her hair, snapping her neck backward before slamming her head into the floor again. She fought to concentrate but felt herself losing the battle to remain conscious. With the next blow, the room went black.

Carmen woke to the sound of the shower running. She was cold, and her head was pounding. She opened her eyes to darkness and froze, suddenly remembering why she was lying naked in her hallway. She listened, afraid to move, fearing that her attacker was still in the house. She had no idea how long she had been unconscious, so in fear, she continued to wait.

Quietly, Carmen slid her hand between her legs, not knowing what to expect, and was surprised to feel no pain or soreness. Oddly, it felt perfectly normal.

After what had to be thirty minutes but felt like an eternity, Carmen struggled to her knees and began crawling to her bedroom. A sharp pain ripped through her wrist making it difficult to move quickly, and when she finally managed to stand, her legs felt like Jell-O.

She made her way back into the bathroom where she quickly closed and locked the door. The candle she'd lit earlier had already burned down. She turned off the shower and stood still, listening for any other sounds in the house. Finally feeling that she was alone, she turned on the light and looked in the mirror. She was horrified by what she saw.

Staring back at her was a face she barely recognized. Her lips were bloody and swollen, and her face was badly bruised. But even more disturbing, the head belonging to the swollen face was completely bald!

Carmen grabbed her head in shock. She tried to scream, but the resulting sound amounted to only a loud gasp. Panic-stricken, she looked around the bathroom and spotted her lounger. She dressed quickly and pressed her ear to the door. Still silence.

Gathering the nerve to unlock and open the door, Carmen slowly crossed the bedroom to the phone at the side of the bed. She retrieved the receiver and tiptoed quickly back to the sanctuary of the bathroom.

Carmen dialed as fast as she could, but her hands were shaking so badly that she had to start over three times. Finally, she heard the ring at the other end, then a connection.

"Carmen! Where have you been? I've been calling you for over an hour!" Pierre chastised.

"Pierre! Please . . . come quickly. I've been attacked!"

"Attacked? What are you saying?" Pierre asked, unsure of what he had heard.

"Yes! Attacked! Pierre, please come now!" Carmen said with as much alarm as she could depict in a whisper.

"Are you okay? Have you called the police?"

"No! Pierre, please!" Carmen begged.

"Okay. I'm on my way!"

Pierre arrived in thirty minutes, making the forty-seven-mile drive in record time. He rang the doorbell, and when there was no immediate response, he used his spare key to let himself in. Met with total darkness, Pierre quickly turned on the light in the foyer and glanced around cautiously.

"Carmen! Carmen, it's Pierre."

Carmen opened the bathroom door and noticed light in the hallway.

"Pierre?"

"Yes, where are you?"

She walked slowly in the direction of his voice, looking from side to side, still not totally convinced that her attacker had left. She spotted Pierre standing in the hallway and staring back at her as if he were seeing a monster.

"Oh my God! Carmen!"

Carmen collapsed into Pierre's arms and began crying uncontrollably.

He helped her to the couch and held her, waiting for the initial wave of emotion to subside.

"Carmen, what happened? Who did this to you? And why haven't you called the police?"

"I was in the shower and someone attacked me. I didn't know anyone was in the house. I tried to fight, but whoever it was just kept pulling my hair and slamming my face into the floor until I guess I passed out. It was awful, and when I finally came to and got to the bathroom, I saw myself and my hair. Oh my God, Pierre, my hair!" Carmen grabbed her head and began crying again.

"Did they . . ." Pierre couldn't finish the sentence.

"No, I don't think so," Carmen said.

Pierre heaved a sigh of relief. Recuperating from the attack would be hard enough without throwing rape into the equation.

"We have to get you to a hospital," Pierre said.

"No! I can't have anyone see me like this! Look at me! Pierre, if this gets out, I'm ruined." Blood continued to drip from her lip, forehead, and under her eye.

Pierre glanced around the room and spotted Carmen's bag on the kitchen counter. He checked the contents. Her wallet and the other items in the bag seemed undisturbed. Her car keys were still on the counter.

"Carmen, I get that you're worried about your career, but I'm worried about you. Look at you!"

Still sobbing, Carmen tried to gain her composure. "I just don't understand. Who would do this to me?"

"I don't know, honey, but the longer we wait to call the police, the more we're going to have to explain later. We can't clean you up because the police will need whatever DNA evidence they can gather."

"What if this is about Drew?"

"What?" Pierre asked as he began to check the remainder of the house. He quickly checked the office, guestroom, and finally Carmen's bedroom. In the bathroom he ran cold water on a towel and headed back down the hallway.

"What were you saying about Drew?" he repeated, handing her the towel.

"I've been sleeping with him for the past four months," Carmen said.

"You hussy! How could you not tell me you were sleeping with Drew Peteers?"

Pierre noticed the door leading to the garage was slightly ajar, but when he peeked into the garage, Carmen's Maserati and everything else seemed in place.

"He's married!" Carmen protested as she began dabbing the cold towel across her face.

"No shit!" Pierre agreed. "This is a fucking PR disaster! No wonder you didn't want to call the police."

Although Pierre knew that they should call the police, he also knew that once the story of the attack became public, he would not be able to protect Carmen from the onslaught. News that the Tresses model had been beaten and shaved completely bald would create a media frenzy, and the financial payday for the gruesome pictures could be worth millions.

Pierre grabbed a hooded jogging suit and tennis shoes from Carmen's closet and darted back to the kitchen. "Put this on. We have to get you to the hospital." He handed her the clothes and went to pour her a glass of wine from the bottle he had seen in the kitchen.

Carmen dressed slowly and accepted the wineglass without question. She sipped carefully, trying to maneuver the glass around her swollen lips. She wasn't sure if it was real or just her imagination, but the wine seemed to relax her.

"We'll call the police from the hospital," Pierre said, handing Carmen her bag in exchange for the empty glass.

Carmen pulled the hood over her head and tightened the drawstring to make sure it fit snugly around her face. She looked at Pierre, her eyes searching for assurance that she looked less disturbing with her head covered.

Pierre nodded and smiled sympathetically. It was difficult to look at her. He glanced away looking at his watch. It was nine o'clock. "Let me get some pictures."

Carmen looked confused. "Whaaaaaat? Pictures? Are you crazy?"

"Listen, if anyone is going to profit from this, it's going to be us! I know it sounds crazy right now, but trust me, photos are always important." He retrieved his iPhone and asked Carmen to remove the hood. Too weak to argue, she relented and stood silently as Pierre took several shots.

Once done, Pierre led her gently down the hallway. Carmen watched as he set the alarm before they exited the house. Quickly they made their way to his car and headed the short distance to the hospital.

"Now when we get there, I'm going to need you to allow me to do all the talking. Victims shouldn't speak. The more you say, the more they'll want to investigate. Got it?"

Carmen could only manage a nod. Her head was throbbing so badly that she was having a difficult time concentrating. She was trying to recall details of the attack, but the pain kept interrupting her thoughts. She still couldn't believe what had just happened.

At the hospital she remained silent as Pierre took over. It was during times like this that she was glad to have Pierre on her side. While she remained in the car, Pierre made special arrangements to ensure her privacy. Once inside, she was led to a private room where she was greeted by a specialist, a private nurse, and a detective ready to take her statement.

Within the hour Carmen was examined and x-rayed revealing multiple bruises, contusions, a badly sprained wrist, and one hell of a concussion. The doctor had concluded from his examination that there were no signs of rape or any sexual assault, which she suspected, but was relieved to have it confirmed. Within moments, the bruises to her face were treated and her wrist was carefully wrapped to stabilize her sprain. Although she was reluctant, Carmen agreed to a mild sedative to ease her pain. She felt comfortable allowing Pierre to handle the final questions from the police and do whatever he was going to do regarding the press.

She waited a moment for the sedative to kick in. She knew she'd have more questions to answer in the morning regarding her attack, but for now, all she was craving was the rest she so desperately needed. Her mind raced with thoughts of who could have attacked her. Although she knew she hadn't acquired many friends in Los Angeles, she'd made it a point not to make any enemies either.

Carmen pulled her cell phone from her bag and checked her missed calls. There were two. The first one was from an anonymous caller, who Carmen immediately assumed was Drew. She smiled at the thought of Drew, then panicked at the thought of how she would explain to him what had happened to her. Although she knew her bruises would eventually fade, it would be an eternity before her hair grew back. As she rubbed her hand across her peach-fuzzed scalp, tears welled in the corners of her eyes. *What am I going to do now?* she thought. She couldn't imagine Drew being so shallow that he wouldn't like her now that her hair was gone, but then again, she could not have imagined her own insecurity and the shallowness *she* felt about what she now thought of herself.

Carmen wiped the tears from her eyes, trying to concentrate on the now blurred second missed call in her phone. Her face became stony as she saw the number that belonged to her ex. She cleared the number only to notice that someone had left her a message. She prayed that it was Drew, and then held her breath as she retrieved the message. It was a woman's voice on the opposite end of her phone.

"Did you actually think I was going to let you get away with this? I warned you about betraying me, but you didn't listen. I will not share what's mine. When I said "til death do us part,' I meant it. Now you've got two choices: either leave Drew alone or leave America in a body bag."

Tears flooded her eyes as she replayed the message over and over again. Carmen wasn't sure if it was the sedative kicking in or the chilling revelation of whom she now knew with all certainty was her attacker, but she was dizzy and almost drunk with emotion. The question in her mind was no longer about what she was going to do, but rather how fast she would be able to get out of dodge.

9

You Forgot About Dinner . . . Again!

"*What* the fuck do you mean you're not going to make it to my game, Ev? It's the fucking playoffs. Win or go home, remember? If we lose there isn't another game. That's it, season over!"

"You guys have a perfect record, honey. Come on, it's not a big deal! You make it seem like I'm trying to go fucking shopping when I'm just doing my job." Eve kicked her Uggs off and tossed them in the corner of their room near Chase's gym bag.

"You wouldn't have to go away this weekend if you had taken your ass to the office this week instead of running around town the past few weeks playing mother hen to them damn wives. What, you thought I didn't know?" Chase took off his shirt exposing his perfectly chiseled chocolate chest. "Eve, I'm your husband, and for the last couple of months you've really been putting everything and everybody else before me."

Chase was right, and Eve knew it. She'd devoted the last few weeks of her time and energy to either work or the wives. She'd missed three games and hadn't made it home for dinner with Chase in over two weeks.

"Babe, I'm sorry. Until now, I hadn't even thought about the fact that I'd been so insensitive."

"You have been," he pouted as he sat on the edge of their bed and went through his practice bag.

Eve tossed her work files aside and kneeled down in front of him. "I'll figure out a way to make it to your game this weekend, I promise." She stroked the side of his face with her hand.

"What else?" he said flirtatiously.

Eve took the hint. "I could . . ." She unzipped his pants exposing his already erect penis. She didn't bother to finish her sentence and instead, allowed her mouth and tongue to complete it for her.

Chase moaned as Eve pleased him orally. While she pleasured him, she realized that the two of them hadn't made love in over two weeks. It was that kind of neglect that Eve knew led to problems in relationships, especially relationships with athletes. For every night she didn't fuck her man to full satisfaction, she knew there was some thirsty groupie bitch that would be more than willing to do it for her.

The mere thought of someone else fucking her man made her fume. She pulled Chase's dick out, fully exposing it, and began to suck him harder. As he lay back on the bed, Eve went to work, handling her man as if he were a Big Gulp from 7-Eleven. She felt it was her duty both as a woman and a wife to make it impossible for any groupie to compete with her. Before he had an opportunity to cum, she removed her clothes, fully exposing every inch of her naked body, and positioned herself on top of him. The butterflies tattooed on her back were about to take flight, and she smiled in anticipation of what was to come.

"I want to ride you," she moaned, resisting his offer of help. She gently moved his hands, preventing him from gripping her waist. "No!" she demanded with a sultry grin. "I got this," she teased, while placing his rock-hard love fully inside her.

"Aaaaaaaaaaaaaa!" she screamed, expressing how good he made her feel.

Their bodies were rhythmic as her pussy led his dick in a tango of pleasure. Holding nothing back, Eve was wild with passion.

"You forgive me?" she whispered as she squatted up and down on him, and then hovered above him, allowing the wetness of her center to drip slowly down the tip of his dick before resuming her stroke.

"Oh yeah . . ." Chase managed between moans, fighting to control his need to cum inside of her. "I . . . Ewwwwwwwwwwwwww, Eve!" he muttered unable to complete his thought.

"You ready to cum, baby?" She moved her hips faster.

"Ewwwwwwwwww, I don't want to buuuut . . ." Chase grabbed Eve's hips, ignoring her earlier command and navigating her direction to suit his own needs.

"You feel it, baby? Is it wet enough for you?"

Chase licked her breasts. "It's good."

"How do you want it?" she quizzed, wanting to make sure she gave it to him exactly the way he liked.

Eve placed her hands on top of Chase's, which were still on her breasts. "Squeeze 'em," she ordered.

He obliged.

"Harder!" she yelled as her body began to tingle with satisfaction.

Eve knew Chase was close to climax, but she didn't want their lovemaking to end. She slowed the rhythm of her stroke, toying with him.

"I want to taste it," he begged.

"Okay," Eve whispered, removing his hands from her breasts and replacing them with her own. She licked her nipple, motioning Chase to take charge.

Eve submitted as Chase lifted her off his dick and turned her, positioning her pussy over his face as she leaned down to gently lick the head of his dick. He gripped her ass, making her scream with pleasure as he slurped and licked her pussy hard. The sensation was so strong she gasped for breath and struggled to hold her position.

"Take it," he ordered as he gripped her ass tighter and continued to lick her dry.

Finally catching her breath, Eve placed him inside her mouth. Determined to make him cum first, she pulled out all the stops and began to suck vigorously, displaying a perfect combination of spit, tongue, throat, and jaw action to guarantee her victory.

It was obvious that Chase was on a mission of his own as Eve felt her insides start to quiver. She sucked faster, and the two of them fell into rhythm, sending each other into a sexual frenzy. Just as her body was about to succumb to the pleasure, she felt Chase's dick respond, first with just a shudder, then a geyser-like release. Eve smiled and was about to declare her victory when she felt her own body tremble, and then begin to shake uncontrollably as the floodgates opened. She was happily the winner of both producing and receiving the gold.

They both laughed as Eve rolled over to lie next to Chase. They lay in the sticky residue of their lovemaking, both fully satisfied as they allowed their breathing to return to normal. Eve initiated conversation.

"You know how much I love you, right?"

"Yeah," he said, gently smacking her ass.

"And if I've been crazy, it's only because I've just been watching how all these men have been taking advantage of their wives. I hate it!"

"I know. I hear you. But, babe, you've got to know that ain't me."

"I know. It's just hard," she said, flipping her hair, dampened from sex.

"To what? Imagine that you do live in a world where not all men cheat? Because Eve, not all men do. I've got sisters. I've seen them get hurt by dudes that just weren't ready for a real relationship. I've experienced through them what it's like to have your heart broken by some guy who's fucking around. I get it. I know that there's unconquered pussy out there that's constantly being thrown at us. But it's not everybody's story to want to conquer it. Some men really love and only want to be with the woman they chose to be with. And I chose you. You're it for me, babe. You're all I want!" Chase confessed.

"So you're saying you've never ever once cheated on me in the five years we've been married?" She was somewhat embarrassed to ask the question in fear of the answer. "Let's keep it one hundred! We've always been able to talk about everything, and when we got together we promised to lay it all out there. You told me your dirt, and I told you mine. I knew what I was getting into when we got married. I knew, just like every other wife of a celebrity or athlete knows, that cheating and temptation come with the territory. I also knew that I never wanted to ask you a question that I didn't want to know the answer to, so I never asked. I just prayed that you'd never lie to me or put me in a position where I'd look stupid because of something you neglected to tell me . . ."

"Eve, I've never cheated on you." Chase's tone was careful yet confident. "I've never wanted to."

"Chase . . ." Tears formed in her eyes. "You don't have to say that . . ."

"But it's the truth. Listen, I take my vows with you seriously, Eva. It ain't about pussy for me, or just fucking some random chick just to get a thrill. I love you. If I'ma fuck, I wanna fuck you," he laughed.

"You're such an asshole. You know that?" She smiled, knowing that he was telling the truth.

"I'm your asshole, though. I love you. Just you! And I promise I'll try my best never to do anything intentionally to hurt you."

"If you feel tempted to stray, will you please promise to tell me? Give me a heads-up or something. I couldn't stand it if what happened to my mother ever happened to me. I just don't think I could live with that kind of betrayal. That kind of lie would kill me."

"I promise." Chase kissed her forehead. "My turn."

"What?" Eve nestled her head under his chin and wrapped her arm around him.

"Promise me dinner at least three times a week."

"Dinner?" She was perplexed by his request. "What the fuck, you want me to cook?"

He laughed out loud. "No, just be home. Me, you, and a date with the table . . . as a family."

"I'd love that," she said wrapping her arm a little tighter across his body.

The two of them shared a kiss while allowing the coolness of the room to calm their still sweaty bodies. Regardless of the facts surrounding the mess that was going on in the marriages of the other wives, one thing rang true with Eve: She had herself a good man in Chase. If having dinner with him and being a family was what she had to do in order to keep him happy, she would make it her mission to do just that!

10

I'm All About the Exclusive!

Jackie closed her eyes and relaxed in the makeup chair of her dressing room at the KTEL TV studios as Marcus applied her foundation. She'd be on the air in less than an hour, and she needed to be picture-perfect. It's not like she wasn't always camera ready, but when it came down to breaking a story, she liked to add a little extra effort.

Marcus Riley had been her makeup artist for over two years, and he was noted as being one of the best in the business. Although she'd worked with her BFF Ramon for years, when Ray was traded to Los Angeles, Ramon regretfully declined to follow Jackie.

It was moments like this one that she actually wished Ramon was still with her. They had been together since the beginning, and even though she adored Marcus, Ramon knew Jackie and knew how to give her that extra "something" whenever she was about to break a story. She could have used Ramon today because she was about to shock the entertainment industry once again with an exclusive!

"Miss O, what's up with your face?" Marcus asked, concentrating on her left cheek.

"It's that damn kickboxing class," Jackie replied. "The chick next to me kicked when she was supposed to punch, and I caught a foot to the face. Bitch! You know I kung fu'd that ass when I got the chance. Can you cover it?"

"Sure, it's not that bad, but you might want to consider switching to yoga or something. We can't have you on the air looking like a domestic violence victim. You know you be all up in everybody else's celebrity business, and they'd love nothing more than to start some shit about you." Marcus threw up his hands, "This just in: Jackie O'Conner finally met her match. Her husband Ray beat that ass. News at eleven!" Marcus slapped his thigh with the blush brush. "Girl, now that's an exclusive for ya . . . Okaaaaaaay!"

"I wish a muthafucka' would put his hands on me. Fuck an exclusive. I'd report that shit myself. I'm from Inglewood; you know we don't play that. I'll catch that fool slippin', fuck him up, and ask questions later," Jackie protested.

"Stranger things have happened, girlfriend. Trust me, I've seen it all." Marcus smacked his lips. "You have no idea how many wives I know who spend tons of money on makeup just to cover bruises they got from their punk-ass husbands."

"Please," Jackie said, opening her eyes. "Ray may be a lot of things, but that kind of crazy ain't never been one of them. Besides, my mama got her ass beat from my daddy for years before she finally shot his ass. Ray knows I got it in me; he ain't crazy."

"Oh, girl, did your daddy make it?" Marcus asked.

"Yeah, he lived. It was just a flesh wound."

"Are you serious?"

"As a fucking heart attack. I told you I'm from Inglewood, and that was a step up for my family because my mama's from Watts!" Jackie laughed.

"Excuse me, Miss Inglehood, I forgot who I was talking to! Now be still so I can get these lashes on straight."

Jackie laughed to herself at Marcus's Inglehood remark. She was proud of her roots. She knew that being from Inglewood carried the stigma of being ghetto or rough around the edges, but she didn't care.

It was that stigma that had fueled her passion to succeed. In high school, she had developed a love for journalism. She was in awe of Oprah Winfrey and what she had managed to accomplish, so Jackie had set her sights on something similar. In fact, it was Oprah's success, not only as a woman, but as a *black* woman, that had inspired Jackie to become the success that she now was.

Jackie had been ruthless in pursuit of her dream to become a news analyst, although there were a few times when that dream had almost been derailed by her other ambitions. Her marriage, for instance, was one of those ambitions. Ray O'Connor had been her high school sweetheart and the love of her life for as long as she could remember. Their grandmothers were childhood friends, making them like family from birth. As far back as she could recall, Ray had been a part of her life. It seemed only natural for them to date eventually. And although her mother was a bit more lenient than Ray's mother, allowing her to date earlier than him, she waited until it was okay for him to date, and then sank her teeth into him deep. They continued to date through college even though Ray went to Miami while Jackie attended Spellman College in Atlanta. Jackie's reputation for dealing with a bitch who tried to brush up on her man was well known throughout Miami and the entire Tri-State area.

Even though she'd suspected infidelity on Ray's part throughout their college years, everyone knew that when she touched down in Miami and made it to campus, that cheating shit came to a close. She'd beat enough bitches' asses for them to think twice about fucking with her man.

Ray and Jackie married as soon as he was drafted into the NFL, immediately sweeping her into a lifestyle of the rich and famous that was new to both of them. While Ray succumbed to the stereotypical behavior of a professional athlete, Jackie struggled to maintain her identity and focus. She took jobs with local newspapers, sometimes working with technicians and camera crews just to be a part of the action. In doing so, she learned the ins and outs of the business from the ground up. She wanted to be a journalist more than anything, and nothing, not Ray's cheating, not two kids—nothing—was going to stop her.

Ray was traded three times, but for Jackie, his trade to the Leopards turned out to be a blessing in disguise. She found herself back in the Los Angeles area, her old stomping ground and the place where she not only felt safe, but where she felt at home. Here, back among family and friends, she wasn't afraid to take risks. She pitched her celebrity entertainment segment to the executives at KTEL, and they agreed to a three-month trial. Nearly three years later, Jackie was at the top of her game, and her segment was at the top of the ratings.

Maybe she was a little ghetto and just a bit rough around the edges, but so what? She didn't mind getting down and dirty if it meant she would be the one breaking a story, and she had no problem straddling the fence between right and wrong if it resulted in an exclusive. Her motto was "by any means necessary," and *any* was the key word.

"So I hear you've got another exclusive," Marcus said, gently blowing her lash.

"Yes," Jackie smiled, hardly able to contain her excitement.

"Girlfriend, I hope they're paying you what you're worth."

"I do okay!" Jackie chuckled.

"*Okay?* Oh no, honey, don't even try it. *I* do okay, and you and I both know they're paying your black ass royally."

"Just call me your majesty!"

They laughed and high-fived each other.

"Plus, you're married to that fine-ass Mr. O'Connor. I don't even know why you bother to work."

"I love what I do," Jackie said. "There's nothing like getting a good celebrity story and sharing it with an audience. Besides, I refuse to be one of those women that rely strictly on her husband's money. Child, you've seen those wives parading around town in cars with license plates that read stuff like HIS MONEY, or MRS. 85, or WIFEY 52. People think that kind of bullshit is cute, but I think it just strips them of their identities and gives the rest of us a bad rep. Well, I'm telling you now, I ain't going out like that. I need my own shit!"

"I guess, but, girl, this exclusive story shit can be dangerous. What if you pissed off one of them celebrities and they came looking for you?"

"I can handle myself, Marcus. Like you said, I'm Inglehood." Jackie opened her eyes and raised her hand for another high five. "Besides, these muthafuckas don't want to step to me. And for the most part, I do right by my sources. Trust me, I have more allies than enemies."

"I hear you, but, girlfriend, I'm not talking about your sources. I'm talking about your *subjects*!"

"Oh, they *really* don't want to fuck with me! Remember, I'm the one with the camera and the microphone. I don't mind putting your ass on blast, and I have thousands of listeners."

"All righty, then!" Marcus responded. "All done, missy, now knock 'em dead!" He completed her makeup with his ceremonial flick of the brush across Jackie's forehead. Marcus held up a mirror for Jackie to see the finished product.

Her close-cropped hair framed her face perfectly. Her smooth, dark skin, large, expressive, chestnut-brown eyes, and full lips all complemented one another. She was cute, and on a good day, some would say that she was actually pretty. Today was a good day.

"Beautiful as usual," Jackie said. "And I can't even see the bruise. Thanks, Marcus."

"My pleasure, Miss O. But when you get a chance, you need to put some aloe vera on that," he added as he packed up his makeup kit, snapped it shut, and headed to the next station.

Jackie glanced at her watch. She had twenty-five minutes before the broadcast. Feeling the familiar rush of anxiety, she leaned back and closed her eyes again. It was her ritual before every broadcast to take a moment, breathe, and just pray. As she felt the nervousness subside, she smiled, thinking it would surprise those close to her to learn that after all these years, she still got a case of the jitters before every broadcast. It was always temporary, going away the minute the cameras started rolling. Jackie welcomed the nervousness, however, because it gave her an edge and kept her job exciting. Just a little anxiety kept her alert and on top of her game, and today was no different.

"Mrs. O'Connor, can I get you anything?"

Jackie opened her eyes. It was Shawn Taylor, one of the staff assistants.

"Yes, my usual, please," Jackie replied. She knew Marcus would be furious with her, but she'd have him touch up her lips before going on the air.

Shawn returned with a cup of warm tea and lemon and placed it on the table next to Jackie. La Shawn "Shawnie" Taylor was a referral of Jackie's by way of Shawn's grandmother.

Shawn, like Jackie, was a Los Angeles native with her roots stemming from Carson, California. She reminded Jackie so much of herself when she was just getting started, and reminded her also of her vow to pay it forward any chance she could.

"Thanks, Shawnie. How's school?"

"Great, I have one more semester, and then I'm finally done."

"Remember what I told you," Jackie said, stirring her tea and winking at Shawn. "Look me up when you're done, and if you're still interested in journalism, I'll hook you up."

"Thanks, Miss O. I won't forget." She smiled and scurried away just as quickly as she had appeared.

Jackie was impressed with Shawn and thought how nice it would've been if someone had offered her a helping hand when she was struggling to get into the business. Now that she had some clout, she wanted to give back. She had presented the idea of a mentoring program to The Wives Association, but it was shot down. Queen Bee Eve stated that it wasn't the right time, which was bullshit to Jackie, but whatever. To date, the association was Eve's baby, and now was not the time to go against her. Jackie wasn't accustomed to playing second-string to anybody, and if she had anything to do with it, Eve wouldn't always be the one calling the shots.

Jackie pulled out her notes for a last-minute review. While she always had a copy readily available, she prided herself in reporting her stories with as little reading as possible. It gave her stories a more personal touch and was part of her signature style.

Jackie looked up and noticed Sandra Harris, the show's executive producer, hurrying toward her. From her body language and the expression on her face, Jackie was sure it was about the exclusive. She sighed in anticipation of a confrontation.

Jackie respected Sandra. She thought she was a great producer, but they frequently bumped heads. It was as if Sandra saw her as a threat to her position, and no matter how many times Jackie assured her that she didn't want her job, Sandra still didn't seem to get it.

"Morning, Jackie," Sandra said, eyeing the notes in Jackie's hand.

"Hey, darling. Good morning." Jackie sipped her tea and smiled politely. She shook her head as she gave Sandra a quick once-over. You'd think with all the money she made, she'd do better than Target eyeglasses, a Supercuts pageboy, and what appeared to be cheap JCPenney pumps.

"Good morning? Well, aren't you the cool cucumber today! I don't understand how you do it, J."

"Do what?"

"Get these stories, and not just stories, but exclusives!"

"Sandy, you know me, and you know that I take my job seriously. I do my homework. You said it yourself. It's what separates a good journalist from a great one. That, plus the fact that I have great sources is how I do it."

"Good try, Jackie, but this is not Marcus you're talking to. I've been in this business a long time, and I know that there is a thin line between sources and insider information. I also know there's an even thinner line between getting an exclusive and being inclusive. I've watched you. You're a great journalist, and true, you do your homework, but you and I both know there's something else going on here."

"It's called luck," Jackie shrugged.

"Nobody's that lucky. You've managed to have at least one *exclusive* breaking news story every year for the past three years. Some journalists go their entire careers and *never* have a breaking story, let alone an exclusive. How do you explain that?"

"I guess they're *unlucky*," she laughed.

"It can't be that simple," Sandra said, folding her arms in frustration.

"So what are you saying?" Jackie replied, raising an eyebrow.

"Come on, Jackie, you know exactly what I'm saying. As executive producer, I have the responsibility of maintaining the integrity of our show and our stories. I have people to answer to. When the big boys upstairs ask me how we got the exclusive, *luck* is not what they want to hear."

"I can respect your position, Sandra. But just like you have people to answer to, so do I, and if I start revealing where I get my information, my sources will dry up like an open tube of Krazy Glue." Jackie sipped her tea. "And when has there ever been a question about the integrity of my stories?"

"Your point is well taken," Sandra said, adjusting her glasses. "But I'm sure you see my point too. If you were in my shoes, you'd be asking the same questions."

"Which is why I'm not in your shoes. You do you, and I'll do me."

"You doing you makes it hard for me to do me."

"Well, me doing me has our ratings at the top."

Jackie got Marcus's attention and gestured that she needed her lipstick freshened. He grabbed the tube from his case and darted to her station. Jackie could almost feel Sandra's eyes glaring at the back of her neck as Marcus smoothed on a fresh coat of lipstick, and then headed back across the room.

Jackie turned to Sandra. "So what do you really want from me, Sandra? Because you and I both know this whole 'the boys upstairs are concerned' business is bull."

"I want assurance that your suspicious success is not going to result in a scandal for this station or this show one day. I have to be able to tell the folks on the twelfth floor that they have nothing to worry about, and if that means verifying your sources, then that's what I'll do. It's what a good producer does."

"I can appreciate that," Jackie said, glancing at her watch. "But as a good producer, you also know that good *journalists* never reveal their sources. Not *even* to you! Now, if there's nothing else, I, just like you, have a show to do. Excuse me." Jackie turned and headed for the newsroom. She smiled as she took her mark at the news desk and prepared for her cue. She loved having the upper hand, and the more successful she became, the more success she craved. This was truly just the beginning in her career, her love, and her life, and nothing, not even a nosy-ass producer, was going to get in her way.

the ability to work and listen, making sure to filter what was interest-ing and what could be dismissed as embellishment. With Brandon, she could count on at least half of the conversation being embellished, allowing her to get a considerable amount of work done while the two of them talked.

". . . I told Jeremy something fishy was going on. And you know I can smell fish a mile away! He said I should mind my own business, but I told his ass right back that if he didn't . . . oh shit! Oh shit!"

Eve paused. These last exclamations did not quite fit the story.

"Brandon, what's wrong?"

"Wait, hold on, girl! Let me turn up the TV."

Eve shook her head and laughed to herself.

"Giiiiiirl, somebody done beat up the Tresses girl! Daaaaaaaaaaamn, look at her! Jeremy! Oh my God, come here quick!" Brandon shouted. "That poor child is tore up from the floor up."

It took a moment for Brandon's comments to register, but suddenly, Eve was all ears as she realized what she was hearing. Guilt followed by immediate fear enveloped her. "Wait, what did you just say?"

"I said somebody beat up the Tresses girl. You know, that model chick from those commercials . . . what's her name?"

"Carmen Garza," Jeremy chimed in from the background.

"Yeah, that's her. The supermodel with all that hair! It's on the news right now. Girl, they're saying she was attacked . . ."

Eve sat up in her chair so suddenly she spilled her tea all over herself. "Damn it!" She began to search desperately for the remote. She felt the burn from the hot tea as it began to scorch her skin, but she ignored the pain and continued her search.

"What channel?" Eve shouted into the phone before putting it on speaker in order to widen her search. "Brandon, what are they saying?"

"Oh damn . . . Girl, whoever attacked her cut off all that pretty hair of hers. The bitch is *bald*!"

"Bald?" Eve's thoughts immediately flew to Callie and their conversation over lunch. Her heart raced as she dug her hands into the couch. "Brandon! Brandon!" she screamed into the phone.

"Oooooh! Sorry, girl. I just can't believe it. Who would do that to the poor child? Pretty as she is it's probably some jealous wife. Or better yet, probably the model that applied for the job and didn't get it. Jealous bitches will do that sort of thing. The cameras couldn't get a good look at her because she had her hands up to her face and a coat thrown over her head, but you can definitely see the bruises on her hands, and her face looks like a damn American flag, all red, white, and blue! I bet it was some jealous—"

"Brandon, I gotta go!" Eve yelled.

"Wait, I didn't finish telling you—"

"No, Brandon, really, I have to go! I'll call you later!" She hung up without waiting for a response. Frantically she tossed the couch cushions onto the floor. When she still didn't see it, she got down on all fours and peered under the couch. Nothing! In frustration she leaned over the couch to search the kitchen counter. There it was!

"Finally," she said, flipping the channels in search of the story. It was everywhere: ABC, NBC, CNN, FOX, every outlet with the same story. The headline read: "SUPERMODEL ATTACKED." Eve turned the volume up.

"…reports indicate that supermodel and official Tresses hair-care spokesperson, Carmen Garza, was attacked last night by an unknown assailant or assailants. According to the Laguna Hills Police Department, the Argentine beauty, known for her luxurious locks, was reportedly taken to Orange County Cedar Hospital, and police received a call at approximately 11:30 P.M. Thursday night.

"Upon arrival, police spoke with Miss Garza's manager who confirmed the attack. Detective Edward Montoya reported that details were sketchy, but that the victim appeared to have been beaten about the face and had bruises on her hands and legs. According to Montoya, Miss Garza was heavily sedated at the time and was unable to give a description of her attacker or attackers or provide any details. 'The victim was understandably upset,' reported Montoya. 'Miss Garza has been released from the hospital, and we intend to speak with her later today. At that time, we should be able to gather more information and continue our investigation."

Eve stood speechless as her mind raced back to her advice to Callie. If Callie was behind the attack, could she be considered an accomplice for planting the idea in her head? Eve fought hard to shake off the spirit of worry yet felt defeated by the failed efforts. She pressed mute on the remote and grabbed her cell phone, quickly dialing Amber's number. As it rang, Eve watched clips of Carmen leaving the hospital holding a coat over her head. The bruises and bald head were obvious despite her discretion. Eve exhaled deeply. "Damn," she whispered.

She waited impatiently as there was no answer after three rings on Amber's phone. Finally, after the fourth ring, Eve remembered Amber didn't have her phone. She hung up and quickly dialed the number to her secret BlackBerry.

"Hey, Evie. What's up?"

"Am, where are you?"

"On my way home. I've been shopping all day for Sean's party. I think I'm finally finished getting supplies."

"I can't believe that muthafucka' still hasn't given you your phone back. What the hell is he waiting for?"

"I don't know, and honestly, I really don't care. I'm just glad we're on speaking terms again."

"I've gotta give it to Sean. The way he's managed to turn his bullshit cheating around on you is beyond me. *He's* the one who cheated, and *you're* the one who's groveling. Go figure!"

"Um, excuse me. Did you purposely call to hurt my feelings and make me feel like shit, or was there something else you needed?"

Eve shook her head realizing her own words. "Amber, I'm sorry. I didn't mean for that to come out so harsh. I just hate the fact that you're going through this. You deserve better. I was completely insensitive, though, and I'm sorry."

"I know. And you've been great to me and Olivia. It's just that even with you working hard to get me insurance through the association, Sean is my husband, and although he's hurt me by cheating, he is and has been my life for all these years. My whole identity is wrapped up in him and our lifestyle. And to be honest, I don't know that I'm ready to give it all up."

There was an uncomfortable silence for a moment until Amber spoke again. "Eve, you still there? Clearly you didn't call to listen to me go on about Sean?"

"Right! And no, obviously you haven't heard the news." Eve turned her attention back to the television screen.

"Girl, you know my car radio is always set to Radio Disney. What's the news?"

"It's about Callie. Have you talked to her?"

"No. Why? What's going on?"

"I think . . ."

Eve heard Chase coming down the hallway.

"Am, I gotta go, but get to a television or Google Carmen Garza on the phone as soon as you can. I'll call you back in a minute." Eve hung up quickly, making sure she turned the television off before Chase entered the room. The last thing she needed was for Chase to suspect that something else might have her attention or serve as a distraction to their relationship.

Chase stood in the doorway. "Hey, babe, whatcha doing?"

Eve forced a smile as Chase made his way to her. "Just wrapping up my morning calls," she said, returning a kiss to Chase's lips. "You taste good."

"You taste like Chai," he joked.

"Sorry, babe," Eve blushed. "You off to practice?"

"Yeah, Coach is making us all come in a lot earlier and stay a lot later ever since we made the playoffs, but I promise to be home by dinner, okay?"

"Okay! Who knows, maybe I'll even make us something special."

"If by 'making' you mean ordering takeout, then I guess I'll consider that special." Chase popped a bagel into the toaster.

"You knew I couldn't cook when you married me," Eve said playfully. "I'll order the sea bass from Daily Grill that you like so much. That's pretty special, don't you think?" Eve took the strawberry-flavored cream cheese from the refrigerator along with the protein shake she had made for Chase before he came downstairs. Like clockwork, she grabbed the bagel and creamed it, then handed it to him.

"I love you," Chase declared as he took the shake and bagel from her hand.

"I know." Eve wrapped her arms around his waist, leaning her head against his chest.

Their embrace lasted only a moment before it was interrupted by the ringing of Eve's phone. She sighed as she glanced at her phone. It was Amber. She knew what it was about.

"Don't worry, take your call. I know you've got to do your thing, especially since you're going to be with me all weekend."

"All weekend? What are you talking about? The game is on Sunday, isn't it?"

"Yeah, but we're playing in Dallas, remember?"

Eve chewed her bottom lip. She'd forgotten. In addition, she'd promised her boss that she would come in on Saturday to meet with the new recruits. "Baby, I already told George I would work this weekend," she whined.

"Eve, what part of the playoffs don't you understand? It's win or go home! I need you there, Ev."

"And I'll be there. Just on Sunday."

"Ev . . ." Chase protested.

"Babe, it's not like I can stay with you anyway. I'll go to work on Saturday and fly out the first thing smoking Sunday morning. I'll be there for kickoff, I promise."

She could tell that her argument wasn't as convincing as she needed it to be. And it didn't help that her cell phone kept ringing.

"I'll see you tonight," Chase said dryly as he headed for the front door.

Eve thought of following him, but feared anything else she said would only make things worse. "Love you!" she shouted, hoping Chase could feel the sincerity of her words.

She listened as the front door closed, then waited, making sure he had left. She'd hoped he would've responded to her last words but figured now her actions would have to make up for what her words could not. She reached for her phone and before she could dial the first number Amber was calling her again. Without hesitation, she answered.

"What the hell?!" Amber yelled into the phone.

Eve laughed out loud. "I'm so sorry," she apologized. "I had to see Chase off—"

"Girl! Oh my gosh! Do you think Callie could have done that to that poor girl?"

"I don't know, but . . . wait! Did you say that poor girl?" Eve quizzed.

"Did you see her? Fucking Drew or not, that girl didn't deserve a beat down like that."

"That's debatable. But I hear you. Has anyone heard from Callie?"

"I haven't. But then again, I don't have my phone, remember?"

"The news reports of Carmen's attack looks exactly like the conversation we had with her last week at lunch. Surely, she couldn't have taken us that seriously, could she?" Eve leaned back in her chair and thought back to the discussion she had had with Callie. Either Callie had taken her seriously, or this was the biggest damn coincidence since the murder of Robert Blake's wife.

"Well, without my phone, I don't have her number."

"Never mind, I'll call her. Listen, until I get to the bottom of this, I'm gonna need you to keep our little lunch discussion with Callie a secret, okay?"

"You don't have to worry about me. I've got too much of my own shit going on to be worrying about someone else's drama," Amber replied. "I can count on you to come early tomorrow for Sean's party, right?"

"Yeah, I'll be there. However, you do know that with Chase and Ray needing to leave early on Saturday to head for Dallas, we may not be able to stay late."

"That's fine. I just know I couldn't get through the night without you."

"Don't worry, I've got your back," Eve responded as she turned off the television. "I'll see you tomorrow."

"Thanks, Eve."

"Talk to you later." Eve hung up the phone and placed it on the counter. She realized again just how important it was to have each other's backs. With Amber's marriage on the rocks, and now her own marriage hanging in the balance, in addition to Callie being a potential fugitive, Eve knew the ladies had to stick together more than ever. And if that was going to happen, Eve knew that she'd have to do what only she could: work to put all the pieces back together.

12

The Party Must Go On!

Amber made her way around the house, checking to make sure that everything was in order. As much as she dreaded continuing with Sean's birthday party, she had invested far too much time, energy, and money not to go through with it now. In addition to the invitations that had gone out over a month ago, Amber had invited her in-laws, who were driving up from the Bay Area just for the occasion, and there was no way she was going to let on to Sean's parents that there was trouble in paradise.

Tami Jackson, Sean's mother, had never been a fan of Amber's and had questioned her intentions with Sean from the beginning. From the moment they started dating, Tami watched Amber like a hawk. Although Sean wasn't an only child, he was Tami's only son, and she had invested a lot in him. Tami made sure Sean went to the best schools her husband's money could provide. Having come from money herself by way of her parents, Tami was no stranger to wealth. Both Tami's parents were Stanford graduates, and although her mother was a housewife, she made sure that her Stanford business degree went to full use by running their family like a multimillion-dollar corporation.

Tami followed in her mother's footsteps as she too graduated from Stanford. To her mother's dismay, Tami met and married Sean's father, Sean Sr., directly out of college. But, like her mother, she ran the household with an iron fist, making sure that Sean and his two sisters, Shaniece and Shauna, abided by her rules.

When Amber came on the scene, it was just after Sean's breakup with his mother-approved girlfriend, Courtney Collins. To Tami, Courtney was the epitome of a perfect girlfriend, and she made sure that Amber knew it. Amber *also* knew that her mother-in-law held her responsible for Courtney and Sean's breakup, a fact that was partly true. Amber also knew that Sean was suspected to have had a girlfriend when the two of them hooked up back in college, but it was never confirmed, especially by Sean.

It wasn't until Sean's parents showed up for one of his football games with Courtney in tow that she discovered the truth. Once confronted, Courtney completely rescinded. She didn't even put up a fight for Sean, stating that if he thought so little of her that he could cheat on her with the likes of Amber, he deserved her.

As Amber made her way from the foyer, through the living room, and down the long hallway to the family room where the party would take place, she looked over the years of memories that rested in the frames that were scattered about the house. Although Amber was certain she was never considered the favorite for Sean, she knew that after more than ten years together, she wasn't ready to give up on their marriage.

She paused as she took in the décor of the family room. "Wow!" she said aloud as she looked at the black-and-gold-clad room. Amber had put a lot of work into the planning of the party, and it was evident in every aspect of the room. From the flowers to the chairs, from the lighting to the candy fountain, nothing was left undone. She smiled to herself as she smelled the fresh cut floral arrangements that were strategically placed throughout the room.

Amber checked in on the servers who were preparing the hors d'oeuvres and pastry trays for serving nearly two hundred guests. The buffet meal offered seven varieties of delicious Cajun-style entrées, including Sean's favorite rosemary jerked chicken—only this time Sa'Myra would not be preparing it, or anything else, for that matter. Amber smiled. Even with the issue of Sa'Myra hanging over her head, she felt good about the work she had put into Sean's party. And if she continued at the rate she was going, a true reconciliation was sure to be right around the corner.

Amber looked at the clock. It was 7:30 P.M., and with her party starting promptly in an hour, she knew she needed to hurry and put the final touches on her outfit before her guests arrived. She knew Sean would be upstairs getting ready and wanted to give him as much space as he needed to avoid a confrontation. The past few weeks had been strange as they barely spoke to each other. And although Amber tried her best to keep the peace, the mere fact that Sean walked around as if his indiscretion didn't matter at all while stripping her of her cell phone and limiting her credit-card usage was starting to wear her down.

It wasn't until she let on that she was throwing Sean a big thirtieth birthday bash that he started treating her worth a damn. Although his conversations were short, his attempts at sex with her grew more and more persistent each day. Some nights it was as if her objections didn't matter to him, because he'd climb into bed butt-ass naked, lift up her nightgown, and place himself inside of her. Only because they were married, and only because it wasn't forceful, did she not claim that it was rape, but it sure as hell wasn't love. Most nights, she'd just lay there and let him shift her from one position to the next until he was satisfied. When he was done, she would pull her gown back down and force herself to fall asleep. Amber rationalized her submission by telling herself that his acts of passion must mean that he was sorry, and that by wanting to have sex with her, he was showing her that he still cared. Either way, she prayed that this storm would quickly pass so that life as she once knew it could start again.

Amber made her way up the stairs and into the bedroom she shared with Sean. She saw his reflection in the full-length mirror that rested in the corner of their room. The moment he noticed that she was in the room, he slowly approached her. Amber held her breath as he drew near.

"That what you wearing?" he asked while circling her.

"What, you don't like it?" she asked, ironing out her dress with her hands.

"Nah. I think you should wear the red one I like."

Amber forced a smile. "It's your birthday," she said, unzipping the back of her black Herve strapless dress. The dress fell to the floor leaving her in only her black La Perla thong and studded Jimmy Choo platforms.

"Bend over and place your hands on the bed." Sean's voice emulated that of an attacker, and Amber wasn't sure if he was being seductive or if he was acting out a scene from *Law and Order SVU*.

"Honey!" she responded playfully, "our guests will be here—"

Before she could finish her sentence, Sean had slipped out of his pants and underwear. He held his hard dick in his hand, and the look in his eyes confirmed just how serious he was about his request.

"Babe," she whispered, unsure of how she should feel. "I, umm . . ." Amber didn't know whether to be afraid or just to submit.

"Don't you think I deserve a birthday present?" Sean asked, gently pushing her down on the bed.

Amber sighed softly and waited, positioning herself for Sean to take her from behind. She wasn't prepared for the sharp pain when, without warning, he shoved his dick into her ass, then gripped her tightly by her waist as he began banging himself in and out of her.

Her moans were both from pleasure and pain. He knew she wasn't a fan of anal sex but insisted tonight be one of the nights she obliged him.

"Sean," she mumbled. "Sto . . . p." Her voice was pleading.

But instead of stopping, he leaned over, placed both hands tightly on her shoulders, and began pounding himself inside of her even harder.

She screamed and began crying softly, but it didn't seem to matter. It was clear to her that Sean had an objective that he was determined to accomplish.

"Fuck!" he said as he pulled his dick out of her ass, flipped her over, and forced her to her knees. "Suck it!"

"What? Sean, no, please," Amber begged turning her face away.

"Damn, Amber, you're gonna make me lose my hard-on. Come on, baby, hurry!" he pleaded, stroking himself.

Confused, Amber opened her mouth, allowing Sean to place himself inside her. She cried as she began sucking him off. Although she had pleased Sean orally plenty of times before, this felt forced and degrading. He moaned, stroking in and out as if her mouth were a pussy. Amber swallowed, and then nearly gagged as the taste of anal juices and semen slid down her throat. She closed her eyes and cried some more.

Within moments she felt his release in her mouth.

"Awwww, yeah, babe, that's *exactly* what Daddy needed," Sean said, continuing to stroke in and out.

Amber swallowed the gush of sticky residue that rested in her mouth while wiping the tears from her eyes.

He grabbed her by her waist and pulled her forward. Kneeling, he slipped her thong down, and then off. He opened her legs and kissed her softly on her pussy, then gently fingered the hairs away from the lips.

"What, you thought I was gonna let you pleasure me without me hooking you up?"

Amber searched his face for answers she couldn't find. She wasn't sure what this was, and to be honest, she didn't exactly know how to handle it. "Sean?" she managed to mutter. "What is this all about?"

Sean, however, didn't bother with words, and instead, did laps around her vagina with his tongue. He sucked and licked her just as hard as he'd just fucked her moments prior, until finally she completely gave in to him. As her body went limp from the oral pleasure, any thoughts of confusion she'd ever had about their reconciliation were erased. At the moment, she was completely convinced that only a man who truly loved her would please her like this. And just as Sean used his actions to speak louder than words, after tonight's party, Amber would be on a mission to do the same.

Amber beamed as she made her way down the stairwell to the front door. Gloria had beaten her to the punch, and she saw her in-laws as well as Eve and Chase coming through the door.

"Well, look at you," Eve raved as Amber made her way to them. "Girl, you know I've always loved that red dress. And you are certainly wearing the hell out it."

The two exchanged kisses to the cheek and laughed as Amber greeted the others.

"I must admit, this is the best I've seen you look in a long time." her mother-in-law said, giving her a quick once-over. "It's about time, is all I'll say."

"You look great, Amber," Chase joined in. "And happy!"

"Why wouldn't she be happy? Hell, she doesn't work, has no real skills, and she gets to live this fabulous life compliments of my baby," Tami chimed in. "I'd say *happy* was an understatement. *Ecstatic* seems more appropriate, if you ask me."

"Good thing no one did," Eve responded, pulling Amber away. "Chase, would you mind getting us some drinks from the bar? I'll have my usual, Ty Ku Soju, please."

"Sure thing," Chase replied, relieved to get out of the cross fire.

Amber made sure that Chase was out of earshot before she spoke. She didn't want to give Chase the impression that when the shoe was on the other foot, Eve would ever speak ill of his family—not that she had to. Unlike Sean, Chase always stood up for Eve. His love for her was obvious to everyone who came in contact with them.

Amber knew Chase from USC but hadn't seen him after he'd been drafted and left school. Her thoughts drifted back to the time of her baby shower seven years earlier. It wasn't until her baby shower that Eve finally revealed who the man in her life was.

"I didn't want to steal your thunder," Amber remembered Eve saying when she showed up at her baby shower waving her copy of Sister2Sister magazine featuring Chase and Eve as the hottest new couple.

"Chase Landon! You're dating Chase Landon? What the hell happened to your no-dating-athletes' rule? Does your mother know? How long have you two been an item? And why are you just now telling me?" Amber asked in a rapid interrogation.

"Well, damn, don't ask me too many questions all at once," Eve joked.

"This isn't funny, Ev. I can't believe you didn't tell me."

"You sound mad." Eve sounded puzzled. "You're my best friend. I thought you of all people would be happy for me."

Amber sat on the bottom step of her then almost empty house. "It's just that it's Chase Landon."

"He's from your alma mater," Eve replied, searching Amber's face for the root of her concern. "Wait! What's this about?" Eve scooted close to Amber. "Is this about me dating an athlete, or is this about which athlete I'm dating? You got a problem with Chase?"

"Of course not!" Amber said, placing her hands on the swollen baby-filled belly. "I'm just concerned is all. You've always been so adamant about getting involved with an athlete. You practically ran me through the coals when I told you I was getting serious with Sean, and you didn't let up even after I told you I was pregnant and that we were getting married. But yet, you come in here waving an article in my face and expect me to what? Do cartwheels?"

"*Wow, I'm sorry. I didn't think about it like that. I guess I was pretty hard on you. But that's not why I chose not tell you about Chase. To be honest, it all just kinda happened so fast, that I . . .*" *Eve twirled her ponytail around her hand before twisting it into a bun.* "*As much as I resisted, Chase just won me over. It only took a week for me to know that it really didn't matter what he did. I'd fallen madly in love with who he was. I love him,*" *Eve whispered, wiping a tear from her eye.*

"*Ev . . . Chase . . .*" *Amber was hesitant. She'd never seen her best friend so genuinely happy.*

"*Yeah?*" *Eve beamed with excitement.*

"*About Chase . . . from what I knew about him from school, he seemed like a cool person.*"

"*Glad to hear it. For a minute there it sounded like you were going to tell me something bad about him. Girl, I couldn't take that.*"

"*Well, there is something. If you want to call it that!*"

"*What?*"

"*You know Sean and Chase weren't exactly friends in college.*"

"*Why?*"

"*I didn't get all the details.*"

"*Probably over some broad. You know how men get down,*" *she said with a grin.* "*I'm sure by now all's forgiven. Hell, it's not like they run in the same circles. Sean plays basketball, and Chase is football.*"

"*And they're both ballers. Athletes! You'll be surprised just how small this circle really is,*" *Amber warned.*

"*Damn, Amber, you make it sound like a fucking cult.*"

Amber laughed. "*Something like that. It's not just our men we've got to think about, it's their families—mothers, fathers, exes, kids, baby mamas, the whole nine. But don't worry, you've*

got me, and like always, we'll ride this train together." Amber
hugged Eve. "I'm happy for you. And no matter what, I'll
always be there."

Amber felt Eve shake her arm and realized she had drifted into
a daydream. She looked back at Sean's mother who was now making
her way up the stairs, probably en route to her bedroom to find Sean.

"Can you believe her?" Amber said, shaking her head.

"Girl, don't even worry about Mrs. Tami. Like you once told me,
there's a very fine line between mothers and their ball-playing sons,
so don't even bother with trying to fight that battle. Take it for what
it's worth and know that I got you," Eve said, trying to comfort her.
"Besides, you're too damn good to be stressing over his evil-ass mama
anyway."

"You're right. I don't know why I'm even tripping. We've never
gotten along, and to be honest, I'm really tired of trying. Nothing I do
seems to work anyway. I mean, look around. This house is perfection.
I've given them an extraordinary grandchild who I practically raise
alone because Sean's working most of the time. I threw this party for
their son. But do you think I get any credit for any of that? No!"

"So stop trying to impress her stuck-up ass." Eve rolled her eyes.
"Fuck her! And you know I try never to disrespect anyone's mother,
but in her case . . ." Eve began to laugh.

Amber smiled. "Ev, you so crazy."

"No, I'm just keeping it one hundred. Besides, she's the crazy one
not to appreciate you. After all the shit Sean's put you through, both
of them should be kissing your ass right about now."

"About that," Amber said slyly, "Sean and I . . . well, let's just say,
I think we're going to be okay."

"You fucked him?" Eve pried.

"Is it actually called fucking when you're married?"

"Hell, yeah! Now don't get me wrong. Chase and I make ourselves lots of love, however, there are those occasions where I don't

need nothing tender. Sometimes, I need him just to catch me completely off guard and fuck the shit out of me."

"Really?" Amber blushed.

"I'm talking pussy-sore-after-fucking kind of fucking," Eve laughed.

"Eve!" Amber exclaimed.

"Oh, for goodness' sake, Amber. You were always a bit prudish," Eve teased. "So let me guess you fucked—" She cleared her throat. "Excuse me. I meant . . . so, you gave your man some 'I forgive you' coochie?"

"It was weird, because at first I wasn't sure what was happening. But then, the way he handled me when it was my turn for pleasure . . . I don't know, but it made me feel as if things between us would be okay, you know?"

"Listen, you know me, and I don't judge anyone. I've been swayed a time or two over some good dick myself. And if you feel like you and Sean are on a road to recovery and you can forgive him, then you have my support."

Amber hugged Eve and smiled. "Thank you."

"Don't thank me. I wasn't the one who fucked you into forgiveness," Eve joked. "Come on and show me the rest of the decorations in the house before Mama Evil finds you and starts in on you again. I swear she's gonna make me kick her old ass."

Amber laughed hard as she led Eve toward the family room. Eve was truly like the sister she never had. It was moments like this that she knew no matter what hand life dealt her, with Eve by her side, there wasn't anything that she couldn't conquer or endure.

"You ready to get your party on?" Eve asked, taking Amber by the hand.

Amber squeezed Eve's hand tightly. "Absolutely!"

13

A Picture Is Worth a Thousand Words

"*The* three of them, they played all day. They kicked and passed the ball. Once Little T had learned to share, football was fun for all," Callie quoted as she read the last page of her son's favorite children's book, *Little T Learns to Share.*

"Mommy, Mommy, read it one more time, pleeeeeeease!" begged her five-year-old son, Dominic.

Callie kissed Dominic on the forehead. "Not tonight, sweetheart. But maybe tomorrow, okay?"

"What about me, Mommy?" Donatello, her youngest, pleaded. "You'll read it to me too, right?"

"I'd never leave you out, Donnie, darling. But right now, I need you two boys to go to sleep." Callie lifted herself from their embraces and made her way out of Dominic's bed. She reached down to pick up Donatello and place him securely on the top bunk.

"Why does Drew-Drew get to stay up until nine? It's not fair," Dominic whined. "Dominic, when you turn seven, I'll move your bed time up to nine as well, but as long as you're five, you'll go to bed at eight o'clock just like Drew did when he was your age."

"I want to go bed at ten hundred o'clock," Donatello protested.

"Wow, that's really late!" Callie laughed as she made her way to the door of their bedroom. "Love you."

"Love you too, Mom!" they said in unison.

Callie closed the door, then walked across the hallway to her oldest son's room. Peeking her head in, she watched for a moment as Drew Jr. played soccer on his Xbox. Although he had his father's name, he looked more like her.

"Twenty more minutes on the game, then wash up for bed, okay?"

"But, Mom, I still have a whole hour before it's time for me to go to sleep."

"I realize that. Yet didn't we just discuss appropriate bedtime behaviors?"

"Yeah, yeah, I know . . . do something constructive like read a book before bed. But, Mom, *Oliver Twist* is so boring!" he complained.

"It's a classic! Now, *haga como su dicho,*" Callie instructed.

"*Sí, Mamá.*"

Callie blew him a kiss, then closed the door to his room. She stood in the hallway for a moment contemplating her next move. The cherry hardwood floor was cold to her freshly French manicured feet. Her heart pounded as she neared the door to her private meditation room. The last forty-eight hours had been a blur as she struggled with the decision she'd made.

She went inside the room making sure to lock the door behind her. An array of torn and scattered pictures of Carmen Garza covered the light lilac plush carpeted floor—a reminder of the fit of rage she was in just days before. Her stomach soured as she could still see the images of Carmen's and Drew's naked bodies entangled in passion in those hateful pictures. Hot tears showered her face as she thought about all the years she'd put into her marriage only for Drew to continue to take advantage of her in this way. Three kids, two teams, and four moves later, she still couldn't believe he had the audacity to cheat on her. She knew it wasn't about her looks, because just like most of the women he cheated with, Callie was a former beauty queen whose parents had pretty much promised her to Drew's family upon conception and the realization that they were, in fact, having a girl. Although arranged marriages weren't exactly common in Brazil, there was often an understood oath among families of status that if the gender and ages allowed, the families would try to make it happen. Callie and Drew were no exception.

She placed her hands on her belly and took a deep breath. Her eyes glanced toward the positive pregnancy test that lay tossed in the corner near her prayer chair. Although she tried to pray her negative, vengeful thoughts away, she knew that with her heart being broken like it was, her words were falling on deaf ears where God was concerned. Repentance would have to be her saving grace because her actions were about to be catastrophic.

She picked up the pregnancy test and placed her free hand over her mouth.

She remembered staring at it and the pictures of Carmen and Drew for hours before her emotions finally took over. Regardless of Eve's discovery of a loophole in her prenup with Drew, she knew that in order for him to change and stop cheating on her, she'd need to do something drastic, something she knew would definitely hurt him as much as he'd hurt her.

"My God, what have I done?" she whispered, burying her face in her hands. As her body slid to the floor, the guilt of her actions enveloped her. She couldn't believe she'd allowed things to go that far. The memory of what she'd done haunted her, even though she tried desperately to go on as if nothing had happened.

As she pulled herself off the floor and made her way to the door, she realized that even though only she and God knew what had actually transpired, eventually the truth would come out. She took another deep breath, then placed the pictures of Carmen and Drew, along with the pregnancy test, in the nearby desk drawer. Although she wasn't a fan of secrets, she knew that until she could sort through the details of just how she was going to tell Drew about her vengeful actions, this would be one secret that would definitely be well kept.

14

All's Well That Ends . . . Awful!

$\mathcal{E}ve$ and Chase worked their way around the room, talking and laughing with some of basketball's elite. Even though they hadn't been at the party long, Eve knew Chase had practice early the next morning due to playoffs, so their time at the party would definitely be limited.

Her eyes circled the room as she noticed all of the women from the association having a good time with their husbands. She smiled as she thought about the work the ladies had put into getting the association off the ground. Although it took effort for the women to relinquish control of things, such as bank statements, their husband's schedules, known mistresses, their own personal indiscretions, past affairs, private savings and stashes, and so on, once they saw how the information would work to their benefit, they were better able to trust Eve in supplying them with the proper insurance they'd need should their marriages fail.

She had her legal team of advisors combing through everyone's prenup looking for anything that could protect them in the event of a problem. She felt good about her progress and felt the bond between all of the ladies growing stronger and stronger with each passing week. They'd even started having weekly meetings just to check in and update each other on their goings-on. And for the first time in her life, Eve actually felt secure in her female friendships.

Even Jai, who had been the most resistant to the requests of the group, started coming around. Jai was adamant about her marriage being one of sincere trust and genuine love, and she didn't agree that the women needed to plot and plan ways for them to come out financially ahead in case of divorce. Eve reminded Jai that her confidence came from the security of knowing that she had initiated her own prenup, especially since the bulk of her and her husband Tony's wealth rested in her hands. Eve also convinced Jai that although her marriage seemed picture-perfect, The Wives Association was not just about plotting and protecting, but that it was also about sisterhood and support. And since Jai was an expert entrepreneur and was in the strongest position to support the association financially, she could really help the ladies perfect their investments by teaching them how to become financially independent, ensuring them the same level of confidence she had.

"Hey, now, there's the birthday boy," Jai said as Sean finally made his way to where the couples were.

"It's about damn time," Jackie joined in, taking a swig of her beer. "How in the hell are you going to show up to your own damn party an hour late? Where have you been?" she joked.

Eve smiled, placing her hand on Jackie's shoulder before removing the beer from her grasp.

"I know you didn't just take my goddamn beer away," Jackie snapped.

Eve ignored her question and shifted her attention to Sean. "Happy birthday, Sean! How does it feel to be the big 3-0?"

"To be honest, it feels pretty good. What's weird is being thought of as a vet now in the league."

"Well, no matter how grown you get, you'll always be my baby," Tami doted while kissing Sean on the cheek.

"Thanks, Ma," he replied with a smile. "Y'all having a good time?"

The group all chimed in with praises for the exceptional food and décor.

"I can't take any credit for this. All this is compliments of my lovely wife, Amber."

"Well, Amber, you did a great job. The place looks great," Ray said, taking a handful of rosemary chicken wings from a passing server.

Sean slipped his arm around Amber's waist and kissed her on the cheek. "That's my girl," he said, smiling before kissing her again.

Eve made note of the time and wondered where Callie and Drew were. All the other couples had long since arrived, and Eve was beginning to wonder about her friend. As the couples continued in their small talk, Eve excused herself for a moment to check around the house with hopes that she'd just missed Callie and Drew in the crowd. When she didn't see them, she returned to where Chase was standing.

"You okay, babe?" Chase asked, noticing the look of concern on Eve's face.

"Yeah, just wondering where Callie and Drew are is all."

"Who knows. Maybe one of the kids got sick. I mean, with three kids, they definitely have their hands full," Chase offered as an excuse.

Eve nodded her head. Chase had a point. She was so busy thinking about the incident with Carmen that she hadn't even thought about Callie's children.

"Fellas, join me for a drink, would you?" Sean insisted as he led a group of men to his man cave.

"You mind?" Chase whispered to Eve.

"I was just about to ask you the same thing. I know how you feel about Sean."

"I ain't trippin'. Besides, that was college. I'm not the kind of dude that holds a grudge. That's some bitch shit. No offense."

"So, you're calling me a bitch?" Eve asked slyly.

"Babe, no, I—" Chase tried to explain.

"I'm kidding, Chase. I know what you meant. I'm just glad you're being such a good sport about this."

"Hey, what a man won't do for a game of pool and a sixty-dollar cigar."

Eve kissed Chase on the cheek, then watched as he followed the other men down the hallway. She waited until they had disappeared before turning to the other ladies.

"Has anyone heard from Callie?" Eve asked.

They all shook their heads no.

"She's probably somewhere trying to keep tabs on that cheating-ass husband of hers," Jackie responded. "You know word on the street is that Drew was the one getting it in with ole' girl!"

"Who?" Jai asked, puzzled by the accusation.

"That damned Tresses model that got attacked not long ago," Jackie reminded the ladies. "You know I was the one who broke that story. Callie's ass better be glad we're cool and that she's a part of this association or else I would have let that shit leak. Because that little tidbit of information would have taken my exclusive from good to fucking-award-winning."

Eve gave Amber a hard look. She didn't realize that Jackie had, in fact, broken the story on Carmen days ago, and now she wondered why Jackie didn't confide what she knew about the situation to the association.

"You mean to tell me you knew about Drew and Carmen and didn't tell us?"

"Are you fucking kidding me? Association or not, the story hadn't broken, which means I couldn't say anything to anyone. I can't reveal my sources, and you know that."

"That story ran almost a week ago. You could've told us about Drew so that we could've warned Callie."

"Warn her? Callie fucking knew Drew was cheating on her. Hell, she told us that shit, remember?"

"You don't think Callie had something to do with Carmen's attack, do you?" Jai asked.

"That's ridiculous. Callie wouldn't hurt a fly," Amber said.

"Shiiiiiiiit, it's those quiet ones you gotta watch. Besides, as fine as Drew's ass is, I'd fuck a bitch up too if I found out he was sleeping around with some random-ass hair model," Jackie said.

"You see, this is exactly how rumors get started. Callie is one of us, so let's not stir up any gossip about one of our own. It's about facts and factors, ladies, and from where I'm standing, all of this chitchat is neither."

"Well, I don't know about the rest of you, but I do know that when the bitch your man is fucking suddenly gets attacked and you don't answer your phone for a week, the FACT of the matter is you look GUILTY as hell," Jackie claimed.

Everyone except Eve laughed. She had noticed a familiar face walking through the door and wasn't happy about it. Her disapproving expression must have been obvious as Eve noticed the other ladies looking in the same direction. She knew from the tears welling up in Amber's eyes that she could now see what Eve had.

"Oh, no, the fuck she didn't," Jackie said, placing her newly copped beer down.

The ladies stood frozen as they watched Sa'Myra charge through the door like she owned the place.

"What is *she* doing here?" Jai asked, shocked that Sa'Myra had the audacity to show up at Amber and Sean's house. "And how did she get through security? You *did* take her off your frequent visitors' list, didn't you?"

Eve watched as Amber's face went from chocolate to ghostly white. "Amber, you did take her name off the list?"

Amber shook her head no.

"Fuck it, let's go! I'll beat this ballsy bitch's ass for you," Jackie said while taking a long, deep swig of her beer.

"You can't fight her here," Eve protested.

"The hell you say!"

"I can't breathe," Amber wheezed.

"You don't need air in order to beat that ass. Besides, girl, I got you," Jackie insisted.

"Amber, calm down. I'm sure there's a logical explanation as to why she's here." Eve struggled to believe her own words.

"I swear, hoes be winning!" Jackie shouted loudly.

"Jai, watch her!" Eve said, referring to Jackie. "And whatever you do, don't let Jackie get anywhere near Sa'Myra. I'm gonna handle this."

Eve darted after Amber who was now in full pursuit of Sa'Myra. When she finally caught up to her, it was too late. Sa'Myra had already begun to cause a scene.

"Sean!" Sa'Myra yelled across the room.

"What the hell are you doing?" Amber asked.

"My attorney just notified me that Sean still hasn't taken the paternity test. If he thinks he's getting out of providing support to me while I carry his baby, he's got another think coming."

"I already told you we'd take care of it. But that doesn't give you the right to come here, especially tonight," Amber said, trying to diffuse the situation.

Eve positioned herself between Amber and Sa'Myra. Although Sa'Myra wasn't showing any signs of pregnancy, she wanted to make sure there was no room for Amber to slap the baby out of her belly.

"Do you think I give a damn about this little party of yours?" Sa'Myra placed her hand on her hip and looked around at the small crowd that had begun to settle around them. "Ooooooh, I get it. You think things are over between me and Sean."

Amber stood her ground. "They are!"

"Really? Then how do you think I knew about tonight?" Sa'Myra snapped. "Oh, hey, baby!"

Eve turned her attention to Sean who had just entered the room.

"Baby?" Amber questioned. "Sean?" Her eyes filled with tears.

"You heard me. What? You thought we'd stopped fucking because you found out about me? No, boo-boo! Your precious husband's been banging my back out ever since. Matter of fact, I was just with him last night. Tell her, Sean."

"Sean, baby, now you know Mama don't like no mess. What the hell is going on here?" Tami asked emerging from the stairwell.

"Amber, come on, let's go." Eve grabbed Amber's hand and tried to pull her away.

Amber resisted and instead directed her full attention toward Sean and repeated her question. "Sean?"

"Amber, I didn't—"

But before he could finish his sentence, Eve stopped him. "Sean, don't do this here and for damn sure, not now!" She turned back around to face Amber. "Amber, honey, go upstairs and pack a bag. You're coming home with me and Chase tonight." Eve watched as Amber immediately did what she said.

"Who the fuck are you?" Sa'Myra asked Eve.

Without saying a word, Eve turned quickly around, allowing her hand to personally introduce itself to Sa'Myra's face.

"Oooooh, shit!" Jackie shouted from crowd.

"You got two seconds to get the fuck out of here," Eve said, pointing her finger in Sa'Myra's face.

Sa'Myra screamed as she clutched the side of her cheek with her hand. "You crazy bitch! I can't believe you just slapped me. Sean! Aren't you going to do something?"

Eve watched as Sean stood still. Chase and Ray immediately escorted Sa'Myra out of the house.

"Eve, let me explain," Sean pleaded.

"No! There's nothing to explain, Sean. First you cheat on her and get that little skank pregnant. Second, you try to flip this entire situation on Amber as if it were all her fault. Then, to add insult to injury, you're still sleeping with this bitch behind Amber's back while she's busting her ass to throw you this fucking party."

"Now, you wait a minute," Tami chimed in. "My son has been nothing but good to Amber."

"No, ma'am, your son is a fucking asshole. And I'm convinced that's all thanks to you." Eve made eye contact with Jackie and Jai who were now standing just a few feet away. "Jackie, hand me my purse, and Jai, would you go upstairs and help Amber gather her things?"

The two ladies moved quickly as Eve took account of the room. All that could be heard were gasps and whispered remarks. She cleared her throat as she took her purse and coat away from Jackie. "So sorry you all had to witness that. Guess it's clear to everyone that Sean and Amber have several things to work out. Thank you all for coming out tonight, but this party is officially over."

Just as Sean reached out to Eve, she snatched her arm away. "Don't you dare touch me!" she protested. "Chase, get the car. We're leaving."

Chase walked back out of the house as quickly as he'd walked in. Eve stood at the bottom of the stairs waiting for Amber. Even though it'd only been a few minutes, to Eve, it seemed as though it was taking Amber forever. When she finally arrived at the top of the stairs with her bag, Eve met her halfway.

"Chase is waiting for us downstairs." Eve took Amber's bag from her hand. "Don't worry, I took care of that bitch for you."

"Where's Sean?" Amber asked.

"Who gives a fuck!"

"Do you want me to get him before you leave?" Jai asked.

"Jai! Hell, no." Eve rolled her eyes as she dragged Amber through the crowd of people that had just begun to make their way out of the house. "We're out of here, period, point-blank!"

Eve shut down the slew of people that tried to say something to Amber. Her only agenda was getting her out of that house safe and sound. Just as Amber and Eve made it to the door, Sean reached for Amber's arm.

"Amber, please," Sean pleaded.

"Please *what*?" Eve snapped.

"Eve, it's okay," Amber replied. "Sean, I really don't have anything to say and quite frankly, I don't want to hear anything you have to say right now."

"There's got to be something I can do."

"No, Sean, there isn't."

Eve placed her hand on Amber's back and ushered her out. She stared Sean up and down as she made her way through the door. She didn't know what was worse—the fact that he allowed Amber to throw him this elaborate party or the fact that all the while, he was still cheating on her with that gold-digging whore Sa'Myra.

"Eve, there's got to be something you can do to help me," Sean begged. "The thing with Sa'Myra was a mistake."

Eve cut her eyes at Sean in sheer disgust. "You can't be serious."

"Eve, she'll listen to you. You're her best friend. Come on, Eve, it's my birthday."

Eve watched as Chase helped Amber into their car. Once she knew Amber was secure, she turned to face Sean. She stood face-to-face with him for a moment before speaking, then leaned in to make sure he could hear her. "You're right. It is your birthday, and you do deserve something special. So let me tell you what I'm gonna do for you."

Sean stood in anticipation with traces of hope beaming from his eyes.

"Come here," Eve signaled with her finger.

Sean leaned in close. "Thanks, Eve, I'll do any—"

Before Sean could finish his sentence, Eve kneed him in the groin. "Happy birthday, you bastard!" she said as she darted to the car.

Eve knew that her little stunt didn't help matters at all and would inevitably cause her best friend Amber further grief. But she didn't care. With The Wives Association finally in full swing, she'd make sure Amber was protected both emotionally and financially. And if Sean tried to make things hard for her, she'd make sure he'd get more than just a hard knee to the balls. Next time, Eve would make certain to nail his balls to the wall.

15

Not Our Business!

"*There* are fresh towels and soap in the bathroom. Feel free to help yourself to anything in the kitchen if you're hungry. Sandy said Olivia ate at the sitter's, but there's plenty of snacks, just in case. I'll make sure Sandy gets you and Olivia anything else you may need in the morning," Eve said as she stood in the doorway of the guest bedroom that Olivia had picked out to stay in for the night. Eve's five spare bedrooms were each decorated by color, and since Olivia's favorite color was pink, it was no surprise to Eve that she'd picked that one.

"Are you sure this room is okay? I mean, if you want us to, we can take the downstairs room. That way, we won't disturb you and Chase."

"Girl, don't worry about it. What's the point of having this big-ass house with all these rooms if I can't have my guests feel comfortable in any one of them? Besides, Olivia picked this pink room, so anything my godbaby wants, she can have." Eve blew a kiss to Olivia who had made herself comfortable on the pink and green queen-sized canopy bed.

"Mommy, this is the room I always pick when I get to spend the night with Auntie Eve. She says this room is just for me," Olivia cooed.

"Livie, why don't you be a big girl and go brush your teeth

for me? I'll be there in a minute to help you with your pj's, okay?" Amber scooted Olivia off the bed and waited until she was in the bathroom.

"Thanks for making the arrangements to have Olivia dropped off over here tonight. She doesn't know what's going on with me and Sean. So far, we've been able to keep all of this from her. I don't want her in the middle of this. I can't imagine what Sean might have done if he'd gotten his hands on her first." Amber pulled the covers back on the bed.

"Sean would never hurt Olivia, would he?" Eve questioned.

"No, nothing like that!" Amber removed the pillows from the bed. "The worst thing Sean would've done was keep her from me and use her as leverage to get what he wants from me. He can be so spiteful at times." Amber kicked off her shoes.

"Well, good thing she's here and safe. Let's talk more in the morning, okay?"

"Okay."

Eve closed the door behind herself as she walked across the hall to the master suite. She opened the door to the bedroom and found Chase sitting on the bed, peeling off his socks and shoes. Eve stood in the door frame for a moment and watched her husband. He wore a combination of exhaustion and frustration on his face as he stuffed his pin-striped socks into his chocolate-colored leather Prada loafers.

"Need some help?" Eve asked.

"Nah, I'm good," Chase replied dryly.

Eve stepped slowly out of her own silver-studded Manolos, releasing a sigh of relief as her heels found comfort on the plush beige carpet.

"Crazy night, right?" Eve said, as she moved in close to Chase and sat next to him on the bed.

"I know what you're trying to do, and I gotta be honest. I'm not interested." Chase rubbed his hands across his head.

"What are you talking about?"

"Really?" he cut his eyes to her.

"Chase, you saw what happened. What did you expect me to do?"

"Nothing! That's what I expected you to do. For once, why couldn't you just mind your own fucking business?" Chase rose from the bed and entered the bathroom.

"Amber is my best friend, Chase. You mean to tell me that if the shoe was on the other foot, you wouldn't have done the same thing?" Eve followed him closely.

"No, I wouldn't have. Men don't do that kind of shit, Eve. We don't walk into problems that don't belong to us, and we damn sure don't create them. Unless a fight is about to break out, we stay cool and stay the fuck out of other people's business." Chase removed layers of clothing starting with his jacket and working his way down to his pants.

"Well, I'm not a man, and clearly we handle things differently," Eve shot back. "What the fuck is the problem with me being loyal to my friends? Ever since I started my association, you've done nothing but complain. Either I'm spending too much time with Amber or I'm spending too much time with my coworkers. It's always something with you. What the hell is it? Are you jealous because I've actually taken the time to make some friends in L.A.?"

"That's classic, Eve! And you can try to spin this shit around, but we both know this isn't about me. This is about your fear of abandonment and your need to try to control everything and everybody. It's pathetic."

"So I'm pathetic now?" Eve began to tear up. "That's rich. So what? Because I care about the people in my life, I'm a control freak?"

"You don't get it, do you?" Chase threw up his hands. "How long have we been talking about starting a family, Eve, huh? We've been together almost six years, and no matter how I try to get you focused on our family, you're always too busy taking on new clients, or starting some new club, or volunteering for some new cause. Meanwhile, you haven't seen your mother in almost three years.

"You never put forth any real effort to connect with my family and, if that isn't enough, you clearly never had that conversation with your doctor to stop taking your pills. But you wonder what the fuck *my* problem is? Well, here's the short answer: it's *your* priorities!"

Eve withdrew from her arrogant stance and leaned against the basin. In the six years that they had been together and the five years they'd been married, he'd never spoken to her like that. For the first time in their relationship, Eve found herself at a loss for words.

"You don't consult me about anything. We're supposed to be a team, Ev. And what do you do, day in and day out? You not only call all the plays for this family, but you go out for every pass, solo. Did it even dawn on you, when you impulsively invited your girl and her kid to stay at our house indefinitely, that your husband is in the playoffs? No, you didn't, because that would've been too much like right. The most important time in my career, and what do you do? You bring drama into our house. Drama that I warned you about. Drama that I asked you not to get involved in." Chase turned on the shower and grabbed a towel before entering. "But do you listen? Hell, no!" Chase closed the glass shower door.

"I'm sorry!" Eve shouted out, hoping that Chase could hear her through the running water. She studied Chase's silhouette through the steamy glass door. He was right. She hadn't taken into consideration any of the things he'd mentioned. It hadn't dawned on her how neglectful and selfish she had been throughout the years. Although her relationship with his family was very civil, she never extended herself more than she needed to as it related to them. She never initiated visits with them, nor did she have them over to their house often. In her mind, since her relationship with Nadia was estranged, she didn't feel comfortable allowing herself to get close to his family. Her passion for various projects had always been her calling card for success. She never realized that it had also been the root of her problems with her husband, her in-laws, and her mother.

"Chase," Eve called out to him again, but he didn't respond. In one swift motion, she slipped out of her dress and made her way into the shower with him.

"Eve, seriously, I don't feel like—"

Ignoring him, she wrapped her arms around his waist, kissing him softly on his chest. "Hold me, please," she begged. "You're right. And I'm sorry."

Eve felt Chase's resistance but didn't give in. Instead, she held on to him tighter. "I want to."

"You want to what?" Chase sounded annoyed.

"Start a family." Eve looked into his eyes. "I'll stop, I promise. I'll stop meddling. I'll stop putting others before you, and I'll even stop"—water poured down her face but Eve continued—"taking the pill." She wiped the water from her eyes, waiting for Chase to respond.

Although his words never came, he did return her embrace, giving her a ray of hope that she'd be given another chance. As she stood in the shower, locked in his arms, she thanked God for her husband. He was and had always been the man of her dreams, and given the opportunity, she was now even more determined to reciprocate and make all of his dreams come true.

16

Runaway Wife

Eve was awakened by the sound of Chase's snoring. After their argument the night before, she was glad to see him sleeping so soundly. She smiled as she listened to the grizzly-bearlike snores ring from his mouth. With the Leopards advancing to the next level of the playoffs and being considered serious contenders for the National Bowl game, Eve knew his snores were usually an indication of his nerves. The idea of the two of them starting a family was a lot to digest, especially all at once. In addition, the fact that Eve had opened their home to Amber and Olivia, forcing Chase to be on his best behavior despite the fact that he didn't want them there had really begun to take a toll on him. Eve knew that as long as Amber needed to stay with them, she'd have to be on her p's and q's where Chase was concerned. Although she wasn't normally accustomed to being passive, she knew in order to keep the peace, she'd have to play her position and make sure Chase was straight in every possible way. If he said jump, she was more than prepared to become Michael-freaking-Jordan in order to keep him happy.

Eve gently rolled out of the bed, making sure that she didn't wake Chase. It took an hour of persuasive lovemaking to get him to agree finally to allow Amber and Olivia to stay with them. Her jaws hurt from all the dick-sucking convincing that was needed in order for him to say yes indefinitely. In addition to allowing him to use her body as his own personal pogo stick as she rode him frontward, then backward, until he was completely sexually satisfied, she also had to agree to officially stop taking her birth control pills so that the two of them could start on their own family immediately. Although she and Chase never had issues sexually, it was only on special occasions that she allowed him to just have his way with her. Eve liked being in control and took pride in giving out her sexual tricks and favors to Chase when she deemed them necessary. Last night was certainly one of those nights, and Chase took full advantage of playing on and with every inch of his personal playground.

As she readied herself for her six o'clock run, she thought about inviting Amber to come along with her. Eve threw on her workout clothes and running shoes, then made her way across their spacious bedroom, tiptoeing all the way to the door and shutting it behind her quietly.

Once in the hallway, she moved across the hall to the guest bed-room. It was during times like these that she regretted not going with her original floor plan where the master suite was on the first level instead of placing it upstairs with the other four bedrooms. Eve justi-fied her choice in floor plans on the notion that when she and Chase agreed to start their family, the baby's room wouldn't be so far away. It was for that reason alone that she insisted that all the bedrooms be on the same level, with the exception of a small guest room on the first floor which rested just off the kitchen.

Eve opened the door to the room Amber chose for her and Olivia to sleep in and found them cuddled comfortably in the bed together. Amber had the nanny drop Olivia off at Eve's house directly after the party with the plan of having Sandy, Eve's housekeeper, go over to their house later in the day and bring back some more of their belongings. Since the situation was so fresh, Amber wasn't sure how long she was actually going to stay with Eve, even though Eve knew that once she took care of Chase, Amber could stay as long as it took to reach a resolution.

Eve gently closed the door, opting not to wake her. The last thing she needed was for Olivia to wake up only to find her mother gone and her left in the house alone with Chase. Eve smiled to herself. *He'd flip the fuck out,* she thought as she made her way down the stairs to the kitchen. She reached in the refrigerator for a bottle of water that she tucked into her sports fanny pack that rested around her waist.

She chose to leave through the French doors next to the breakfast nook. Eve knew it would be a lot quieter than using the front door or exiting through the garage. She cleared the night alarm so that it would not announce her leaving, opened the side door, and slipped outside. Realizing she had left her keys upstairs, she considered going back into the house, but the thought of skulking back upstairs and down again was not appealing.

"Oh, well," she said as she closed the door behind her and began her morning stretches in the driveway.

Her routine two-mile run normally took less than an hour, but Eve had a lot on her mind, and she wanted to use this time alone to sort things out. She jogged at a slower gait, allowing herself to think. She hated not being on top of things. Wheeling and dealing and making shit happen was what she did, and she was good at it. But as she scrolled through her mental library, she couldn't remember the last time she had felt this uncomfortable about handling a situation. Maybe part of the problem was that it was not one situation, but several. Eve mentally scrolled through the issues she had on her plate. The highlights alone were overwhelming. There were the current situations with Amber and with Callie, and, of course, the whole idea of starting a family with Chase. Then there was her job, The Wives Association, and the other ladies in the group, not to mention the fact that she'd been so busy with her life that she hadn't taken any time out to check in on her mother and her store. For the first time in her life, Eve was beginning to question whether she had taken on too much.

With The Wives Association finally off the ground, and with Amber, who was supposed to be serving as co-chair, finding her marriage in ruins, Eve had been taking the bulk of the responsibility on all by herself. She thought about asking Jackie to help out, but she was hesitant because Jackie always seemed just a bit too eager to take over the association rather than just taking on a few new responsibilities. Jai, on the other hand, didn't seem remotely interested in taking on a leadership role. And she had made it very clear to all the ladies in the beginning that beyond the financial and business support, she was confident in the strength of her marriage and didn't see the need for the association, at least as it pertained to her life. She made it clear that it was only the strength of her friendship with each of the ladies and the extra incentive of an even tighter bond that kept her there at all. Her only commitment was to their friendship, and if the association provided comfort for the other ladies as it related to that, she was all in.

Eve pushed forward with a strong stride, making her way down the winding hill from her house, her heart pounding hard in her chest as she controlled the rhythm of her breath. The issue that gave her most concern was how to handle Sa'Myra.

Eve had taken it upon herself to have Sa'Myra checked out and immediately discovered that in terms of pregnancy scares and baby-daddy drama, she'd been down this road before. Eve learned that Sa'Myra had not only been pregnant before but that she'd also had two children by two different celebrities as well as two abortions by two others. Her MO hadn't changed a bit. With her, it was always the same story: she'd get hired on as the family chef and within months, she'd sink her claws into the arms of someone else's celebrity husband. Sa'Myra was a pro who didn't just prey off athletes. The only prerequisite she had was that the husband had to make seven figures or higher. He had to be rich, and he had to be married to his wife for at least seven years, preferably ten. Eve guessed that Sa'Myra was hip to the laws that allowed wives a certain entitlement to assets regardless of any prenup, ensuring her a hefty payday either way.

"Clever bitch," Eve said aloud as she picked up her pace.

So with one comedian, two actors, and one television producer already victims of her plan, Sa'Myra could officially add an athlete to her résumé. Eve discovered that Sa'Myra was getting $20,000 a month for the two kids she already had, and with Sean's new $60-million contract extension, she would have officially hit the gold-digging jackpot.

Eve wasn't overly concerned though, especially now that she knew Sa'Myra was so easily motivated by money. All she really had to do was figure out where to cast her line in order for Sa'Myra to take the bait.

Eve reached the bottom of the hill where she usually made a left turn to begin the circle back toward her house, but today, she decided to keep going. The run felt good, and she wasn't ready to end her solo therapy session. She ran for another fifteen minutes before deciding to head back.

She knew what she needed to do in order to feel like she was back in control, and as she trekked up the hill, breath heavy and legs burning, she was fueled with the motivation to do whatever was required.

Eve smiled as she neared her house. She glanced at her watch; it was almost 7:30. Although she'd been running for over an hour, she wasn't tired. In fact, she felt refreshed, rejuvenated, and ready to tackle everything on her plate. She cooled down by walking the last one hundred yards home, gathering her thoughts each step of the way.

As she made her way along the side of the house, Eve heard Chase and Amber conversing through the sliding door off the kitchen. She eavesdropped while taking off her shoes and adjusting herself before going in the house.

"This was never supposed to happen. If anyone were to ever find out that—"

"They won't, I promise," Chase replied.

"Then there's Olivia. I can't fathom putting her through this."

"We'll do whatever is necessary to keep her out of it," Chase said.

"I know," Amber said. "I want to make sure I never have to have that conversation. It'll kill her."

"Which is exactly why you can't let that happen. No matter what, Olivia should always be your first concern."

"I know. Whatever I do is always in the best interest of everyone involved."

Eve smiled. She knew she was wrong to be eavesdropping, but Chase had never been a big fan of Amber's, and the fact that the two of them were having a civil conversation, even if it was about her problem with Sa'Myra and Sean, was a good start.

Eve made her way to the French doors. From where she was standing she could see Amber leaning against the kitchen counter with her head down. Eve couldn't see Chase, but she saw his hand rise to push Amber's hair away from her face. *Such a softy!* Eve thought as she slid the door open and entered the kitchen. "Good morning, you two!"

Chase and Amber turned, obviously startled.

"Babe, you scared the shit out of me!" he said.

"Me too," Amber said, clutching her chest.

"Sorry," Eve replied, smiling widely. "I was actually enjoying the fact that the two of you were having a friendly conversation for a change." She sank into a nearby chair allowing her shoes to fall from her grasp.

"Conversation?" Chase asked.

"Yes, I could hear you from outside," Eve said.

"Mommy!"

"Olivia's awake," Amber said and hurried from the kitchen.

Eve walked to the counter and selected a hazelnut coffee. She placed it in the coffeemaker and turned to Chase who kissed her on the cheek.

"I know this isn't the best time for Amber, but if this whole mess somehow brings the two of you closer, it would really make me happy. She's a great person, and if you give her a chance, I'm sure you'll see that she's really a sweetheart."

"Anything for you, Evie."

"Thank you, baby." Eve kissed him softly on his thick, full lips.

Chase pinched Eve's chin as he stared into her eyes. "If being nice to Amber gets me all this goodness and puts this smile on your face, I'll make it a point to be more cordial."

"I love you, babe. And about last night . . ."

Chase cupped Eve's ass with both hands. "Awwww, you want some more, don't you? I knew it," he teased.

"Ummmmm, no, not what I was going to say at all. What I was going to say was that I heard you." Eve smiled. "And I promise, the next time something like this happens, I'll check with you before involving you in other people's drama." Eve placed her arms around his waist. "Thank you though for being so supportive."

"It's not like you gave me much choice. You've got her and her daughter staying here with us. Trust me, it would be a lot easier to get along and be supportive if she wasn't under our roof. Besides, I don't know how many more nights of quiet fucking I can take. You know big daddy likes to make you scream."

"Oh, you wanna hear me scream?" Eve playfully rubbed her breast across Chase's chest. "I thought last night was kind of hot! I mean, every time I felt the need to scream, I put your dick in my mouth." Then she put her hand down Chase's sweats. "But if you need to hear me scream . . ."

"You better stop playing," Chase laughed as he backed away from Eve's grasp. "Besides, unless you want your girl and her daughter walking in on me fucking you on top of this counter, you might want to keep your hands to yourself."

"Whatever," Eve said, playfully smacking him on the back of the head as he left the room.

Eve poured her coffee into a cup and headed upstairs to check on Amber. Although it had just been a few days and wasn't an ideal situation for anyone, she was grateful for the opportunity to help. For Eve, the issue was never about who and how she was going to help out a friend, it was more about finding and creating a healthy balance that didn't allow her the opportunity to make the issues of others a problem for herself.

17

Don't Make Me Come Over There!

Eve shredded a stack of papers that rested on the desk in her office while talking to Jackie on the phone. The two of them had fallen behind on their plans for the Leopards' team road trip to San Francisco for the playoff game. Paula, the Leopards Wives' Association president, had suggested renting a party RV and inviting all the wives, girlfriends, and baby mamas to tag along. Eve shot down the notion that she'd even consider being a part of such a tacky ordeal, yet for the sake of unity, she offered to cover the expense of the rental as a gesture of good faith. Jackie was also forbidden to ride in the RV as Eve insisted her loyalty be to her and their own association.

"I still don't see what the big idea is, Eve. Hell, just because we've got our own shit doesn't mean we shouldn't participate in the team's events. Besides, I've been on one of those party buses and, if I remember correctly, I had myself a ball."

"Drunk does not translate into fun."

"Shiiiiiiit, I don't know who you've been partying with, but every time I'm lit or even a little buzzed, oh, best believe some serious fun is being had," Jackie laughed to herself.

"Well, it's too late now; I've already told them we'd meet them there. Plus, I bought our tickets and they're nonrefundable."

"Of course they are," Jackie mocked. "Fine, whatever. I'll meet you at the airport. You just better make sure I get my beer."

"Promise," Eve assured her.

"And I better have fun. None of this work or Wives' Association agenda shit either. I'm already gonna be on edge, hoping the Leopards win."

"All right, all right," Eve whined. "Hey, Jackie?"

"Yeah?"

Eve turned off the shredder and leaned back against her custom-made plum leather chair. "I need a favor. And I need you to promise me you'll just say yes."

"Eve, what the hell is going on?" Jackie scoffed. "You're always pulling this crap with me. First, you needed me to cozy up to Paula in order to secure you a copy of her personal files pertaining to the Leopards Wives' Association, so you could have a blueprint for our own group—which, by the way, cost me five unbearable nights of dinner at that bitch's house. And you know Paula's ass can't cook to save her life."

"She should've hired Sa'Myra's skanky ass for herself instead of pawning her little gold-digging friend off on Amber."

"You know Paula's too damn cheap for that. And ever since Donté got moved to second-string, that ho is watching every dime coming in and going out of that house. You know she pulled her babies out of St. Joseph's Academy and put their little asses in public school."

"No, she didn't!" Eve clowned.

"Yes, the hell she did. Damn shame too. You and I both know those ain't the cutest kids in the bunch. They needed that Ivy-League education because ugly and dumb ain't a good combination."

Eve burst into laughter. "Jackie, don't talk about the babies." Eve couldn't contain herself. "That's just wrong. You know the rules: babies and old people are off-limits."

"Maybe to you, but hell, I call 'em like I see 'em. And since we've both seen them gremlin-looking kids, you know I ain't lying," Jackie laughed. "Anyway, back to you. You're just about out of favors with me. Hell, it's about time I started cashing in on a few favors of my own."

"Jackie, you know I got you. And didn't I just hook you up with that new Hermes wallet to go with the bag Ray bought you for Christmas?"

"Bitch, please. You and I both know good and damn well that you and Chase got invited to have lunch with Johannes Burges, the owner of Hermes, after you donated all that money to that Parkinson Research Project he chairs. I know for a fact that he gave you a bag full of goodies as his way of saying thank you. My guess is that that wallet was one of the things in the bag."

Eve snickered. "And I used it as my way of saying thank you to you! Come on, Jackie, I need your help."

"What is it this time?" Jackie surrendered.

"It's Callie. I'm really starting to worry about her. It's been almost three weeks, and no one has heard from her or Drew since Carmen's attack. I know you broke the story. And I know you know Carmen and Drew were having an affair. Can you tell me anything about the attack that's not being reported? Do they suspect anyone? Was the attacker male or female?"

"Eve, I can do a lot of things, but when it comes to violating the integrity of my job, I have to draw the line. Listen, I'm concerned about Callie too. And yeah, word is floating around that Carmen and Drew were having an affair, but until there is more evidence to support that and Carmen cooperates with the police to make an official statement about the attack, it's all speculation. Other than that, there's not much more I can tell you. What I will say is this: if, and I do mean *if,* Callie had something to do with this, it would be in her best interest to surface soon." Jackie sounded sincere. "Now, I know you're very resourceful. And if I were you and I were wise, I'd use whatever tools necessary to get in touch with Callie and have her ass make some kind of statement, quick."

"I hear you. Thanks, Jackie," Eve sulked.

"Listen, I've got to go. Ray took the girls to the movies, and I've got a few more things to wrap up before they get back. I'll see you Sunday at the game, okay?"

"Yeah, sure."

Eve hung up the phone only to pick it up again. She scrolled through her cell phone until she came to Callie's number, then dialed it from her landline. Unlike before, when the phone would ring a couple of time before going to her machine, this time it went straight to her voice mail. Eve listened to Callie's thick Brazilian accent on her message. At the beep, she decided to leave her own.

"Callie, it's Eve again. I'm worried. I've left you countless messages, and you haven't returned any of my calls. I've seen the news, and I can't help but wonder if you . . ." Eve paused before finishing her sentence. "No matter what's happened, I've got your back, okay? Don't make me come over there!" Eve threatened jokingly. "But seriously, call me."

Eve placed the receiver back on the base and pressed her head firmly against the headrest of the chair. She pulled her Louis Vuitton day planner out of the desk drawer and flipped to the page marked emergency contacts. She scrolled her finger down the list until she got to the name Eugene Frankel. Eugene had been the investigator that she'd been working with at one point to help her find out who her father was. She hadn't spoken to him in months but knew that now was as good a time as any to play catch-up. Eugene had made wonderful strides in narrowing down who Eve's father could be based on her DNA, birth records, and approximate date of her mother's affair, so Eve hoped he could be equally as successful in helping her with Callie.

Even though Eve had just promised Chase she would stay out of other people's business, until she knew Callie was safe that would just have to be a promise she'd have to break . . . at least for now.

18

Anonymous Caller

Jackie checked the time on her phone. She still had a couple of hours before Ray and the girls would be home and knew exactly how she wanted to spend her spare time. She pulled off her plush leopard bathrobe, exposing her naked, curvy, Beyoncé-like frame. She studied herself in the mirror, admiring her own reflection. Inch by inch, she examined herself starting from her head and working her way down to her toes. Although she'd had a little work done reshaping her ass after her second daughter, Jackie prided herself on her natural and authentic African American beauty.

At thirty-six, Jackie could give the average twenty-five-year-old a run for her money. Her rich caramel skin was flawless, and her super short Halle Berry-inspired coif set her apart from the typical long-haired, light-skinned trophy wives that sat in the stands with her week in and week out. Although Jackie was cool with most of the wives on her husband's team, she hated the fact that most of them were only with their men for material gain.

Every Sunday she listened to countless conversations about the latest Louboutins, Louis Vuittons, laser surgery, or Lamborghinis, and wondered how in the hell had any of these women managed to perfect phoniness like they had. The main reason she gravitated to Eve like she had was because, outside of supporting causes with a real purpose, which she usually spearheaded, Eve never fraternized with the other wives.

Eve was a woman of substance, and Jackie appreciated that. They could talk about anything intelligently and actually push and inspire each other to do more where their families and communities were concerned. Jackie's competitive nature was always piqued by Eve's aggressive demeanor, which often got her into trouble. When she would push too hard, Eve never seemed to mind. In fact, in most cases, Eve seemed to welcome the challenge.

Jackie ran her hand across her flat stomach and positioned herself so that her breasts perked up. Her own nakedness was making her horny, and she knew just who to call to satisfy her appetite. She left her bathroom and walked across the spacious bedroom decorated in red and black until she reached the bed. Jackie pulled her cell phone out of her purse and smiled as she dialed the number. While the phone rang she allowed her body to spread across the newly purchased Ralph Lauren Collection red and black checkered comforter. The thousand-count cotton was cold against her skin, but she knew the sound of her lover's voice would quickly heat her up.

"Hey, you," Jackie flirted when she was greeted with a hello. "I have the house to myself for a couple of hours, and I was wondering if you wanted to come over?"

"Where's your husband?"

"He took the girls out."

"You know we're playing Russian roulette coming to each other's houses while our spouses are away. Do you ever worry about getting caught?"

"I try not to worry about my life, period. Besides, I told you that was the whole reason for me joining Eve's Wives' Association. Hell, with all the attention and information the group is drumming up on Ray, it practically makes it easy for me to do my own thang. And right now, I'm trying to do my thang with you," she toyed.

"I like the sound of that."

"That muthafucka' doesn't have a clue. He thinks after all these years I still only have eyes for him. Dumb ass! Honestly, I can't stand the touch of him anymore," Jackie scoffed.

"I wish it could just be me and you, without all the secrets and the lies."

"Well, it can't. You and I both know what that would do to our kids and our families. Besides, we agreed, this is the only way," Jackie insisted.

"I know. It is what it is."

"And what it is is a great fucking arrangement. So, are you coming over to fuck me, or are you going to sit over there and pout?" Jackie laughed. "My pussy is getting dry."

"We don't want that, now do we?"

"No, we don't," Jackie giggled. "Wait! I didn't even ask. Can you get away from the family for about an hour?"

"Yeah, I can get away, but I'ma need more than an hour with you."

Jackie placed her finger inside her vagina. "Trust me, baby, as wet as I am, this won't take long at all."

"Well, let's not waste time talking. I'm on my way."

"I can't wait," Jackie moaned with anticipation, sliding her finger in and out of her wet pussy. She closed her phone shut and rolled her eyes in delight at the pleasure she was giving herself. Needing more, she reached into her nightstand drawer and pulled out her vibrator.

"Atta boy, Jo Jo! Help mama get started," she teased as she turned the thick pink vibrator on and adjusted the speed to her favorite level. Jackie licked her lips, spread her legs wide, and arched her back before placing the vibrator inside her. She figured a little foreplay wouldn't hurt while she waited for her friend to arrive. And since her lover also lived in the plush hills of View Point, lived less than five minutes away, she knew her wait wouldn't be long at all.

19

What Does the Bitch Want?

Eve struggled to keep her balance as she maneuvered her way through the side garage door and into the house. True, it would have made more sense to make two trips to the car instead of trying to carry three bags of toys while shouldering her purse, but she was exhausted, and one trip was all she had in her.

"Shit!" she cursed as her purse slipped from her shoulder and ripped one of the bags from her hand. She bent down sideways and managed to retrieve them both, twisting the straps of her Chloe bag and the handles of the Toys 'R' Us bags tightly around her wrist.

It had been almost three weeks since Amber and Olivia had moved in, a fact that she was thrilled about, but one that had started to put a real strain on her marriage. So, rather than make any more uncomfortable trips to Amber's house whenever she or Olivia discovered that they needed something, Eve decided to just take it upon herself to go out and buy whatever was needed, and today, Olivia needed toys. Even though Eve was convinced that Olivia was playing the "guilty parent card to the max," but rather than suggest that to Amber, she decided that after breakfast she'd be on a mission to buy enough "kid shit" to keep Olivia happy for months.

Bracing the door with her foot, Eve stumbled into the house.

Determined not to stop until she had deposited the goodies in Olivia's presence, she headed down the hallway. She stopped at the bottom of the stairs to steady herself, then started the precarious ascent, teetering on her five-inch pumps. Once upstairs, Eve headed down the hall to the guest room where she found Amber and Olivia lying on the bed quietly watching television.

Amber looked up to see Eve standing in the doorway winded and slightly disheveled but victoriously holding three bags of toys and her purse.

"What in the world?" Amber chuckled as Eve slowly slid to the floor allowing the contents of her bags to spill onto the floor around her.

Eve removed her shoes and began massaging her feet. "Five-inch pumps and Toys 'R' Us are not a good combination," she declared.

Olivia had been glued to the television yet the sudden commotion got her attention. Seeing the toys, she bounded from the bed and rested herself next to Eve. "Auntie Eve, what is all this?" she shrieked with delight.

"It's toys and dolls and—" before Eve could complete her sentence Olivia grabbed the fallen Etch A Sketch.

"Is this for me?" Olivia asked eagerly.

"Yes," Eve said breathlessly. "All of it's for you."

Olivia's eyes were wide with excitement as she began turning the knobs on the sketch board.

"What do you say, Livie?" Amber reminded.

"Thank you, Auntie Evvvvvve." Olivia almost sang her gratitude as she leaned in and gave Eve a hug.

"You're welcome, Livie." Eve struggled to her feet leaving Olivia to explore the assortment of toys on the floor before her. Then she motioned for Amber to follow her, and she turned and headed down the hallway, tossing her shoes into her bedroom as she passed by.

"Livie, you stay here and check out all the nice toys Auntie Eve bought you and Mommy will be right back, okay?" Amber instructed as she followed Eve down the hall. "You really didn't have to do that, Eve," Amber insisted.

"Yes, I did. Trust me, I couldn't stand to see you make one more unnecessary trip to get Candy Land, her iPad, or another damn American Girl doll," Eve said heading down the stairs.

"I know it's been a little ridiculous, but Livie's having a hard time with this. She's used to her own room, her own bed, and her own toys," Amber apologized following close behind.

"No need to apologize. Besides, that's what godmother-honorary aunties are for, right? To be honest, Chase and I have been talking about starting a family of our own and having Olivia around is definitely good practice for our own child. I only hope that we can produce one as cute as Livie."

"Oh, please. You and Chase are both good looking, so you should have nothing to worry about."

Eve led them down the stairs and into the breakfast nook where they took a seat at the table across from each other.

"Have you talked to Sean?" Eve asked.

"Only to talk about Liv. He misses her, and she keeps asking when we can go home."

"Well, that's what I wanted to talk to you about. I've been thinking that maybe you should contact Sa'Myra and tell her you want to negotiate some kind of settlement. I've done some digging, and this is not the first time she's been in this position. From what I've gathered, she's been pregnant a few times before and has a couple of kids. Girl, she's a cold piece of work, that woman. I heard she even got paid $50,000 in hush money not to tell some producer's wife that he was cheating."

"How do you know this stuff?" Amber asked shaking her head in amazement.

"It doesn't matter how I know. Just consider it an added benefit to being a part of The Wives Association. Besides, the sooner we get that bitch Sa'Myra out of your life, the sooner you get to go home."

"Goodness!" Amber said in anguish as she held her head i hands. "How did we get into this mess?"

"Well, I would love to say that if you had listened to m never hired the bitch in the first place you wouldn't be in this But the truth is Sa'Myra has a history of positioning herself tc advantage of vulnerable rich people. Unfortunately, you and Se the profile perfectly."

"And we fell right into her trap," Amber sighed rubbing temples.

"Yeah! But I say it's about time that somebody dealt with hei accordingly. And that somebody is going to be you. Offer her mo but only if she agrees to have an abortion and not go public with t shit. See if she still threatens to have the baby once you dangle so Benjamins in her face." Eve leaned back in her seat. "I say call her blu

"But what if she's not bluffing?"

"Oh, believe me, she's bluffing, but she won't back down until sl hears the right price."

"So you think we should just pay her?"

"Trust me; in situations like this, money is almost always th answer. The only question is, what or how much does the bitch want.

"Sean's not going to like this."

"Sean doesn't even have to know. By the time he figures out what happened, you and Olivia will be back home, and this will all seem like a bad dream."

"More like a nightmare," Amber groaned.

"True, but the point I'm trying to make is that it will be over, and that bitch will be out of your lives forever," Eve stated profoundly.

"You know what? I'm in. Tell me what I have to do."

"Call her ass and set up a meeting."

"Cool. I'll do it first thing tomorrow," Amber said.

Eve grabbed the phone from the kitchen counter and quickly scribbled something on the pad next to the phone. "Call her now. Here's her number."

"Right now?" Amber quizzed.

"Yes, right now." Eve handed her the phone.

"Okay," Amber said picking up the piece of paper. She paused a moment, then looked at Eve. "Wait! Where the hell did you get her number from? Or is this just more perks from our esteemed association?"

"Bitch, just dial the damn number and quit with the third degree," Eve laughed.

Eve watched as Amber slowly dialed the number. She had to admit that it would have been a difficult phone call for her too if the shoe was on the other foot. When Eve suspected ringing, she motioned for Amber to put it on speaker.

"Hello?" Sa'Myra sounded as if she had been asleep.

"Sa'Myra, it's Amber Jackson."

"What do you want, Amber?" she snapped.

"I was hoping to talk to you about resolving our current situation."

"Anything you want to say to me you can say to my lawyer," Sa'Myra said coldly.

Amber glanced at Eve, not sure how to respond. With a circling of her finger Eve signaled Amber to continue.

"I was hoping that wouldn't be necessary," Amber replied, regretting the words the moment they escaped her mouth. She looked at Eve who confirmed her concern by rolling her eyes and shaking her head in disapproval.

"Necessary? Of course it's necessary. Unless you . . ." Sa'Myra paused. "Again, what do you want, Amber?"

"Okay, no more beating around the bush. How much is it going to cost for you to terminate this pregnancy and leave my family alone?" Amber was becoming angry.

"You're assuming that I *want* to terminate the pregnancy."

"No, but I am assuming that there is a price that would convince you to consider it."

"How much are you offering?"

"I have no idea what the price of fetal blackmail is, but I figured, based on your past experiences, you could come up with a number." Amber was hoping that this personal dig would not go unnoticed, and by the silence on the other end, she was pretty sure that she had touched a nerve.

Eve smiled and gave Amber a nod and thumbs-up.

Feeling that she had the upper hand, Amber continued. "By your silence, I'm going to assume that a negotiation and settlement are not impossible. So, I'd like to propose a meeting. Meet me, face-to-face, woman-to-woman."

"Alone!" Sa'Myra demanded. "'Cause frankly, I don't trust your ass."

"Well, I'd have to say the feeling is mutual . . . but fine," Amber confirmed. "You pick the time and place."

"Starbucks on Wilshire and Bixel at two o'clock tomorrow," she said without hesitation.

"Perfect!" Amber said. "Tomorrow, at two then."

"This better not be a setup either," Sa'Myra snapped. "And bring your checkbook," she shouted before hanging up.

Eve and Amber stared at the phone, and then looked up at each other.

"Did that bitch just hang up on me?" Amber asked.

"Yep," Eve laughed. "That's an old-school power move," she chuckled. "I gotta hand it to her, though, she's slick with her shit. But hell, it's not like you invited her to tea."

"I know, but she didn't have to hang up in my face," Amber said shaking her head. "The bitch has balls!"

"True, but you held your own. I was checking you out. You strapped on a pair yourself. They may have been tiny little balls, but hell, at least you had a pair," Eve laughed.

"Whatever!" Amber said laughing aloud.

"So, two o'clock tomorrow it is. You okay going by yourself?" Eve asked slapping the table.

"Honestly, I think I'll be okay. It's not like I'm scared or any-thing."

"Good, but just in case, take a box cutter," Eve suggested making a cutting gesture. "You can slice and dice that bitch if she gets out of line," she joked. "But real talk, she can forget about that checkbook shit. You let her know that whatever you two decide will be put in writing, and she won't get a damn dime until you have proof that she's actually gotten the abortion."

"You think it will be that simple?" Amber asked.

"We'll find out soon enough. Once we know what the bitch wants, I'll get the papers drawn up."

Amber took a deep breath. "Thanks, Eve."

"No need for thanks. I'm sure you'd do the same for me."

"I wouldn't have to," Amber laughed. "We know you woulda already handled the situation."

"What you mean is that it would have never happened. I told you not to hire that bitch. Next time you'll listen."

"There won't be a next time. My next chef will look like Emeril," she managed a laughed.

"After this, you shouldn't want another chef even if he looks like Colonel Sanders! Hell, I think now is as good a time as any to learn to cook."

"Right!" Amber agreed. "I don't know what I'd do without you, Eve."

"Yeah, yeah, whatever. Don't go getting all soft and teary eyed on me. I'm not in the mood for no *Color Purple* patty-cake shit. The sooner I get you and Livie out of my house and back at home, the sooner me and my man can start walking around the house naked again!"

"You don't fool me, Eve Landon. I know you. You can pretend to be a bad ass all you want, but there's a shitload of toys upstairs that says otherwise. In fact, let me get my ass upstairs and make sure my baby hasn't overdosed from toy joy!"

"Whatever, heffa. Just because I love you doesn't mean I'm not sick of you and that spoiled, rotten godchild of mine," Eve laughed, giving Amber a hug before she left the room.

Eve leaned back in her chair and listened as Amber's footsteps faded. Although she'd never admit it to Amber, she actually enjoyed having them stay at the house. L.A. was Chase's home, and Eve was actually starting to look forward to coming home to a family she and Chase would create.

She looked at her phone and thought about calling her mom. The strain on their relationship had gotten completely out of control. Eve knew her mother's position as it related to her marriage; however, she never thought it would go as far as a five-year grudge. Outside of the occasional holiday, Eve and Nadia barely spoke. And despite the numerous plane tickets she'd sent to her mother with the request of a visit, Nadia always sent them back with a note that said the same thing each time: "SAVE IT AND USE IT FOR YOURSELF WHEN HE BREAKS YOUR HEART. BECAUSE, TRUST ME . . . HE WILL."

Eve took a deep breath and placed her hands on her belly. Secretly, the thought of a baby gave her a lot of hope. Although her mother never expressed an interest in grandchildren, she hoped her getting pregnant would be the thing that changed her mother's mind and lured her back into her life.

Her thoughts were interrupted by the ringing of her cell phone. Eve answered it without looking to see who was calling her.

"Hello," she answered.

"Eve?"

"Callie!" Eve responded surprised. "I've been calling you for over two weeks. I've been over to the house, but no one's there. Where have you been? Better yet, where are you?"

"I don't have a lot of time to talk. I took the boys to my mom's house in Brazil. I'm at the airport now, headed back to the States. The police want to question me tomorrow, and Drew is in Mexico for a game. Do you think you can be with me when they do?"

"Absolutely! What time?"

"I don't know. But I'll call you when I get in. I've gotta go."

"Okay," Eve said ending the call.

Eve rose from the table and placed her iPhone gently down on the counter. She couldn't believe the turn of events that had transpired since the ladies had formed The Wives Association just a few months ago. Already there had been an issue of infidelity, and now with Callie, a possible felony charge lingered over their heads. Even though she knew there would be a need for the association, she never imagined that it would look like this. As the president of the organization, Eve knew that the bulk of the responsibility lay in her hands, and although she was more than willing to do whatever it took to protect her friends, she was beginning to question whether or not she would actually be able to do it.

20

Unusual Suspect!

"*Now* you're sure you're going to be all right meeting Sa'Myra alone?" Eve pressed Amber as she handed her the keys to her white Range Rover.

"I'm good. Stop worrying, I'll be fine. This isn't my first time at the rodeo, Eve. Remember, I was the one beating bitches up in defense of you when we were little. I can handle her," Amber responded assuredly.

"I know, I'm just not comfortable with you going alone," Eve confessed.

"It's just like you said. Sa'Myra is motivated by money, and right about now, she's looking at me like I'm her own personal bank. She's not about to mess up her big payday. Trust me!"

"You're right. I just can't stand this, though. The mere fact that we even have to deal with shit like this is beyond belief. I see why my mom had her strict no-athlete policy. This is enough to drive a person insane. The audacity of these hoes." Eve used her hand to fan her face. "It makes me hot with anger."

"What are you gonna do? It's the life we chose. The life of an athlete's wife! And once you have kids, there's really no turning back. You better think about that before you decide to get pregnant."

"I know. Unfortunately, Chase is past the thinking stage and has officially entered into the making stage."

"Really?" Amber asked surprised. "How do you feel about that?"

"I love him. And to be honest, I think Chase would make an amazing father. The fact that he doesn't have any kids is a freaking miracle, especially in this day and age. How many athletes do you know without kids? Hell, besides Chase, I don't know any, and I deal with all kinds of athletes on a daily basis. Even the new recruits have at least one stray out there. But Chase is different; he doesn't have any. He's rare, and that's special. The fact that he's been so patient with me makes me wanna give him a slew of babies. Can you imagine a bunch of Landon kids running around?"

"I can imagine the kids, but I can't imagine you as their mother," Amber teased.

"What?" Eve barked. "So what are you trying to say, I wouldn't be a good mother?"

"Girl, you never even played with dolls when were kids."

"Shut up! Me not playing with dolls has nothing to do with my potential parenting skills. Instead, it had everything to do with there being a lack of Latina dolls to choose from. I was just very particular about what my baby should look like, that's all. And blond hair and blue eyes wasn't it."

"Ummm-hmmm." Amber shook her head. "I better get out of here if I'm going to make it all the way to Wilshire on time. What time were you meeting up with Callie?"

Eve checked the time on her Cartier watch. "Shit, I need to be leaving right now myself. You've still got my spare phone, right?"

Amber waved it in the air. "Got it right here."

"Perfect. Call me the minute you're done," Eve instructed as she watched Amber get into the SUV.

She watched as Amber pulled out of the driveway before darting into the house to get the keys to her Bentley. Within a flash, Eve had emerged from the house with her keys, purse, and Chanel shades in tow, ready to take on whatever the day would bring.

She hopped into the car and pressed the automatic start button. Before pulling out of the garage, she sent Callie a text message indicating that she was on her way. She set her navigation to Callie's address and backed out of the garage. Callie and Drew lived in Brentwood, which was approximately half an hour's drive from her house, giving her plenty of time to make it there before three o'clock. Eve wasn't sure what she was walking into, but trusted that she would finally get all the answers to her questions.

She exited the gates of the Playa Vista Estates community anticipating her meeting with Callie. Callie had been sketchy with the details of exactly what she needed Eve to do, but as president of The Wives Association and one of Callie's best friends, no matter what it was, Eve knew that she was absolutely, positively going to do it.

"Thank you, Mrs. Peteers. We'll be in touch," Detective Rollins concluded. "By the way, Mrs. Landon, me and the fellas at the station will be rooting for your husband in the big game on Sunday. We're all huge Leopards fans down there in Orange County."

"Thank you, Detective. As a matter of fact . . ." Eve went into her purse and pulled out two tickets to Sunday's Leopards game. She handed them to the detective on his way out the door. "If you're not working on Sunday, perhaps you and your partner can make it to the game."

The detective beamed with excitement. "Wow, these are on the fifty-yard line! You always keep tickets like this on you?"

Eve smiled. "Actually, no. I'd just gotten those from my husband for another couple we know, but I can always get them some more. You should definitely come and enjoy yourself."

"I will. Thanks." The detective shook Eve's hand. "And hey, tell your friend to try not to worry. I'll personally see to it that we get to the bottom of this." He handed Eve his card. "I wouldn't normally say this, but it's not a bad idea for your friend to have an attorney present if we need to speak to her again. It has been my experience in dealing with celebrity types that it's just best to be prepared, ya know?"

"Thank you, Officer. I'll let her know." Eve turned and looked toward Callie who had already made her way back to the front door of her house. Not even a fifteen-hour flight from Rio de Janeiro could make her look bad. Only Callie could take some basic black sweats, a pair of classic brown Ugg boots, and a man's white dress shirt tied at the waist and make it look like a ripped-from-the-runway ensemble. Her naturally sun-kissed skin was a little more tanned than usual, but that was probably due to the fact that her mom's house rested on the beach in Rio, compliments of Drew's last contract.

Eve met Callie at the door and noticed something different about her. She reviewed her once again, trying hard to pin-point the change, when it struck her.

"Oh my God, you cut your hair!"

"Yeah," Callie replied subtly. "I actually did it just before I left. I was going to surprise you guys at the next meeting, but then all this happened and . . . you know." Callie ran her fingers through her neck-length locks.

"Damn, how many inches did you get cut off?"

"Almost fifteen. I donated it to Locks of Love, of course. It's kinda refreshing. It's definitely easier to manage, that's for sure. Drew hates it; he prefers long hair, which is probably why I cut it to begin with," Callie snickered. "It obviously didn't stop him from cheating, so what's the point?"

Eve walked closely behind Callie through the living room, down the hall, and into her bedroom. "Well, I like it. But hell, you could have shaved your head bald and still looked amazing. I swear you make me sick," Eve grinned.

"Excuse my room. I know it's a mess, but I left in a hurry and told Maria not to come to the house until I got back."

Eve surveyed the room and wasn't sure what Callie was talking about. With the exception of a few clothes tossed about near her opened suitcase, everything else in the room was perfectly intact. "Um, yeah, this place is a pigsty," Eve said sarcastically. "You gonna be okay?" she asked, taking a seat next to Callie on her bed.

"I really don't know. You heard them, Eve. They think I actually did this to that woman."

"It is a crazy coincidence though, don't you think?" Eve frowned.

"Wait a minute! Eve, you can't possibly believe I'm *guilty* of this, can you?" Callie probed.

"All I know is that one minute you're showing us pictures of Carmen and Drew fucking, then I'm advising you to beat that broad up and cut off her hair, and the next minute Carmen's on the damn news black, blue, and bald. Either that's one hell of a coincidence or . . ." Eve speculated.

"I'm guilty," Callie whispered.

"I didn't say that," Eve explained.

"No, but that's what you're thinking, isn't it?"

"Callie, I'm not gonna lie to you. The shit looks bad. But if you're telling me truthfully you did not do this, then I'll have no other choice but to believe you." Eve pursed her lips together. She watched as Callie walked over and kneeled down in front of her. She placed her hands on top of Eve's with tears in her eyes.

"I need you to believe me."

Eve squeezed Callie's hand tightly. "Okay, then," Eve sighed heavily.

"What do we do now?" Callie asked, hoping Eve had a solution.

Eve scratched her head and thought for a moment. "Well, I've certainly made a friend in that Detective Rollins, but I honestly don't know how much leverage those playoff tickets give us. We'll have to do something else, or, like he suggested, get you a lawyer." She rose to her feet and began pacing the floor. "What does Drew have to say about all of this?"

"Nothing yet! He doesn't know I'm being questioned. The funny thing is I'm not sure he even knows I know about Carmen. Or at least if he does, he hasn't let on that he knows," Callie confessed.

"Why did you take your boys to your mother's then? You mean to tell me he didn't say anything about that?"

"It's carnival in our country. The boys go every year. Guess you could say it's perfect timing, huh?"

"When are you going to let him know that you know?" Eve asked.

"He's back from Mexico tomorrow. I'll speak to him then. In the meantime, I've got a little money stashed away. I don't know if it's enough for what I'll need, but I'm sure it'll be enough to at least retain a lawyer until I can sort things out with Drew."

"Put together what you have, and I'll talk to the other ladies about pulling together the rest. That was the whole point in forming the association, remember? To have each other's back during times like these." Eve gave Callie a hug. "Don't worry, girl, we'll get you through this."

Callie rested in Eve's embrace. "Thanks, Eve."

"That's what we do." Eve patted her on the back. "Listen, I've gotta get going. Chase is expecting me back before he gets home. He'll shit bricks if he makes it home before me and is left alone with Amber and Olivia."

"What are they doing at your house?" Callie asked as she walked Eve out.

Eve dug around in her purse in search of her keys. "Girl, it's a long story. And quite frankly, I wouldn't feel right telling you about that drama right now anyway. You've got enough on your plate without worrying about Amber and her issues."

"I hear you." Callie forced a smile.

"You gonna be all right here tonight by yourself?" Eve asked, praying for a positive response.

"Yeah, I'll be fine. It's not often that I have the house to myself. I think the quiet will do me some good."

"Whew!" Eve said laughing. "Chile, I was hoping you said that.

If I brought one more person home with me, Chase would file for divorce and put my ass out for sure."

Callie laughed out loud. "We wouldn't want that now, would we? I'll be fine. I'll call you tomorrow."

Eve waved good-bye and got into her car. Her eyes followed Callie back into the house as she watched her through the rearview mirror. Once Callie was out of sight and secure in the house, Eve exhaled. The last few weeks had been exhausting, and she honestly didn't know how much more drama she could take. She promised herself that once things were situated with Callie and Amber, she and Chase were going on a long and much-needed vacation. As she felt the knots tighten in her shoulders, she knew it was time that she started putting herself first. Normally, it would be at Chase's suggestion, but this time, she didn't need anyone telling her anything. As soon as things settled down, she was going to go away . . . far, far away!

21

Come the F@*! Home!

"*And* Auntie Evie got me this new toy called an Etch A Sketch. It's really cool, Dad. I've already drawn a butterfly, a house, and even a car . . . well, it started out as a car, but I shook it and kinda messed it up, so I turned it into a ladybug instead. I can't wait to show it to you," Olivia doted.

"I'm glad you like all your new toys, princess," Sean replied.

"Daddy, can I ask you a question?"

"May you ask me a question," Sean corrected.

"Daddy!" Olivia whined.

"I'm sorry, princess. Yes, you may ask me anything."

"Why are we still here? What did you do to Mommy that makes her not want to come back home?"

"It's complicated, baby. But trust me, Daddy's doing everything he can to convince Mommy that he loves you guys very much, okay? It won't be long now, I promise."

"Did you send her some flowers? Girls really like flowers, Daddy," Olivia suggested.

"No, I hadn't tried flowers yet, princess. You think that would work?" he asked.

"Yeah, flowers are pretty. Mommy likes pretty things."

"What about you?" Sean asked. "Is there something pretty Daddy can buy you?"

"I want a new bike!" Olivia declared.

"Didn't you just get a bike for Christmas?"

"OMG, Daddy! That was last year. Besides, that bike is for babies. I'm seven. I need a big-girl bike now."

"Excuse me, big girl," Sean laughed. "I'll get you a new bike on one condition!"

"What?" Olivia asked eagerly.

"I want you to draw me one of your beautiful pictures so I can hang it up in my locker at work."

"You got it. I love you, Daddy!" Olivia said.

"I love you too, princess. I'll try to call you tomorrow. Put your mom on the phone for me, okay?" Sean requested.

"Mommmmmmy!" Olivia sang Amber's name as she handed her mother the phone.

"Go upstairs and play. I'll be up in a little bit." Amber held the phone to her chest and waited until Olivia was out of sight. She looked down at the notepad containing bullet points from her meeting with Sa'Myra and sighed.

"Sean," she said dryly.

"I haven't seen Olivia in over two weeks. How long do you plan on keeping my daughter hostage over there, Amber? This shit is getting ridiculous."

"I'm not trying to keep Olivia from you, Sean. I'm just not ready to come home, and I feel it's in Olivia's best interest if she stays here with me." Amber's tone was calm.

"I wish you would just tell me what it's going to take to get you to come home. I mean, damn, Amber, I've apologized. I've given you your space for two whole weeks, and you still haven't come home," Sean contended.

"Are you serious? This from a man who's cut off my credit cards, taken my phone, the keys to my car, and has practically forced me to stay with my best friend at her house with our daughter because he's too goddamn selfish to just leave us in the house alone for a minute?" Amber couldn't believe her own words. Under normal circumstances she would have never stood up to Sean like that, but after her meeting with Sa'Myra, and Eve finding that loophole in her prenup, she no longer cared about sparing his feelings.

"Who the fuck do you think you are talking to like that?" Sean snapped back. "What? Your little friends got you over there feeling like you're entitled? You think this is your own little personal waiting-to-exhale moment or some shit? Let me remind you of something, Amber. You don't have a whole lot of choices. If you leave me, you don't get shit but the little money I decide to give you. And if you think for one minute I'ma let you take Olivia from me, you got another think coming," Sean protested.

"Are you finished?" Amber asked.

"Whaaaat?"

"Are you finished? Because if you are, I'd like to remind you of a little something as well. Eve's lawyers found a loophole in our prenup. It's a little something called a morality cause."

"And? That doesn't mean shit. And it damn sure doesn't make it void just because I cheated."

"You're right; it doesn't protect me if you cheat. But it does entitle me to 30 percent of your net worth should you conceive a child with another woman during our marriage."

"What the fuck are you talking about?" Sean asked puzzled.

"I suggest you have your attorneys review the fine print. Now, don't quote me, because I don't have exact figures, but by my calculations, that puts any potential settlement right around close to twenty million dollars. I wouldn't exactly call that 'nothing,'" Amber said matter-of-factly.

"So, is that what this is? You ready to talk lawyers and dollars and cents?"

"No, actually, I'm not, Sean. I'm just tired of you bullying me. Saying stuff like I don't have choices when in fact I do! And right now,

I choose to stay here and take whatever time I need in order to figure out my next move."

"I'm not gonna wait forever," Sean swore.

"And I'm not asking you to. I'm just asking for you to give me a minute and let me sort some things out, okay?"

"I wish you would just come the fuck home!" he whispered.

Amber knew that was Sean's sick and twisted way of saying he missed her, and deep down inside, she missed him too. Before the situation with Sa'Myra, she and Sean had had a pretty good marriage. It had been her dream to marry an athlete and live the life of a trophy wife, and Sean had more than made it possible for all her dreams to come true. Even though she wasn't ready to forgive him, Amber had no intention of giving up on her marriage. "I'll have Olivia call you tomorrow," she responded.

Amber hung up the phone and focused her attention back on the dollar amount Sa'Myra had requested to make herself and her little "situation" disappear. As she studied the number on the yellow sheet of paper, she realized that she'd placed a higher value on restoring her marriage than Sean had placed on her getting out of it. Even if it meant manipulating her way into getting greater respect from Sean, in an effort to maintain the lifestyle she had become accustomed to, she would. Amber had worked too hard and sacrificed too much to throw it all away now. In order to come out on top, she was prepared to do whatever it took to maintain her position. And as she looked at the figure that rested on the sheet of paper in front of her, she realized that if going home and repairing her marriage was even an option, it was definitely going to come at a high price.

Eve exited her bedroom and almost collided with Olivia who came bounding down the hallway singing.

"Whoa, slow down," Eve said, laughing, as she wrapped her arms around Olivia. "What are you so excited about?"

"I just talked to my daddy, and he said if I draw him a pretty picture he's going to buy me a new bike!"

"A new bike? Wow, I guess that *is* exciting. Where's your mom, honey?"

"Downstairs. She's still talking to my daddy. I'm gonna go draw him a picture," Olivia announced proudly.

"Okay. Well, go ahead and draw your picture. I'm sure it will be very pretty."

"I know," Olivia said already heading for the bedroom. "My new bike is going to be pretty too!"

Eve laughed as she watched Olivia disappear into the bedroom. She loved having a child in the house and was excited at the thought of Chase and her getting started on having a child of their own. Even though it hadn't been long since she had stopped taking the pill, every time she and Chase made love, she secretly hoped that they were successful in their quest.

Eve rubbed her belly and made her way down the stairs. She laughed at her own silliness and the thought of actually desiring to be someone's mother. She walked into the kitchen whistling the tune "Rock-a-bye Baby," when she spotted Amber seated at the table, scribbling on a tablet and sipping a cup of tea. Eve made herself a cup of tea and joined Amber at the table.

"So, I hear you talked to Sean," Eve said.

"If you call what we did talking," Amber chuckled.

Eve glanced down at the tablet. "Two hundred fifty thousand dollars? What's that?" she asked curiously.

"That's the magic number to make Sa'Myra go away," Amber sighed as she scribbled over the number until it was no longer legible.

"I told you that bitch was motivated by money, but shit, I guess I underestimated her. I guess it was all about the Benjamins!"

"No shit! And after talking to Sean, I don't even know if I want to go back to his cheating ass. As far as I'm concerned right now, his ass is not worth two dollars and fifty cents, let alone two hundred and fifty thousand dollars."

"True, but it's not Sean you're paying for. You've got your dignity, your reputation, and most of all, your daughter to think about."

"That's still a lot of money!" Amber shook her head in disbelief.

"It is," Eve agreed.

"She rattled that number off as if she was just ordering another Frappuccino."

"Did you counter?"

"Yes, but it didn't do any good. She wouldn't budge. And no matter how much I tried to reason with her, she held her ground. Said she wouldn't even consider a lower figure. It was almost like her life depended on that exact dollar amount, and nothing I said even mattered." Amber cupped her forehead in her hand.

"That's what happens when everyone knows what you're worth. Sa'Myra knows Sean has that nice contract so she's going in for the kill. I mean, this chick ain't bounced a ball, set a pick, put up a shot, or nothing, but she's going all in like her ass signed the contract. These hoes should be agents the way they negotiate these deals."

"What gets me is she acted like she was doing me a fuckin' favor. It was all I could do to keep from slapping the shit out of her smug ass," Amber recalled.

"Well, I'm glad to see you made it through the meeting without making a scene. I can't have you and Callie both getting hemmed up by the police."

"Oh, we made it through all right. And to add insult to injury, the bitch walked out and left me hanging with the bill!"

"Are you fucking kidding me?" Eve laughed.

"Glad you find it funny," Amber said fighting back a smile.

"Bitch, you know that shit is funny."

"Whatever."

"So what's next?" Eve asked.

"I don't know. How in the hell am I going to come up with that kind of money without going to Sean?"

"Aren't you forgetting something?" Eve asked raising an eyebrow.

"What?" Amber replied confused.

"The association. We didn't spend all that time and effort for nothing."

"But two hundred and fifty thousand dollars is a lot of money. The ladies are going to flip."

"Hey, you heard our last financial report. The money is there. Two hundred and fifty thousand dollars is barely shopping money."

"So you're saying we should agree to her number?"

"She didn't give you much of a choice! You said so yourself. She wouldn't budge. The last thing you want is to give her time to think that she's got you by the tits. Listen, if you don't move on this quick, she could come back with an even bigger number. We want her to think she's just dealing with you. If she finds out the association's got your back, that bitch is going to the well!" Eve got up and poured herself another cup of tea. "So, how did you guys leave it?"

"She said call her when I was ready to talk details for an agreement."

"Then let's call her," Eve said confidently.

"Before we go to the association?" Amber asked.

"Why wait? Let's find out everything we're dealing with so that we can have our facts straight when we bring this to the group. Two hundred and fifty thousand dollars will be a good test for the association. Let's see what we're made of." Eve handed Amber the phone.

Amber pulled Sa'Myra's number from her purse and started dialing. She placed the phone on speaker and waited while it rang. Sa'Myra picked up on the second ring.

"Hello?"

"Sa'Myra, it's Amber."

"So I take it you're ready to settle?"

"I want to get the details so I can have an agreement drawn up."

"Let me guess, you've got me on speaker phone, don't you?" Sa'Myra asked sarcastically.

"Excuse me?" Amber quizzed.

"Don't play with me, Amber. Everybody knows you don't make a move without your girl Eve. So, just so we're all clear on our earlier conversation, here's the deal. I'm willing to have the abortion upon signature of your agreement to pay me the two hundred and fifty thousand dollars I asked for."

"So you're serious about that amount?" Amber asked.

"You heard me. Two hundred and fifty thousand. We all know what Sean makes. That's pennies to you and him. Two hundred and fifty thousand and that's my final offer."

"How do we even know its Sean's baby?" Amber asked defiantly.

"Do you *really* want to play that game? Trust me; two hundred and fifty thousand is a gift compared to eighteen years of child support, college tuition, medical bills . . . need I go on?" Sa'Myra barked.

Amber started to speak, but Eve placed a silencing hand on her wrist.

"You're right," Eve said to Sa' Myra. "That is pennies to them. I'll have the papers drawn up immediately and have them faxed over to you tonight."

"Good," Sa'Myra agreed. "Soon as I get the agreement, I'll schedule the appointment."

"Just like that, huh?" Eve scoffed. "All of this for a check?"

"This ain't personal, ladies. It's business. And speaking of business, make sure you come with a cashier's check. I don't trust you bitches."

"Whom do we make the check out to?" Amber asked.

"What do you mean to whom? Me, of course."

"Now who's playing games?" Eve laughed. "You don't trust us? Well, bitch, we don't trust you. We'll make the check payable to your attorney in care of you."

There was silence on the other end for almost ten seconds. "His name is Carl Thornton," Sa'Myra finally replied.

"Fine, we'll call you when we're ready," Eve said.

"Damn, Eve, if I didn't know any better, one would think I fucked your husband," Sa'Myra chuckled sarcastically.

"Boo, if you had fucked my husband I would have kicked your ass and we'd be talking about two hundred and fifty thousand *stitches*," Eve replied. "Don't get it twisted. The smart thing for you to do is sign this agreement, take your money, and shut the fuck up."

"Whatever. You'll get a text message with my fax number in a minute," Sa'Myra huffed.

"You do that," Eve sneered, slamming her phone down. "Stupid bitch! How dare she go there with me?" Eve stared at the phone, then focused her attention back on Amber.

"Now you see what I'm talking about?" Amber drummed her freshly manicured nails on the table. "Two hundred and fifty thousand dollars," she sighed in dismay.

A few seconds went by and a sly grin crept across Eve's face. "Yep, like she said, that's pennies to you and Sean." Eve jumped up from the table excited. "Follow me!"

"Eve, what's going on?" Amber asked, grabbing her pen and pad.

"Trust me, I just thought of something that will give little Miss Sa'Myra exactly what she's asking for."

22

Non F'N Factor!

Eve drove down Highland Boulevard in the heart of Hollywood bypassing the star-paved sidewalks, bold lights, and bright colors of the Chinese, Kodak, and El Capitan theaters before arriving at her destination at Musso and Frank twenty minutes early. After a long night of research, phone calls with lawyers, and drafting out Amber's settlement agreement with Sa'Myra, she had contemplated canceling her lunch with Jackie and Jai, but knew that the situation with Callie couldn't wait on her ability to get in a full eight hours of sleep. She pulled into valet and relinquished her keys to Eric, the valet superintendent.

"Good evening, Mrs. Landon."

"Good evening, Eric. How's the family?"

"Fine, ma'am. Thanks for asking. I'll park you up front as usual."

"Thanks, my dear."

Eve reflected on how she had been coming to Musso and Frank since her first visit to L.A., and in all those years, Eric had been the only attendant to valet her car. From the parking lot to the kitchen, the restaurant was famous for the professionalism and longevity of its staff. For decades, the operation had run like a well-oiled machine, boasting class and a rich history of celebrity clientele. Eve looked forward to coming to the restaurant just to see what actors or writers would be dining on any given day. She would watch and listen as heads would swivel back and forth and the hum of conversation would rise with the arrival of each notable celebrity. She smiled at the thought of how things had changed, because now heads turned and people whispered when she entered the room. She and Chase were regulars, and on most occasions, when they came to eat, they couldn't make it through the evening without being interrupted for pictures or autographs.

Eve entered the restaurant and was immediately escorted to the hostess station. As usual, the restaurant was packed with a variety of Hollywood's who's who.

As she sashayed through the aisles, she pretended not to notice the eyes that had now shifted in her direction. She had become social media royalty and knew that her public appearances were being monitored closely by the fashion police. Eve took pride in her ability to avoid fashion citations by making sure all her outfits got a stamp of approval by her stylist friend, Larry "Loves It" St. John. Larry had been assigned to dress Eve the first year she attended the Espy Awards with Chase, and they'd become instant friends. Although Eve wouldn't dare add Larry to her payroll, she made sure that whenever she did any major shopping, he was right by her side in exchange for a few special thank-you pieces, compliments of Chase's Black Card.

"Evening, Mrs. Landon. Your booth is ready. Follow me please."

Mario led the way as Eve followed him through the maze of white tablecloths, china place settings, and crystal stemware. The aromas of beef, chicken, and fish lazily wafted about as she passed tables, but she dared not look down for fear of losing her footing. Falling on her ass in Musso and Frank would be confetti for the paparazzi that took up residence there, so Eve stared straight-ahead, keeping her eyes glued to the back of Mario's red jacket, until they were finally in the aisle next to a row of booths.

As she slid into a booth Eve gave a cursory glance around the room to see if she recognized anyone. She spotted Harold Enberg, a former client, at a center table and made a mental note to call him next week.

"May I take your drink order, Madame?"

"Let's go with your best Pinot Grigio," Eve said.

The waiter left and returned immediately with the bottle of wine. He poured a taste test.

"Perfect," she said and held her glass to be filled.

Eve sipped her drink and continued to people watch. In addition to Al Pacino, she was pretty sure she spotted Johnny Depp at the bar talking with director Gore Verbinski.

She wondered how many deals and agreements were being hammered out throughout the room and how successful she'd be at negotiating her own deal later with Jackie and Jai.

Eve knew she was running the risk of asking the ladies to bend the association's rules with her request, but she also knew that any organization established for the purpose of protecting finances, reputations, and social welfare survived because of the side bars, private agreements, and back room negotiations. Hell, history had proven that even the president of the United States had secret agendas, and as far as Eve was concerned, this was no different. True, it was very early in its existence for The Wives Association to require such dealings, but desperate situations called for desperate measures, and the situation involving the assault on the Tresses model, and the possibility of Callie's involvement, was a ticking time bomb.

While Callie had not admitted it, Eve was sure that she was behind the beating. It was an issue that, if not handled quickly and properly, could bring down TWA before it had a chance to prove itself. It would have been nice, Eve thought, if their first issue could have been something as simple as the takedown of some groupie or the cover-up of some husband's DUI. Either of those problems could have been easily dealt with using only the resources of the inner circle, but breaking and entering and assault and battery were a whole different story.

Eve looked up just in time to see Jai making her way toward the table. She gave her a quick up and down, taking note of the classy green two-piece St. John pant set, the gold Tory Burch sandals, and matching Prada bag. As always, the bitch was impeccably dressed. Her long dark hair was pulled back from her face, a face that was clearly glowing from a recent facial.

Because of Jai's naturally rich olive complexion, it was always difficult for Eve to determine whether she wore any makeup. In conversation, Jai had mentioned using only tinted moisturizer on her skin because she didn't like her skin to feel cakey. Besides, she said, she relied on her signature individual lashes to serve as her dramatic facial accent and thought anything more would be too over the top.

It was true, Jai was a spoiled rich kid, but it could never be said that she did not know how to handle the title or the responsibility that came with it. She could be accused of being born into money, but it could never be said that she took it for granted. Parlaying finances was her forte. She knew how to get the most out of a dollar, and she had a keen eye for potential investment opportunities. It was a talent that made her valuable to the association, and hopefully, Eve thought, a talent that would prove to be resourceful in what she would be proposing today.

"Hey, diva," Eve said, rising to extend a cheek kiss and a hug.

"Hey, girl," Jai responded. She slid into the booth and quickly glanced around.

"Musso and Frank! Girl, I haven't been here in years. My parents used to bring me here whenever we were on vacation. I didn't think it was still open."

"I know," Eve said. "I still come here every few months just for the old-school celebrity feeling. Chase loves it here. You know how his ass loves attention."

Eve poured Jai a glass of wine.

"So who's joining us?" Jai asked.

"Just Jackie, and there she is now," Eve said as Jackie appeared in the doorway.

They watched as Jackie wove her way through tables. She looked good, dressed in skinny jeans that accented her long legs, boots, and an off-the-shoulder sweater. In Musso and Frank, Jackie was in her element, and Eve and Jai observed as she paused at several tables to exchange pleasantries. It took her nearly ten minutes to finally make her way to their table.

"Sorry, ladies," she said quickly hugging Eve, and then sliding into the booth next to Jai to repeat the gesture. "Duty calls. And some folks aren't ever satisfied with just a wink and a wave. Knowing me, I've probably done some kind of scandalous story on half the people in here, so you know I can't afford to pass up an opportunity to try to make amends for some of that shit."

"And good afternoon to you, too!" Eve said with a hint of sarcasm.

"I said sorry. Shit, give me a break." Jackie picked up the empty glass in front of her and poured herself a glass of wine. "Well, damn, y'all heffas coulda ordered a bitch a beer if you were going to drink up all the wine," Jackie joked.

"I did order you a beer . . . bitch." Eve stated.

"Don't start with me, Eve," Jackie laughed.

"Don't pay any attention to Eve," Jai said. "We know you're a hot item right now. Especially with that exclusive you just broke on the Carmen Garza story. Excellent piece, by the way. And you looked amazing."

"Girl, I try," Jackie replied shaking her head. "That shit was sad though. All that pretty hair gone!"

Eve couldn't believe her luck. She couldn't have planned a better segue.

"Speaking of Carmen Garza, you know at some point we're going to have to acknowledge that that's an issue for TWA to get involved in." Eve eyed Jackie and Jai trying to read their initial response to her comment.

"Why?" Jackie asked rolling her eyes.

"Because of Callie, that's why," Eve argued.

"Humph! Are you sure we need to get involved in that?" Jai asked. "She hasn't asked for our help. In fact, she hasn't even admitted to being involved."

"The way I see it, we need to be proactive and prepare for the worst," Eve said. "The association is new, and she probably hasn't even considered that we could be of any assistance."

"Well, I couldn't agree more because I still don't see how we as an association can help her anyway," Jackie said as she waved to someone across the room.

"Of course we can help. What are you talking about?"

"How?" Jai asked.

"Fuck 'how'! 'Why' is the question you should be asking." Jackie paused, then looked directly toward Eve. "Eve, please tell me you didn't bring my ass down here to get involved in this shit with Callie?"

Eve took a sip of her wine and cleared her throat. She was disappointed that her ulterior motive had been so quickly exposed. "Let's keep it one hundred. Callie's going to need our help. I saw her recently, and although she didn't admit it, I'm pretty sure she's either directly or indirectly involved in the attack on Carmen."

"What makes you so sure?" Jai asked.

"Well, I would appreciate it if we kept this among the three of us, but I'm pretty sure it was me that planted the idea in her head."

"Reeeeeally?" Jackie asked surprised. "How so?"

"A few days before the attack I had lunch with her and Amber, and she told us that she had proof that Drew was sleeping with Carmen Garza. She asked what I would do in her situation, and keeping it real, I said I'd beat the bitch's ass."

"That's it?" Jai asked. "Please, how many times in conversation has one of us suggested that a bitch needed her ass kicked? No one takes that shit literally."

"I would normally agree with you," Eve said. "But I also suggested that if she really wanted to get her point across, she should cut the bitch's hair off. Now I'm no psychic, but if Callie had nothing to do with it, the fact that Carmen's attacker cut her hair off has to be one hell of a coincidence."

"No shit!" Jackie said.

"What do you think, Jackie?" Eve asked.

"It's like I said. Professionally, I'm limited in the information I can discuss with you, and I'm not compromising on that. Now personally, I think if the bitch did do it, then hell, she's gonna have be held accountable for her actions. It's as simple as that." Jackie raised an eyebrow.

"I can't believe you're saying that," Eve said.

"Sorry, but that's my honest opinion," Jackie shrugged.

"Eve, exactly what were you expecting to accomplish with this meeting? It *is* a meeting, right?" Jai asked.

"I would prefer to call it a lunch where the topic of Callie and Carmen just happened to come up," Eve said motioning for the waiter to bring another bottle of wine.

"Well, if this is a lunch, I would like to order something," Jackie said picking up a menu. "But if it really is a meeting, then Eve, you're paying."

"Whatever, bitch," Eve said rolling her eyes. "But if I'm paying, I need to get my money's worth."

"Meaning what?" Jai asked following suit and picking up a menu.

"I asked the two of you here for two reasons. One, to get a feeling for what you thought about the Callie and Carmen situation."

"Hmmmmmmp," Jackie huffed.

"And two, to see if you would consider joining me in bankrolling a legal fund."

"Chile, pleeeeeeeeeze," Jackie said shaking her head.

"As far as the situation," Jai interrupted, "I've got to be honest. Until now, I didn't even know there was a connection between Callie and the assault. And as far as bankrolling a legal fund, I guess my question would be how much are we talking about here?"

"Explain to me why we're even considering this. I mean, if Callie, in fact, did beat a bitch down, why should I feel obligated to pay for her legal fees? That is why you're suggesting a legal fund, right?" Jackie asked.

"Yeah, Eve, I agree with Jackie," Jai added. "It's one thing to protect ourselves from outside threats, but do we really want to get involved when a member of the association knowingly breaks the law?"

"Damn that, what's your Plan B?" Jackie asked.

Eve was about to answer when the waiter appeared. She waited as Jackie ordered shrimp linguini and Jai, a Cobb salad. In her head she was trying to formulate her response to Jackie's last question. The fact of the matter was she didn't really have a Plan B.

Eve ordered a ginger avocado salad and poured herself another drink. She eyed Jackie and Jai as she took several sips. "You do realize," Eve began, speaking deliberately, "that if Callie did attack Carmen and we do nothing, the association is going to look guilty of suggesting or condoning it. Either one is not good. It could be construed that that's what our organization is about, and we can't have that. It would undermine everything we are attempting to do. Instead of presenting an attractive package that will entice others to join, we'd be hard-pressed to even keep the inner circle intact."

"Good point," Jai said looking at Jackie for a reaction.

"So your Plan B is to lay a guilt trip on us. Really, Eve, I know you can do better than that." Jackie leaned back to allow the waiter to place Jai's plate on the table, then hers.

"Guilty? I was hoping you'd feel empathy," Eve said accepting her salad.

"Well, if it means we can avoid jeopardizing the association, I'm not opposed to forking over some cash," Jai said. "I assume that's why only Jackie and I are here. It doesn't take a rocket scientist to figure out that we are the three members in the inner circle with our own money."

"Thanks, Jai," Eve said glancing at Jackie who was now busy texting.

They ate in silence until Jackie placed her phone on the table. "I'm sorry," she said. "Where were we?"

"I was hoping that we were in agreement," Eve said noticeably irritated.

"I'm sorry, but I have a problem with putting good money after bad actions. If Callie is guilty, I see no sense in financing her defense. She has a husband who makes a grip, so let him pay. Hell, it's his fault she's in this predicament in the first place. If he'd kept his dick in his pants, his wife wouldn't be sneaking into houses, beating up models, and cutting their fucking braid off. And as far as how the association will look, I say kick her ass out of the organization. There has to be something in all that paperwork we signed that can justify getting rid of her. That way, it will be obvious that we don't condone what she did. That would actually make The Wives Association look pretty good. Bottom line, we solve our problem and we keep our money." Jackie took a swig of her beer and peered over the rim of her glass, making eye contact with Eve.

"So we just leave her out there on her own? That's pretty fucked-up, Jackie," Eve said glaring at her.

"Maybe we should just wait until we know if she really did it," Jai said hoping to ease the growing tension.

"I personally don't care if she did it or not," Jackie said returning Eve's stare. "What's more important—the welfare of the association or the welfare of its individual members?"

"Without its members there is no association," Eve replied.

"All the more reason why we don't need a criminal among our ranks," Jackie shot back.

"You wouldn't feel the same way if it were you," Eve snapped. "For your sake, I hope you never find yourself in this situation."

"What situation? We don't even know if the bitch did it, and you're already polling the jury. Whose ass are we really covering here, Eve? The way I see it, if Callie did beat that ass, the only other person that should be concerned is you. You said so yourself that you're the one who told her to do it."

"Fuck you, Jackie!" Eve retaliated. "You know damn well that's not the issue. How will it look if we turn our backs on her? How can we expect the other members to feel secure?"

"No need to get hostile," Jackie taunted.

"Who's hostile? I'm just trying to get you to understand that our allegiance could be seriously tested depending on how we handle this whole thing."

"Eve's right, Jackie. It would be pretty fucked-up if we just ignored the situation." Jai glanced at Eve hoping to show support.

"Read my lips," Jackie said. "We-don't-even-know-if-she-did-it." She pushed her plate to the center of the table. "I'm done with my lunch. Are we finished with the meeting?" She looked from Eve to Jai for a response.

"I'm finished too," Jai said. "I'll do whatever is best for all involved, but maybe we should table this discussion until we have some concrete information. We may find that Callie had nothing to do with it. Maybe it really is a big, big, big coincidence."

"Well, concrete information or not," Jackie said standing and gathering her things, "count me out." She looked at Eve and pointed to her empty plate. "You got this, right?"

"I'll pay for mine," Jai said opening her purse.

"No, Jai, I got it," Eve said pouring herself another drink.

"Thanks," Jackie said. "And don't worry, what happened here stays here. You wouldn't want word to get out that you're the mastermind behind the Garza assault," Jackie chuckled as she turned to leave.

Eve's first thought was to snatch Jackie by her hair and slam her ass to the ground, but she quickly weighed the consequences of that action and decided against it. Instead, she bit her bottom lip, then took

23

Do Something!

Callie sat in silence as she examined the prayer-inspired paintings that donned the walls of her meditation room. Her eyes were fixed on one in particular, that bared a pair of hands that were symbolic of the hands of the Lord, with a subtitle that read, "RELEASE AND RECEIVE." Although she'd grown up in the Roman Catholic Church as a child, and practiced Catholicism throughout most of her adult life, Callie had converted to Christianity almost immediately after moving to the States and attended weekly services with her boys at Faithful Central Bible Church in Inglewood, California.

Callie had also become a fan of television pastor Creflo Dollar and made it a point to watch him on television every morning. For the life of her, she never understood how people in the United States could take their religion and ability to praise God so freely for granted. In her country, people were often shunned for blatantly displaying their religious beliefs, and oftentimes their relationship with God had to go under a veil of secrecy, never to be discussed with anyone other than the priest who heard their confessions. But here, Callie was free to have an open relationship with God, and viewed that freedom as a luxury that she vowed never to abandon.

She closed her eyes and tried to focus her attention on the Bible a long sip from her drink and allowed Jackie to walk away unmolested. She knew that if there was any chance that she could change Jackie's mind, it would all go out the window if she kicked her ass in Musso and Frank.

"Thanks, Eve," Jai said sympathetically. "The next one's on me," she said sliding from the booth. "Get back to me once you definitely find out what's really up with Callie."

"I will," Eve said. "You do understand where I'm coming from though, right?"

"Yes, and don't mind Jackie. She's hard-core, and she gets off on being difficult, but if Callie needs us to help her out, I'm sure Jackie will come through for her." Jai bent and gave Eve a hug. "See you later," she said and headed for the door.

Eve watched as Jai exited the restaurant. Looking around, she spotted Jackie who had not yet left, and was chatting with a group at a table across the room. She was pissed that she had let Jackie get to her. Eve thought back to the exchange they had just had. She couldn't put her finger on it, but there was something going on there. There were a lot of facts and factors that Eve needed to consider regarding the Callie situation, but in the scheme of things, Jackie wasn't one of them. In fact, as far as she was concerned right now, Jackie was a non fucking factor.

Maybe Jai's right, Eve thought. Maybe Jackie was just getting off on being difficult, but something in her gut told her it was more than that. Eve watched as Jackie finally made her way to the exit. Yes, the more she thought about it, the more she was sure that there was more to Jackie's resistance than just a natural proclivity for being a bitch. Eve wasn't sure what it was, but she definitely intended to find out.

confessions that played softly in the background. As Creflo Dollar spoke the confession aloud via CD Callie whispered along.

"I will fear no evil for thou art with me, Lord; your Word and your Spirit they comfort me . . ." Callie felt tears stream down her face. Although Creflo had moved on to another verse, she repeated that one over and over, hoping that it would cause the fear that resided in her heart to disappear. She opened her eyes to the darkness that lingered in the room. Rising from her knees, she turned on the nearby lamp, and stood frozen for a moment. Her thoughts were scattered as she tried to make sense of the argument she'd just had with Drew. If she'd heard him correctly, which she prayed she hadn't, it almost sounded as if he was accusing her of attacking Carmen also. The gall of him to suggest that her finding out about the affair seemed like a solid motive for an attack, and that if the police suspected her enough to want to question her, then why shouldn't he.

"I'm your wife, Drew. The mother of your children! Do you honestly think I'm capable of something like this?" Callie remembered asking Drew.

"Honestly, Callie, I don't know what to think about you anymore. Ever since you started hanging out with those wife friends of yours, you've become a different person." Drew picked up the photos of him and Carmen and tossed them at her. "What is this? You're spying on me now? Spending my money on a private investigator like I'm some kind of animal you can just cage and trap."

"Why?" Callie screamed out him. "Why do you think I do these things? It's because of *you*, Drew. You and these whores!" Callie picked up the photos and threw them in his face. "I deserve better, and you know it."

"She meant nothing to me," Drew confessed. "Is that what you want to hear?"

"I hate you!" Callie cried out. *"Rompió el corazón."*

He grabbed Callie by the wrists and shook her. "So, I break your heart and you break her face? Is that what you do? You could have killed her."

Callie snatched herself free. "You defend her and not me?"

"You could've killed her!" Drew shouted, his voice echoing in the room.

"I didn't do this," Callie defended, throwing herself to the floor. She placed her hands over her face and wept aloud. "I would never hurt someone like that."

"You would, and you have," Drew said lifting his shirt to expose a scar that went from one side of his body to the other.

Shame covered Callie's face as she locked eyes on Drew's scar. It reminded her of a night she'd just as soon forget. Drew had just signed his first multimillion-dollar contract, and after a night of heavy drinking and celebrating, he and Callie had decided to put an end to what had just been one of the best nights of their life.

It had been obvious from the start of their relationship that Callie's temper was an issue. She had given jealousy permission to run rampant in her life and often looked for opportunities to allow it to explode in any given situation. From meter maids, to store clerks, to flight attendants, Callie had a history of spearheading vicious confrontations which often led to cruel and venomous fights. As Drew excused himself to the bathroom just prior to him and Callie leaving the club that evening, he was confronted by a drunken female fan that met him outside of the bathroom. He struggled to unwrap the woman from his body, but not before Callie caught a glimpse of what she perceived as him engaging in inappropriate behavior. Like a hurricane, Callie unleashed a fury of rage, demolishing everything in sight and leaving both Drew and his female admirer with wounds that required one hundred and fifty stitches for him, and plastic surgery and an undisclosed settlement check for her.

In an effort to keep Callie out of prison, Drew had accepted a trade to a team in London two years prior before accepting his most recent offer a year ago to move his family to the United States.

Things between Callie and Drew hadn't been the same after that. Even though she sought therapy, took medication, and even became a mother, Drew never quite held her in the same regard. And no matter how much she tried to repent of her sins from that dreadful night, somehow something always led her back to a place of remorse.

"Drew, I swear on our babies—" Callie pleaded.

"Don't!" he stopped her. "Don't you *dare* put anything on our boys."

Callie crawled over to him. "Drew!" she pleaded.

Drew threw an unopened prescription bottle at her. "I know you stopped taking your pills."

Callie grabbed the bottle and gasped for air. "It's not what it looks like," she appealed. "I'm preg—" She choked on her words.

"Stop it! Whatever you're about to say . . . stop it!" Drew shouted, releasing his leg from her grasp. "Only because of our boys will I do something to help you," he said walking out of the room and leaving her lying on the floor.

Callie's body ached with sorrow. She didn't know what was worse, being haunted by her past or not being able to believe in forgiveness for her future. She kneeled down once again and clasped her hands together. Then she took a deep breath, allowing her mind and thoughts to catch up to the confessions that poured out of the speakers of her Bose system.

"I am of God and have overcome Satan. For greater is He that is in me, than he that is in the world. In Jesus' name . . . Amen."

24

Reality Is a Bitch!

Eve and Amber arrived at 1200 Wilshire Boulevard with fifteen minutes to spare. They sat in the car in the parking garage of the building while Eve gave Amber last-minute instructions.

"If everything goes well and as planned, we should be out of here in no time," Eve said confidently.

"Why shouldn't it go well?" Amber asked nervously. "We're giving her everything she wants."

"That's true, but I just need you to follow my lead. Let me do the talking, and whatever you do, don't mention anything about money. You got that?"

"For the hundredth time, yes, I got it, but I don't understand it," Amber said shaking her head.

"You don't have to understand it. Just please do as I say," Eve pleaded. "Trust me; it'll all make sense real soon."

"I hope we're doing the right thing. As much as I can't stand the thought of Sa'Myra carrying Sean's baby, is it right for us to offer this chick money to abort it?"

"It's fucked-up, I know, but listen, we're not here to debate or discuss a woman's right to choose. Besides, she's already made her decision."

"I just pray I don't live to regret this. This life already comes with so many secrets," Amber spoke softly.

"I know," Eve said, without looking at Amber.

They exited the car in silence and walked the short distance to the elevators. The register indicated that the law firm of Turner and Thompson was located on the third floor.

"You ready?" Eve asked pushing the button.

"As ready as I'll ever be," Amber replied as the doors opened and they entered the elevator.

Shortly, the elevator doors opened, revealing a reception area that not only looked like it had been decorated in 1970, but from the thick layer of dust that covered the bookshelves, plastic plants, and water cooler in the corner, it was clear that the office hadn't been thoroughly cleaned since then either.

Eve noticed a row of cheap metal frames hanging on the faux wooden paneled wall with several certificates belonging to Carl Thornton in them. Ever since Sa'Myra had mentioned that name, Eve couldn't help but wonder if the Carl Thornton from the certificate could be the same Carl Thornton she briefly dated in Miami during college.

Eve smiled as she thought back to their short-lived relationship. It wasn't that Carl was a bad catch—quite the opposite actually. Carl came from several generations of lawyers, including two uncles, his mother, father, and grandfather. It was just that no matter what she did or how much she tried, Eve couldn't fake chemistry with him. Everything about Carl irked her! His corny little jokes, the way he chewed his food, even how he moved his lips around her mouth when they kissed bothered her. It didn't take long for Eve to end things with Carl, stating that she just wasn't ready to be in a committed relationship with anyone. Although he continually tried to change her mind with flowers, candy, tutoring sessions, the whole nine, she never budged.

To say that Carl was unhappy when she broke it off would be

putting it mildly. About a month after the breakup, Eve and a few of her classmates were reprimanded for using answers provided to them for a test. She would later find out that it was Carl Thornton who had informed the professor, but by that time, they had both graduated, and she had not seen or heard from him again.

Eve still remembered how she had to beg and plead with her professor not to report her to the dean, and how she had paid dearly with a slew of makeup tests and research papers. It couldn't possibly be her Carl Thornton, Eve thought. There was no way she could be that lucky!

Before they reached the reception desk, a tall, handsome, brown-skinned gentleman approached. The brown-skinned cutie was in full attorney attire complete with a navy blue pin-striped suit and a matching tie. Although he was a bit older and a little heavier, there was absolutely no mistaking that the man who stood before her was in fact her Carl Thornton!

"Eve! Long time no see!" Carl said, shaking Eve's hand with a broad grin.

Eve painted on a flirtatious grin and replied, "It's certainly a pleasure to see you again. I only wish it was under better circumstances."

"Do you two know each other?" Amber appeared confused.

"Carl and I went to school together. I was studying to be a paralegal while Carl was pursuing being a lawyer," Eve quickly responded.

"I'd say we did more than that," he rebutted.

"Hey, now!" Amber teased. "What exactly do you mean by 'more'?" she inquired.

"Clearly, this isn't the time or place," Eve interrupted, determined to change the subject. "Carl, this is my client, Amber Jackson."

Carl shook Amber's hand politely. "It's nice to meet you, Mrs. Jackson." He flashed a wide smile. "Well, it's pretty apparent that perhaps we should get down to business," Carl laughed. "Ladies, follow me."

Eve and Amber followed Carl into the conference room where

Sa'Myra and another elderly lady were already seated. Eve and Amber chose seats directly across from them and focused their attention on Carl, who positioned himself at the head of the long rectangular table.

"Can I get you ladies something to drink?" Carl asked.

"No, in fact, Mrs. Jackson and I have another appointment after this, so I would prefer that we move things along quickly," Eve responded.

"No problem," Carl said. "So, let's jump right on in, shall we?"

Sa'Myra grunted and folded her arms.

"Eve, I have already briefed my client on the fact that you and I know each other and the circumstances of that relationship. We are in agreement that there is no conflict of interest, and if you and Mrs. Jackson also agree, we can dispense with the need to address that issue."

Eve turned to Amber who gave a nod of approval.

"Then there's no conflict," Eve replied matter-of-factly.

"Good," Carl said, pretending not to notice how quickly their relationship had been dismissed. "Then let's get this over with."

Carl handed Eve the documented evidence of the abortion performed on Sa'Myra.

Eve checked the document thoroughly. "You do realize that if we discover this document is not legitimate it nullifies the entire agreement, correct?" she said, placing the document in her folder.

"Don't worry, it's legit," Carl said flatly.

He pulled his copy of the settlement agreement from the file he had placed on the table. "I assume you have the original agreement ready for notarizing?"

"Yes." Eve pulled two original copies of the letter from her file and handed them to Carl. "You do realize that there is no need to notarize as long as we both agree that the date and time shown on the faxed document is correct?"

"I know," Carl said. "But humor me. It will make my client happy." He looked at Sa'Myra who nodded in agreement.

Eve watched as he and Sa'Myra leaned in to read and compare the two documents to the one they already had. She felt her heart begin to race when she saw Sa'Myra point to something on the document that caused Carl to frown.

"Oh yes," he said turning to face Eve. "Was it really necessary to include my client's comment about the amount being just pennies to your client?" he asked as if scolding Eve.

"It is what she said," Eve replied remaining calm.

"Same old Eve," Carl said shaking his head as if in reproach.

"Excuse me?"

"You haven't changed a bit. You never were very good at losing."

"It's hard to get used to something you don't do very often," Eve said.

Sa'Myra stirred in her chair. "Can we get back to business?"

Once they were convinced that everything was indeed intact, Amber and Sa'Myra signed both copies of the agreement and handed it to the elderly woman, who turned out to be a notary, to process.

"Everything looks in order to me," Carl said, eyeing the documents.

"Is there anything your client would like to say?" Carl asked eyeing Amber.

"Nothing, except that I expect your client to adhere to the restrictions of the contract. Two hun ..." Amber stopped as she remembered Eve's admonishment regarding any mention of money. "I just want her out of my life and away from my family."

"Amber, I hope there are no hard feelings. Guess this is just a reality of life," Sa'Myra said smugly.

Eve placed her hand on top of Amber's and shook her head urging her not to respond. She felt a twinge of nerves in the pit of her stomach as she pulled the envelope with the check from her file and placed it on the table. Sa'Myra quickly glanced at the envelope.

"Well, looks like we're done here," Eve said, sliding Amber's copy of the agreement into her folder.

Carl extended his hand to Eve. "I want to thank you and your client for not making this difficult. There are no winners, only losers in these situations."

"It's not exactly like we had a choice," Eve responded. "But somehow, I don't feel like we lost."

Eve motioned to Amber, and they stood, turning to leave as Sa'Myra began opening the sealed envelope with a look of triumph on her face.

"Wait a minute!" she yelled. "This is not right!" Sa'Myra's eyes were wide with surprise.

"This check is only for twenty-five hundred dollars! The deal was for two hundred and fifty thousand dollars! What are you trying to pull?" She handed the check to Carl.

"Is this some kind of joke?" he asked, looking from the check to Eve. "Because if it is, it's not very funny."

Amber turned to Eve with a look of total confusion on her face.

"The deal," said Eve, glaring at Sa'Myra, "was two hundred and fifty thousand, and in your own words, that was 'pennies' to Amber and Sean. By my calculations, two hundred and fifty thousand *pennies* is twenty-five hundred dollars. Read the agreement. It clearly states what you asked for, and I quote, 'two hundred and fifty thousand and that would be pennies to you.'"

Sa'Myra stared at Carl, who was now frantically scouring through the documents in his folder.

"The agreement says two hundred and fifty thousand dollars!" Sa'Myra was now standing, palms down on the table for support.

"No, the agreement says two hundred and fifty thousand," Eve repeated. "There is no mention of dollars."

"Can she do that?" Sa'Myra asked slamming her fist against the table and staring at Carl, her eyes wide with anger.

"I'm afraid so," he said nervously. "The agreement is exactly as she said, and unfortunately, there isn't one dollar sign or decimal in conjunction with any of the references to the two hundred and fifty thousand on any of the documents!"

"You have *got* to be kidding me! How did you let this happen?" Sa'Myra was yelling at Carla and stomping her feet. "What kind of fucking attorney are you?"

Without waiting for a response, Sa'Myra turned to Eve. "You bitch! You planned this all along. You knew what I meant! This is not fair!"

"Well, Sa'Myra," Eve smiled, "life is not fair, and as you said yourself, this is a reality of life. Unfortunately, sometimes reality is a bitch!" she snapped, unable to resist being a smart-ass.

Eve quickly gathered her things and grabbed Amber's arm to leave. She turned to Carl with a huge grin. "I assume you won't be validating our parking, so we'll see ourselves out."

As Eve and Amber exited the conference room they maneuvered their way past the small group that had gathered outside the conference room watching the scene. Eve frantically pressed the button to the elevator. From behind, they could hear Sa'Myra screaming expletives in their direction.

"Fuckin' bitches. Both of you! You know this shit ain't right! Amber, I'm going to tell the whole fuckin' world about your scandalous-ass husband, you stank-ass bitch!"

Eve banged her fist against the elevator button repeatedly. "Whatever you do," Eve said to Amber, "don't look back!"

Finally the elevator bell rang and the doors opened. Thank God it was empty! As Eve and Amber stepped into the elevator they could still hear Sa'Myra screaming at the top of her lungs.

"You fuckin' bitches! You won't get away with this. I'm gonna kick both of your asses. Just wait! I'm gonna kick both your asses! You hear me, bitches?"

They turned in time to see Carl holding Sa'Myra around the waist, and with the aid of the notary clerk, struggling to pull her back into the conference room.

"You want to tell me what the fuck just happened?" Amber asked in amazement.

"Sure. You just paid Sa'Myra a settlement of twenty-five hundred dollars to shut the fuck up and go away," she replied releasing a huge sigh of relief.

"Can we do that?" she asked.

"We just did!" Eve smiled.

"But . . . I mean, does this mean I don't owe her any more money?"

"Not a dime."

"No wonder you were so secretive," Amber said scratching her head. "Wait! Have you been planning this all along?"

"Yep, and the shit fuckin' worked!" Eve said as her heart continued to race.

From the moment Sa'Myra had made the comment about the settlement being pennies, she had been setting her plan in motion. She had been careful to cover every detail, checking with partners at the firm, and then double-checking. Finally, all that was needed was to pull it off.

"Why didn't you tell me what you were planning?" Amber asked, still unable to believe what had just taken place.

"Because if the shit had blown up in my face, you would have been in the clear, and besides, in order for it to work, you had to be honest and sincere in your negotiations. I couldn't take the chance that you would get nervous and slip up."

"No shit! And I still nearly fucked up!"

"I know, but you didn't," Eve said, turning off the alarm to her car. "Hurry up and get in. We've need to get the hell out of here . . . quick!"

Once in the car, Eve gripped the steering wheel and let out a victorious yell. "Yes!!!"

Eve and Amber looked at each other in silence. Eve watched as tears began to slowly escape from the corners of Amber's eyes.

"Is it really over?" Amber tried to wipe the tears away with the back of her hand, but they were falling too fast.

"I wouldn't start celebrating just yet, but I think so. I say we give it a few days to let Sa'Myra calm down. I'm sure she's not gonna just tuck tail and run. She'll have the agreement checked for any loop-holes, and when that doesn't work, she'll check to make sure that what we did will stand up in court, but I'd say the hard part is over."

Amber sighed heavily and leaned back against the seat. "Man, did you see how she lost it? I thought she was going to pass out! I guess that really was a reality check."

"Yes, and like I said, reality is a bitch!"

Eve paid the parking attendant and made her way out of the parking structure. As she veered onto the 110 Freeway, she looked over at Amber realizing she hadn't looked that peaceful in weeks. She was happy that she could deliver this victory for her friend.

"I can't believe it's really over," Amber repeated again and again.

Eve smiled. Finally, there was some real peace among them. And with Sa'Myra now almost definitely out of the way, Eve felt confident that even more peace was sure to come.

25

Win or Go Home

Eve sat next to an empty seat in the Baltimore stands and looked down on the playing field. The players were milling around chatting, waiting for the officials to finish reviewing the last touchdown. It had been a spectacular one-hand catch by Chase. He had run another twenty yards after the catch, and then hurled himself over the goal line just as he went out of bounds. The challenge flag had been thrown almost immediately as Baltimore questioned if Chase had successfully stretched the ball over the pylon before going out of bounds. Right now, the score was twenty-seven to seven in favor of the Leopards, and with the first half almost over, Baltimore was trying everything to make sure the game was not about to get out of reach.

Eve looked at her phone. There was a text from Amber. "HOW'S IT GOING?"

"COLD AS HELL," Eve texted.

She read Amber's reply. "THAT'S WHY I PICKED A BASKET-BALL PLAYER. WE PLAY INSIDE! LOL"

"WHATEVER! TTYL," Eve texted back. It was too cold to keep up the conversation.

Eve could see Chase in front of the team bench shifting his weight from one foot to the other and shaking his hands to keep warm. He was having a great game. With three minutes left in the half, he already had one hundred and seventeen receiving yards.

It was cold in Baltimore, and Eve pulled the hood to her snow-white sable fur tighter around her face. It was a frigid twenty-seven degrees, a cold, blistering wind had been whipping her cheeks until they were numb, and now she had to pee. Eve couldn't wait for the game to be over and had come close to not even attending it, and it was partly her fault. Tickets to the playoffs were hard to come by, and that was especially true for the visiting Leopards. Eve hadn't helped the situation either. She waited until the last minute to confirm whether she was actually going to be able to attend.

Eve had been placed on assignment for a major campaign at work and informed Chase that due to the short notice from her boss, she might not be able to attend. It wasn't until two days before the game that she discovered she could still go, and Chase had scrambled, not being able to get her a ticket until the last minute. As a result, here she was, stuck in some random section with a bunch of people she didn't know.

Eve held her head down in an effort to avoid the next blast of arctic wind. Looking down the row, she noticed two other Leopards wives. In Los Angeles, the running joke among the wives was that they should always make an effort to "Leopard Spot," and whenever they saw another wife, they should greet her with the official Leopard's wave.

"Damn that!" she said, shaking her head. "It's too fucking cold to wave." Eve tucked her hands deep into her pockets and snuggled up. She only knew the two ladies by sight, but recognizing her, they waved excitedly. Eve gave them a polite grin, and then turned away. She wasn't about to try to socialize; if anything, she was trying hard to decide whether she could hold her pee.

Eve groaned as she thought about the VIP Press pass she had in her purse. When Andrew Rothberg had found out that she didn't have a ticket, he had gladly relinquished the pass. But after all the effort Chase put into getting her a ticket, she didn't have the heart to tell him she no longer needed the ticket. She could still remember how excited he was.

"Babe!" Chase had come into the house and sprinted up the stairs wearing a huge grin on his face and his hands securely tucked behind his back. "Bam!" he said, revealing the ticket.

"Who's the man, huh?" he asked as he danced around her.

Eve looked at the location of the ticket and frowned. "You got me a ticket in the red zone!"

"Yep! Right where your man will be spending the day all day on Sunday!" Chase gloated.

"Hopefully, you'll be spending it in the end zone," she laughed.

"Oh, you already know what time it is."

"Win or go home," she replied.

"What time is it, baby?" Chase asked louder.

"Win or go home!" Eve yelled.

"That's right! Now I need to go out and buy one of those little skimpy cheerleader outfits and some pom-poms, and I want you on the twenty-yard line shaking that beautiful body of yours and cheering, 'Win or go home! Win or go home!'" Chase was bumping, grinding, gyrating, and waving his arms as if he held pom-poms.

Eve laughed hysterically. "You are so crazy!"

"That's right. Crazy about you, baby." Chase tackled her to the bed and held her tightly.

Eve nestled her head against his chest, knowing full well she couldn't dare mention the VIP pass. She wasn't about to steal his thunder, especially since he had worked so hard to secure the ticket.

A series of boos and groans went up from the crowd as the official on the field announced that the touchdown was good. Chase was right. From her seat on the twenty-yard line Eve had a clear view of the red zone and the Leopards' bench. She watched Chase celebrate with a silly dance as his teammates gathered around congratulating him. It was his second touchdown of the half.

The extra point was good, and Eve watched as the teams made their way to the sidelines. Since there was no immediate activity on the field and the Leopards held a lead of twenty-eight to seven, she decided it was a good time to go to the restroom.

As she made her way through the crowd, Eve admired the array of stylish outfits on a few women that joined her in the line. She laughed to herself as she watched them struggle to walk in their six- and seven-inch heels—a mistake she made once herself and vowed to never make again. Instead, Eve kept it simple and elected to wear an all-black ensemble complete with her favorite wedge Louboutin riding boots, a pair of skintight jeggings, along with a form-fitting turtleneck sweater, and, of course, her winter white fur.

Eve felt her feet continue to numb as she searched desperately for a bathroom. Clearly the directions she had gotten from the popcorn vendor were wrong, and she didn't know how much longer she could hold her bladder. In the distance, she could see the VIP section and knew that if she could just make it over to that area before her bladder burst, she was certain a bathroom would be nearby.

Eve squeezed her pelvic tightly and hustled over to the VIP.

"Good afternoon, ma'am," the attendant greeted her while examining her pass.

"Bathroom, quickly!" she squirmed, unsure of how much longer she could hold on.

"Down the hallway and to your left," he announced proudly, quickly lifting the rope to allow her in.

"Thank you," she said, picking up the pace.

Tears streamed down Eve's eyes as she made her way to the neon-lit W that was less than fifty feet away. She couldn't remember the last time she was this happy to see a restroom and prayed that her bladder wouldn't fail her before she could make it into a stall.

Eve darted past the attendant that was busy putting the finishing touches on a stack of folded hand towels, nearly knocking her down.

"Sorry!" she yelled out as she scrambled to find a vacant stall. She slammed her hand against more than six doors before finding an opened one, which was located all the way in the back. Fortunately, Eve preferred the stalls in the back, a habit she adopted based on her mother's logic of those being the least used and the cleanest. She was barely inside before her pants fell below her waist and warm trickles of urine began making their way down her thigh. She prayed no pee had made its way to her pants, but figured even if it had, it would be a problem that would have to wait to be resolved.

Eve slammed the door shut and with one quick motion, managed to balance and squat, permitting a rainfall of urine to flow from between her legs. The feeling was almost orgasmic as she closed her eyes and moaned with relief. After realizing her flow wasn't ending, Eve reluctantly allowed her body to melt down in the seat. Ordinarily, she'd feel uncomfortable about sitting on a public toilet seat with her bare bottom, but today, she didn't care. The release felt too good for her to be concerned about germs. Furthermore, from the looks of the bathroom, with its gold knobs, ivory bowls, and hand carved bamboo doors, she knew her ass was safe.

Eve heaved a sigh as her bag dangled from her now relaxed hand. "Ewwwww, chile," she whispered with a smile as she continued to breathe in and out. As her body thawed from the warmth of the room, she couldn't imagine fighting her way back out into the cold to return to her seat. Eve had immediately determined that Chase would just have to understand her decision to not return to those god-awful seats.

As Eve enjoyed the comfort of the room, she heard the sound of laughter near her stall. The laughter was contagious as Eve found herself quietly snickering to herself.

What the hell are you laughing for? she thought to herself as she reached for the toilet paper in preparation to finally finish up and flush.

"Stooooop! Somebody could be in here!" a voice said playfully.

"Nobody's here. The attendant just left for her break. Come on, if we hurry up, we can get in a quickie," the second voice encouraged.

Eve quieted herself and lifted her legs slightly off the ground. Although she wasn't sure if she was in the mood to wait out a little make out session by two lovers, she damn sure could relate to the urge for a little quickie in the bathroom even if it was between two women. She and Chase had been guilty of their fair share of bathroom-sex sessions in places far crazier than this. Be it at the Staple Center, Nokia Theater, or at any of the several restaurants located at L.A. Live, a quickie in the bathroom was always a good idea for Eve and Chase.

"Right now?" the first voice asked.

"Yes!"

She sat frozen on the toilet seat, afraid that if she moved it would set off the automatic flush. She felt herself getting moist as the slurping, smacking, and kissing sounds echoed across the room.

"Awww, yeah . . ." one of the ladies moaned. "Come on, baby, eat my pussy!"

"Oh my!" Eve mumbled softly.

The slurping and smacking continued a few moments longer before one woman spoke again. "We gotta stop before somebody comes in."

"Hmmmmm," the other groaned, clearly ignoring her partner's request.

"Shit, that feels good," one of them wailed, taking deep, long breaths.

"Damn, baby, your pussy is wet."

Almost acrobatic, Eve leaned her body forward in an effort to see who was talking. Oddly, she felt as if she knew those voices. As she strained to get a look at their faces, all she could make out was that one of women was wearing a fabulous pair of red snakeskin boots.

"Seriously, we've got to stop. Someone may catch us. This shit isn't safe."

"Okay!" the other woman reluctantly agreed. "I'm good now anyway. I just needed to taste you," Red Boots declared.

"You're so fucking nasty."

Eve scrunched her face in disgust as she heard one of the women licking her fingers and lips loudly.

"Whatever, bitch, you know you like it."

Eve watched as Red Boots leaned in for a kiss. "You know the drill. One minute, then you can come out." Red Boots kissed her again then moved out of sight.

Eve heard the same rustling of clothing and could make out voice number one pulling up and zipping her pants. The door closed as Red Boots exited. Eve listened as voice number one turned and began washing her hands. She could see her reaching into her purse and heard the opening of a compact. Eve strained to see through the crack in the door just as voice number one leaned into the mirror, and she nearly lost her balance when she recognized the reflection looking back at her. It was Paula Andrews, president of the Leopards Wives' Association!

Holy shit! Eve thought. *What the fuck is going on?* It was all she could do to keep from falling off the toilet seat.

Paula washed her hands and freshened up her makeup.

Eve bit her lip as she contemplated her next move. She thought about coming out of the stall and busting Paula out, but what would she say? "I just heard you getting finger fucked by another woman"?

Eve fought the urge and remained with her feet in the air until Paula left the room. Who knew her time in the gym would come in handy for something like this!

When Eve was sure the coast was clear she lowered her feet, grabbed her things, and exited the stall. She still couldn't believe what she had heard and almost seen! Clearly Paula was involved in some kind of lesbian relationship, but with whom? Maybe it was one of the rookie wives since it had been no secret that Paula repeatedly took advantage of them. She had them doing everything from running errands to volunteering to work her charity events, making them earn brownie points with her, but this took sucking up to a whole other level, Eve thought.

Her mind raced as she staggered to catch her balance. "Oh my word!" she said, still trying to digest what she'd just witnessed. All sorts of questions came to mind. This was just the kind of shit she had been telling the association about. It was information like this that had to be handled carefully and used to the association's advantage. One thing was for sure. Before she divulged what she knew, she had to find out who Red Boots was. From the conversation Eve had overheard, it was pretty obvious that this was not just some random meeting.

Eve washed her hands and checked her makeup. If she had had any reservations about going into the VIP room before, they had certainly faded now. She retraced her steps and found her way back to the attendant that had helped her moments prior.

"Excuse me," Eve stated, "do you mind pointing me toward the opposing team's box?"

"Sure thing, ma'am. Go straight-ahead and you'll see a skybox with a makeshift sign that reads Leopards."

"Thank you, love." Eve scurried in the direction of the skybox.

On the way there, she caught a glimpse of the score on one of the nearby monitors. She couldn't believe she'd completely missed half-time and five minutes of the third quarter.

The VIP and Press Room was buzzing with conversation as Eve scanned the room in search of Paula and Red Boots. Although Paula was nowhere in sight, Eve spotted Jackie sitting in the press section of the box representing KTEL.

She made her way over to KTEL's table, bent down, and gave Jackie a hug. She was dying to tell Jackie what she had just witnessed in the ladies' room, but two other people were seated at the table alongside her so she'd have to wait. Besides, until she found out who Paula was involved with, the last person Eve would be sharing the information with was Jackie. She knew how Jackie was when it came to her job, and she wasn't about to let her turn this shocker into one of her exclusives. Too many times Jackie had proven to be journalist first and friend second.

Jackie introduced the two people at the table as Dave and Karen, associates from KTEL. Dave was busy on his laptop, and Karen was involved with texting. They both nodded and smiled politely and went back to what they were doing.

"Did you just come in?" Jackie asked.

"Yes, I've been out in them cold-ass stands representing while you've been in here, warm and toasty," Eve groaned.

"What can I say? My job has privileges. So how'd you get in?"

"Rothberg. My job has privileges too, but my husband is not impressed. I thought I'd get a drink and warm up a bit before I go back to Antarctica."

"I know that's right," Jackie laughed. "If I wasn't working, Ray would insist that I have my ass out there too."

"Well, there's an empty seat next to me if you want to freeze your tits off."

"No, thanks. Take a load off. I'll get you a drink 'cause service is kinda slow. What do you want?"

"What are you drinking?" Eve asked.

"Beer, bitch! What else?" Jackie replied.

Eve laughed. "Girl, you and that beer!"

"What? You know I keeps it all the way one hundred," Jackie sassed.

"Beggars can't be choosers. I'll take a beer, as well," Eve said taking a seat at the table and placing her coat and bag on the empty chair next to her.

As Jackie stood and headed for the bar Eve gave her a quick

once-over. Jackie was well dressed as usual, in a fabulous red cape sweater, tight leather like leggings, and . . . Eve's mouth dropped open and her eyes widened when she got to Jackie shoes. There they were! The bad-ass red snakeskin boots from the bathroom.

Eve looked frantically around the room for Paula Andrews, but she was nowhere in sight. Her eyes darted around the room once more, checking the shoes of every woman she saw. She knew the chances of someone else wearing an identical pair of those red boots were rare, but she looked anyway!

Eve glanced at her phone. She had a text from Amber. "WHAT'S UP, FROSTY? LMAO!" Eve was about to respond when Jackie returned with her drink.

"Here, I got you a vodka and cranberry instead. I told the bartender to make it strong, especially since your ass was stuck out there in the damn cold." Jackie handed her the drink. "Hell, you look like you *need* this bad boy."

"You have no idea how right you are." Eve took a long sip. "By the way, nice boots," Eve complimented.

"Thanks. You like?" Jackie raised her leg for Eve to get a better look.

"Yeah, they're bad."

"I had them custom-made. I can hook you up if you want."

"I bet you could," Eve said under her breath. She glanced down at her phone and noticed she'd missed several text messages from Amber.

"WHAT'S THE MATTER? FINGERS FROZEN?" Amber's last text read.

Just then the room erupted with a combination of cheers and groans. Eve glanced at the wide screen. Chase had scored again and was dancing in the end zone.

She downed the rest of her drink. "I gotta go," she said, standing.

"So soon?" Jackie looked surprised.

"Yeah, I gotta get back to my post of duty. Thanks for the drink."

Eve reached across the table and acknowledged Dave and Karen. "It was nice meeting you two," she said to no response.

"Girl, you know Chase's ass won't mind if you stayed in here."

"You know how spoiled he is. Besides, I don't want to hear his mouth." Eve grabbed her coat and bag and hurried from the room before Jackie could protest any further.

Once outside, Eve took a deep breath. She was trembling with nervous energy as she hurried back to her seat in the stands. As much as she tried to concentrate on the game, she couldn't stop thinking about her discovery.

"Jackie and Paula in a lesbian relationship! What in the TMZ hell have I gotten myself into?" Eve questioned herself as she tried to erase the thought of Jackie tongue fucking Paula out of her mind.

Eve felt her phone vibrate again. She knew it was Amber sending her yet another text to which she quickly typed a reply. "TRYING TO STAY WARM. WILL DEFINITELY CALL YOU THE MINUTE I GET TO THE AIRPORT. YOU WON'T BELIEVE WHAT I HAVE TO TELL YOU," she said, placing her iPhone back in her bag.

She glanced up at the scoreboard which read 35 to 17 in favor of the Leopards. She wasn't sure if it was the excitement from the game or the information that was burning in her mind, but somehow, she didn't feel so cold anymore.

"Win or go home!" she yelled, as she removed the hood from her head and leaned back against her seat to enjoy the rest of the game. Win or go home was right. With the Leopards looking to secure the win and the juicy gossip secure in her mind, Eve couldn't wait to get home!

26

Sudden Change of Heart

Eve drove slowly as she and Amber looked for 1885 Barrington Street. Jai and Tony had just purchased a new home in Brentwood, and it was Jai's turn to host the monthly TWA meeting.

"I don't know why you insist on me not using my navigation. You know good and damn well you're terrible with directions."

"I can't stand the sound of your navigation system. That bitch's voice is so annoying," Amber complained.

"Ummmm, excuse me? We had the car custom-programed using *my* voice," Eve protested.

"Oh, my bad, girl. Damn, I knew that bitch sounded familiar," Amber laughed.

"Forget you. Just for that, I outta put your ass out and make you walk," Eve pouted.

"Quit being so sensitive. You know I'm just playing with you. Now, keep going."

Eve listened as Amber read off the addresses. "Eighteen sixty-seven, seventy-one, eighty-three, eighty-five. There it is!"

Eve turned into the driveway and up to the black wrought iron double gates. Although there was an intercom in place, the gates were open, allowing her to drive up to the circular driveway. Ahead, she could see a row of luxury cars complete with Callie's Porsche Cayenne, Jackie's Jaguar, and Jai's custom-painted purple Range Rover. Eve's stomach fluttered at the thought of what she was going to say to Jackie when she saw her again. She contemplated sharing what she knew with Amber, but by the time she made it home, Amber and Olivia were already in bed, and although the information was juicy, she felt it wasn't worth waking her up about it.

By morning, Eve had had a sudden change of heart and figured she owed it to Jackie as friend to at least talk to her about what she saw, rather than talk about her with someone else.

As she and Amber made their way up the driveway, they marveled at the sight of the house.

"Wow! And I thought her old house was nice," Amber exclaimed. "This is gorgeous!"

Eve agreed the entrance to the house was breathtaking. The driveway encircled a lawn so well-manicured that is looked artificial, and in the center of the lawn was a massive three-tiered marble fountain that was at least fifteen feet high with a cherub carving that rested atop. The serene sound of the tinkling water could be heard from inside the car, tempting Eve and Amber to almost not depart.

As they made their way to the front door, Eve admired the oversized bamboo wooden pots filled with flowers that dotted the walkway. The ladies enjoyed the intoxicating aroma of gardenia and vanilla that greeted their every step.

They laughed as the doorbell belted out a chimed-inspired rendition of "Take Me Out to the Ball Game."

"Welcome, ladies," Jai greeted them with a smile as she held the wooden doors open. "Come on in. Excuse the jeans and tee shirt, but we're still going through boxes. And you know by *we*, I mean *me!*"

"If the outside is any indication of what awaits us inside, then let me go ahead and compliment you now . . ." Eve praised.

Jai pointed out the unfinished foyer that was outfitted with impressive cream and beige marble tiling that led to a double spiral

staircase that served as the platform for a stunning four-tiered chan-
delier that hung from the ceiling of the second level.

"Exquisite, Jai," Amber added.

"Thanks. I love it, but I'm still trying to find my way around. I
keep trying to tell Tony that bigger doesn't always mean better, but
what I can do?" Jai beamed. "Jackie and Callie are already here, so we
can get started. I'll give everybody a tour after the meeting."

Eve and Amber followed Jai down a long hallway covered with
complementary tile that matched the tile in the entrance. They passed
a row of closed doors, which, according to Jai, hosted an office, grand
living and dining room, as well as two master suites.

Eve took note of the Rembrandt-inspired painting that graced
the walls. Although she wasn't an art connoisseur, Eve always appreciated people who regarded art enough to make it a part of their space.

Jai led them into the family room where Jackie and Callie were
already seated and munching on hors d'oeuvres.

"Hey, guys," Callie and Jackie said simultaneously, and then
laughed at their unison greeting.

"What's up, you two?" Amber laughed.

"Hey!" Eve added, trying to avoid eye contact with Jackie. Instead,
she fixed her attention on how small Callie and Jackie appeared on
Jai's peanut butter-colored sofa.

"It's something else, isn't it?" Jackie asked walking over to Eve.
"Girl, and we thought our husbands' football money was something."
She placed her hand on Eve's shoulder. "Shit, if I had known baseball
players rolled like this, I would've invested in a fucking bat."

Eve cut her eyes at Jackie's hand on her shoulder. The thought of
one of those same fingers that had just been inside Paula's pussy, now
resting boldly on her shoulder, sickened her. She forced a smile until
she got a glimpse of Jackie's infamous red boots. She felt the same
knot form in her throat that had introduced itself to her in that skybox
when she discovered Jackie was the one wearing those boots.

"I know, right?" was all Eve could manage as she eased her shoulder from Jackie's grasp. Quickly, Eve walked over to the wall-sized window and admired the view. She took deep, long breaths as she looked at the Olympic-sized swimming pool that was nestled in the center of the backyard. From where she was standing, the backyard seemed to extend forever.

"Are my eyes deceiving me, or is that a perfectly round swimming pool?" Eve asked extending her neck to get a better look.

"Yes, girl! And between you and me, I think the only reason Tony wanted this house is because of that damn pool. He's having the floor of the pool painted like a baseball!"

"Go on, Tony! I ain't mad at him," Jackie chuckled, sitting back down on the couch next to Callie.

"Well, I hope Chase doesn't find out about that 'cause I don't need him getting any ideas," Eve laughed.

Jai grabbed her spiral notebook from the smoked glass coffee table and took a seat at the end of the sectional. "I hate to rush you, ladies, but we need to get through the meeting so that we can eat and take a quick tour of the house. Unfortunately, our fundraising meeting with the mayor got pushed up to seven."

"No worries, let's get started." Eve pulled her agenda from her folder. "The meeting is officially called to order," she announced. "Jai, do you have the minutes from the last meeting?"

"I do, but I have to apologize. My printer hasn't been set up yet, and I haven't had time to type or print them."

"Then I move that we table the minutes until the next meeting," Amber offered.

"Thanks, Amber," Jai said.

"Second," Jackie added.

"Okay, moved, seconded, any objections? Perfect, the minutes are tabled." Eve thought for a moment. "I think, since we have tabled the minutes, I am going to take executive privilege and table any old business until the next meeting. That includes the financial report and any new member submissions. So let's go on to new business.

Any new business?" Eve looked around the room, but no one spoke. "Okay, if no one has any new business, then let me take this opportunity to congratulate us on the great job we did with the mentoring program last week.

"I got a call from the superintendent of L.A. Unified, and they're thinking of incorporating parts of our program into the district's curriculum, so be prepared. If all goes well, we may be called on to speak before the school board. So congratulations, ladies. Give yourselves a hand."

Eve waited until the brief applause subsided. "Well, that's all I have. I guess we can officially say this is the shortest meeting in Wives' Association history," she laughed. "Does anyone else have anything we need to discuss?"

There was silence, and then the ladies all started to giggle.

"Okay," Eve said laughing. "It was obvious that no one, including me, feels like having a meeting."

"I move that the meeting be adjourned," Jackie said, trying not to laugh.

"I second," Callie giggled.

"Moved and seconded. If no objections, it's a wrap," Eve said smiling as she took her seat.

"Actually, I don't have anything to discuss, but I do have an announcement," Amber said softly.

"An announcement? Didn't you hear the meeting is over?" Jackie groaned.

"Only if it's good news," Jai said. "It seems like every time one of us makes an 'announcement,' someone has a crisis."

"Well, I think it's good news," Amber replied with a slight smile.

"Then let's hear it," Jackie coaxed. "Because I'm hungry as hell, and before you got here, Jai informed us that she whipped up her famous jambalaya!"

"I promise to make it quick!" Amber smiled.

"What's the announcement?" Eve asked curiously.

"Well, Olivia and I are going home." Amber sighed as if she was relieved to get the words out.

"Excuse me?" Eve was caught off guard.

"Congratulations! She said she's going home," Callie echoed Amber's words.

"No, I heard her, but wait a minute. When did this happen? What brought this on?" Eve interrogated.

"Sounds like the same question to me," Jackie said. "Would you mind letting her answer at least one of them?"

Eve glanced at Jackie but decided not to respond and turned back to Amber. "Okay, Amber, answer."

"I actually talked to Sean, and he really wants me and Olivia to come home."

"And you're okay with that?" Eve couldn't believe what she was hearing.

"Yes, I am," Amber responded assuredly.

"When did you decide this? The last discussion we had, you still didn't know if you wanted his cheating ass back. And those are *your* words, not mine."

"Damn, Eve, give her a break. If she wants to go home, we should support her," Jai said. She moved closer to Amber and placed a supportive hand on her shoulder.

"I do support her. In fact, no one has done more to support her than I have. I just want to know why the sudden change of heart."

"It's not sudden. I've really been thinking about it, and it's time," Amber offered.

"Time? Time for what? Don't tell me this is because you're staying with me and Chase. I told you, you and Olivia are welcome for as long as you need."

"I know, Eve. And no, it has nothing to do with you and Chase. You've been wonderful. But I have a different perspective now that we don't have the Sa'Myra thing hanging over us, and I realize that I still love Sean. We took vows that said through the good and the bad. I just think we owe it to those vows to try to stick it out."

"I get it, and I'm happy for you, girl. Now can a bitch get some food? I'm ready to eat," Jackie chimed in.

"Jackie, pleeeeease! Can you just get serious for one minute? I don't want to see or hear about you eating anything." Eve paused a moment realizing the verbal attack she'd just administered to Jackie. It was all she could do to avoid looking at Jackie so the visual of her and Paula wouldn't return.

"What the fuck is your problem?" Jackie snapped back.

Eve knew she was wrong and that now was not the time to address her issues with Jackie. She quickly relented and apologized for her outburst. "I'm sorry, Jackie. It's not you. It's just . . ." She paused, trying to gather her thoughts and focus on what she wanted say. She took a deep breath and turned to face Amber. "I just want you to be sure about this, Amber."

"I am sure. Sean and I have already discussed it. It's what we both want."

Eve eyed Amber suspiciously. "Well, if you've actually thought this through, and if it's really what you want, then I'm happy for you, and I wish you only the best."

"Thanks, Eve. Your support is important to me. In fact, all of you have been great, and I really appreciate you having my back."

"Good!" Jackie said, raising her glass. "Then I say we make a toast! Here's to Amber, Olivia, and Sean. May your reunion be blessed and good, and may the sands of time remove all memory of the bad."

They all chuckled and took a sip in agreement.

"Damn, Jackie," Jai said, "that was nice. I didn't know you had it in you."

"I have my moments," Jackie said, popping her collar. "Plus, I figured that was better than what I was going to say."

"Oh, Lord," Callie said. "I'm almost afraid to ask, but go ahead. What were you going to say?"

"Well, Amber reminded us that the vows state through good and bad, and I was just going to add that they also state till death do us part, which means that sometimes you may have to kill a muthafucka'!"

"On that note, I say we all have another drink," Jai said laughing as she led the way across the room to the bar.

Eve laughed and noticed that everyone else was laughing except Amber. She made eye contact and gave Amber a supportive smile. Amber smiled back, but Eve couldn't help but notice that it was a tentative smile masking an actual look of discomfort.

"I don't mean to sound repetitious or doubtful, Amber, but are you *sure* you're telling me everything? I mean, you didn't mention anything to me on the way over."

"Eve, stop overanalyzing everything and just find it in your heart to be happy for me."

Feeling like she had been a little hard on Amber, Eve called for attention. "Ladies, I have a suggestion. In honor of Amber's reconciliation, I would like to suggest that we have a moving party. Just us girls! I'll make breakfast, and we can get started early. What do you say?" She gave Amber a sympathetic grin.

"If it'll get you to shut the hell up, then count me in," Jackie smiled.

"Me too," Jai said. "When?"

"How about tomorrow?" Eve asked, turning to Amber.

Amber hesitated. "Can we make it Saturday? Sean's parents are here until tomorrow, and the last thing I need is to deal with Miss Tami. My housekeeper has already told me that she's been there all week talking shit and rearranging things. I need her ass good and gone before I go back."

"That's probably why Sean wants your ass back. A week with his mama must make living with you seem like Christmas!" Jackie laughed.

"Saturday's good for me," Jai said.

"Not me. I'm sorry, love, I have a prior engagement," Callie reported.

"I understand," Amber said.

"Great! Saturday it is. I'll e-mail you all tomorrow with the details." Eve slapped her hand on the bar. "Now, Jai, is it true? Did you *really* make jambalaya?"

"Yes. I'll have Edna warm it up and set us a table while I show you around." Jai made her way out of the room.

"I'll help," Amber said following Jai into the kitchen.

Eve watched Amber walk away, promising to let bygones be bygones. Although she was trying to accept Amber's sudden change of heart bit, something about her recent decision didn't sit well with her.

Sudden my ass, Eve thought. She knew shit when she smelled it, and something was definitely rotten in Paradise.

Jai returned. "All right, ladies, let me give you a quick tour of the place, and the food should be ready when we finish. Follow me."

Eve quickly finished her drink and placed it on the bar. She had a lot to consider, and it was starting to bother her that between the secret she was keeping regarding Jackie, the defense she was preparing for Callie, and now this bullshit of an excuse she was receiving from Amber, she was slowly finding herself back in a place of feeling completely overwhelmed. As she followed Jai and the others down the hallway, through the foyer to the staircase, Eve chose to focus her attention on Amber. If Amber was lying, it wouldn't take her long to find out why. If Eve was confident about anything, she was confident in her ability to uncover the truth. And with the web of lies that seemed to surround her at the moment, she was determined more than ever to eventually get to the bottom of it all.

27

What Happens in the Dark . . .

"Noooooo," she groaned, kicking the covers frantically. Eve rolled over and squinted at the alarm clock. It read 6:30 A.M. The plan was to have the moving party start with breakfast at seven-thirty, and then begin moving Amber at eight-thirty, but as she tried to focus on actually waking up, she realized that morning had come too soon.

Normally six-thirty in the morning would not have been considered early, but she and Amber had been packing boxes until eleven-thirty the night before, and by the time she had showered and climbed into bed, it had been after midnight. Eve could hear Amber and Olivia laughing and talking across the hall.

"How the hell did she do it?" Eve asked herself. *Maybe when you have a kid God gives you extra energy or something,* she thought, forcing herself to roll over and place her feet on the floor.

"What was I thinking?" Eve said stretching as she made her way to the bathroom. She flipped on the light and closed her eyes instantly. Immediately, she turned off the light realizing it much too bright and her eyes weren't ready to make the sudden adjustment.

Eve made her way to the toilet as she yawned and scratched her ass. She pulled down her pajama pants, allowing them to fall to her ankles, sat, and enjoyed the relief of her first morning piss. With her eyes still closed, she started going over the plans for the day and nearly fell asleep on the toilet until she heard a faint knock on her bedroom door.

"Just a minute!" Eve shouted out while quickly pulling a wad of toilet paper from the roll and wiping herself. She pulled up her pants, flushed the toilet, quickly rinsed her hands, and dried them on her pants as she made her way to the bedroom door.

She opened the door to see Olivia hugging her American Girl doll with a broad smile. "Good morning, Auntie Eve."

"Good morning, baby." Eve playfully tugged on one of Olivia's neatly combed braids that hung down her back. Olivia had thick, curly hair like Amber, hair that Eve didn't envy Amber having to comb every day.

"Livie! I thought I told you not to bother Auntie Eve." Amber appeared from the guest bedroom wearing jeans, a sweatshirt, and tennis shoes, and carrying Olivia's jacket.

"It's okay," Eve said stretching and yawning. "I should have been up half an hour ago."

"I feel bad keeping you up all night," Amber said helping Olivia on with her jacket.

"Don't worry about it. As soon as we finish getting you moved, I have made plans to date myself tonight."

"Are me and Mommy are going home today?" Olivia asked excitedly.

Eve grimaced, then made a fist and bit down on the knuckle of her index finger as Amber made an accusatory face. She had forgotten that going home was supposed to be a surprise for Olivia.

"Let's go, Livie. Daddy's waiting," Amber said as she led Olivia down the hallway. She looked back and made a fist at Eve.

Eve shrugged apologetically. "Bye, Livie!" she yelled after them. As she made her way back into her bedroom she could hear Olivia's faint good-bye followed by "Mommy, are we going home today?"

"Shit!" Eve said flinging herself onto the bed. She rolled over on her back and sighed heavily as she stared at the ceiling. "With all the secrets I've been keeping, you would think that I could keep a secret from a seven-year-old little girl!" she said scolding herself.

Eve grabbed a pillow and hugged it tightly against her body. She missed Chase. He was already in San Francisco for the game, and she had booked a morning flight to join him. She glanced at the alarm clock which now read 6:50 A.M.

Eve leaped up and made her way back to the bathroom where she washed her face and quickly brushed her teeth. She glanced in the mirror and was glad to see that she didn't look as tired as she felt. She quickly dressed in jeans, sweatshirt, and tennis shoes, and pulled her hair into a ponytail with a rubber band she plucked from her vanity tray.

She trotted down the hallway then galloped down the stairs taking them two at a time. She kept trotting until she was in the kitchen. She stopped for a moment with her hands on her hips and took a deep breath as if she was about to run a race.

"All right," she said giving herself a pep talk. "You can do this!"

Eve quickly spooned coffee into the coffeemaker, filled the reservoir with water, and pushed the brew button. Then she grabbed a bag of frozen hash browns from the freezer and a package of bacon and a carton of eggs from the refrigerator. She pulled three skillets and a bowl from the cabinet and balanced them precariously as she shuffled to the stove.

Eve went to work layering the hash browns in one skillet and lining the bacon in another. She had chopped bell peppers and onions the night before and quickly added them to the hash browns. Then she cracked the entire carton of eggs into the bowl, added milk and butter, and then scrambled them furiously. She turned on the burner under the third skillet, rubbed butter in its center, and waited, allowing it to warm.

The smell of fresh coffee began permeating the air. She pulled the pot from the base and poured herself a cup before it was finished brewing. After two sips she could feel her body start to warm, and she stood still for a moment, allowing the hot liquid to do its job.

She turned and looked out the kitchen window just in time to see her neighbor appear in her panties and bra. She watched her crouch down and look from side to side until she was convinced that the coast was clear, then quickly darted across the lawn, retrieved her newspaper from the sidewalk, and dashed back inside. Eve saw the look of triumph on her face and could tell she thought she had accomplished the mission unseen.

"She's crazy as hell. Why doesn't she just put on a robe?" she asked herself. She guessed some people just liked the excitement of taking unnecessary risks, laughing as she remembered how she and Chase had slipped into the movie theater once without paying, strictly for the thrill of it.

Eve checked the skillet by splashing it with a few drops of water before pouring the eggs in it to scramble. She glanced at the clock on the microwave which read 7:20 A.M. Eve gave herself a mental pat on the back after whipping out a complete breakfast quick enough to impress the Iron Chef. She added a plate of bagels and an assortment of cream cheeses, poured a large pitcher of orange juice, and had completed setting the table when the doorbell rang.

Eve opened the door to find Jai and Jackie waiting together. "Did you guys come together?" Eve asked, and immediately realized it was a stupid question.

"Not exactly," Jackie laughed.

"Jackie got here first, and I caught her sleeping in her car in your driveway," Jai joked.

"I was making phone calls!" Jackie retorted.

"Whatever! Come on in. I'm just glad you're both here and hopefully ready to work," Eve said giving them a once-over. She was glad to see that they at least knew proper moving attire. "Jai, what's with the do-rag?" Eve asked referencing the yellow cotton scarf Jai had tied around her head.

"Girl, I just got my hair done yesterday. Need I say more?"

They all laughed as Eve led the way into the kitchen.

"Damn, Eve, you sure you want us to help move? If I eat all this, I won't be able to move anything, including myself!" Jai plucked a bagel from the plate and began spreading it with cream cheese.

"It will give you energy," Eve said. "And I know damn well somebody had better eat because I was in here running around like Aunt Jemima trying to have it ready before you guys got here." She grabbed a plate and scooped on a large helping of hash browns.

`"Looks like you're celebrating," Jai said starting to fix a plate. "Where's Amber?"

"She took Olivia home so she would be out of the way. Sean has a whole day planned for the two of them. By the time they get home later this evening, we should have Amber and Olivia settled back at home. It was supposed to be a surprise, but I opened my big mouth this morning and ruined that."

"What's the matter? Can't wait for them to be gone?" Jackie asked pouring a glass of orange juice. She glanced down at her cell phone and frowned as she read an incoming text.

"No. Actually, it hasn't been bad, but it will be kinda nice to have my house back," Eve said.

Jai wiped cream cheese from the corner of her mouth. "Well, it wouldn't be soon enough for me. Just like you have a rule about only hiring the ugly, I have a rule about friends living in my house with me and my husband. I don't care how close I am to a bitch, she can't stay at my house. I'll help her get a hotel room or something, but my house is off-limits."

"Please, the last thing I have to worry about is Chase and Amber," Eve said chewing slowly.

"You mean you wouldn't let your best friend stay at your house if she needed to?" Jackie asked, looking up from her cell phone.

"No, and my best friend already knows the rules and respects my feelings. That's why we're such good friends," Jai said.

"Sounds like you've been burned," Eve remarked.

"Yep! I had a friend stay at my apartment with me and my boyfriend during spring break when I was in college. I told her to make herself at home and that she could have anything in the apartment that she needed. Turns out she needed some dick."

"Damn, just like that?" Jackie laughed.

"Yep, just like that. I lost a best friend, boyfriend, and a real nice apartment. I learned quickly, though, and that was the last time I let a bitch live with me and my man."

Eve heard the front door open and smiled as she saw Amber appear in the doorway of the kitchen.

"Good morning, ladies."

"Hi, Amber, come and join the party." Jackie tried to take a piece of bacon from Jai's plate, but Jai slapped her hand away.

"Get your own plate," Jai pointed her fork at Jackie in a threatening manner.

"No need to get violent," Jackie said. She glanced at Eve's plate.

"Don't even try it, bitch. All this food, I *wish* you would touch my plate."

"What did I walk into?" Amber asked, hanging her bag on the back of a chair and taking a seat.

Eve handed her a plate. "Here, eat."

"No, thanks, I'm not very hungry. I'll just have some coffee and a bagel."

"Girl, you better fix a plate and eat." Eve was still holding the plate for Amber.

"Really, I'm not hungry. Guess it's nerves," Amber insisted.

"Then eat. You'll feel better." Eve shoved the plate into Amber's hand.

"Damn! Eat the cake, Anna Mae," Jackie laughed as she began fixing a plate of her own.

Amber took the plate and began scooping scrambled eggs just as her cell phone began ringing in her bag.

Eve glanced at the bag wondering if the call was for her. She watched as Amber retrieved the phone, glanced at the caller ID, and shrugged without answering. "That can wait," she said out loud.

"What's that?" Eve asked.

"What's what?" Amber asked, confused at the question.

"That?" Eve said pointing to Amber's phone.

"Oh, my cell phone. Sean gave it back to me this morning when I dropped Olivia off."

Eve held out her hand. "Then you won't be needing mine anymore."

"Oh, right," Amber said, reaching into her bag and retrieving Eve's BlackBerry. "Thanks. It turned out to be a lifesaver. We don't realize how much we rely on these things until we don't have one."

"That's why I have two," Eve said, making her way into the adjoining family room and tossing the phone into her bag.

"Does Chase know about that?" Jackie asked as she texted, not bothering to look up.

"Please, I had two phones when Chase met me," Eve said boldly as she returned to the kitchen. "In your line of work I'm surprised you don't have two."

Jackie looked up. "One phone is enough for me. The line that separates my personal life and my job is very thin. Sometimes I can't tell one from the other," she said.

"That can be dangerous," Eve replied, sipping her coffee and looking over the edge of the cup at Jackie.

Jackie glanced up and smiled slyly. "Fine with me. I like walking on the wild side."

"I guess you do," Jai said grabbing another slice of bacon. "But one of these days you're going to report the wrong thing and somebody is going to whoop that ass!"

"Well, you know what they say. You gotta bring some to get some!" Jackie laughed.

"Well, bring your ass in the back bedroom and get some of them damn boxes Eve and I spent all night packing," Amber laughed getting up and starting to clear the table.

"Right!" Jai said, standing and stretching. "Let's get started. I don't want to be here all day. Good breakfast, Eve," Jai said, licking her fingers and then dusting the bread crumbs onto her napkin. "So where do we start?"

"Eve and I were up until midnight bringing boxes downstairs. We thought it would make things a little easier," Amber said, standing.

"I brought my truck so I can take quite a bit," Jai said.

"Me too," Jackie stated, still typing. She bit a slice of bacon and chewed slowly, concentrating on her e-mails.

"Then I'll use Chase's truck," Eve said. "With that much truck space, we can be done in no time. I'll grab the dolly from the garage, and, Amber, you can use the cart we left in the back bedroom."

"Okay, then Jai and I will work together and you and Jackie can team up," Amber suggested, scooping the last of the leftovers into a container.

Eve turned to Jackie who had pulled out a pad and was now talking and taking notes. "Are you going to help or not?" Eve asked.

"Yes, but this is important." Jackie held her hand up. "Give me about five, ten minutes."

"You're parked in the driveway so we need to load your truck first," Eve stated impatiently.

"Shit, here, take my keys." Irritated, Jackie reached into her purse and tossed Eve her keys.

"You've got ten minutes, and then I'm turning your damn cell phone off until we finish," Eve said tucking Jackie's keys into her pocket. She made her way out of the kitchen and down the hallway to the garage side door. She sighed, not happy about the fact that Amber had arbitrarily paired her to work with Jackie. With what she knew about Jackie, Eve was still uncomfortable with being alone with her.

Eve stood on her tiptoes and strained to reach the dolly from its hanging place. She stretched, pulling at the dolly until it came crashing down. Eve screamed as she managed to barely escape getting hit in the head. "Jackie needs to bring her ass on," Eve fussed realizing she needed help.

She lifted the dolly to its upright position and rolled it into the house. She laughed when she witnessed Jai gingerly lifting only the small boxes. "Can you guys move to the side?" Eve said, rolling her eyes. "I can make two trips to your one at the rate you two are going."

"I don't do manual labor," Jai said checking the fingernail on her left index finger. "Shit! I chipped a nail already! Where's Jackie?"

"Busy being busy as usual. I have her keys so I'll start packing her truck while you guys pack yours, Jai," Eve said.

Eve loaded four boxes onto the dolly and headed back down the driveway, through the garage. She pressed the garage opener on the wall and waited as the door slowly opened. Pushing the dolly slowly, she headed for Jackie's Cadillac Escalade that was parked next to Jai's Range Rover. Unlike Jai, Jackie had not backed in, so Eve carefully maneuvered the dolly between the two vehicles being careful not to scratch their custom-paint jobs. She reached the rear of the Escalade and balanced the dolly with her foot while she searched in her pocket for Jackie's keys. When she managed to retrieve them, she pressed the automatic door opener and waited for the door to lift. She saw that there was a camera bag, tripod, and two boxes already inside.

"Jesus!" Eve complained. "She didn't even bother to clean it out."

She steadied the dolly until she got it to stand upright by itself, then rearranged the camera equipment and shoved the two boxes together. One was longer than the other, so Eve leaned in to reach the box that was farthest from the front. Leaning over the first box, she tugged at it, causing it to fall forward and the contents of the box to spill out. Eve tried to push the garments back into the box while tilting it upright, but it fell over on its side and out came a knit cap and a long braid of hair.

Lifting the cap, Eve discovered that it was actually a ski mask. She frowned as she held up the rest of the outfit which turned out to be a pair of black knit pants and a black hoodie. Eve looked back and forth at the assortment of clothing and the braid of hair and laughed, wondering what kind of cat burglar shit Jackie was carrying around in her trunk. The thought was barely out of her head before she froze suddenly. The reality of what she was looking at hit her like a ton of bricks!

"What the fuck!" she exclaimed staring at the garments and Carmen's cut-off braid. Eve couldn't believe what she was seeing, let alone what she was thinking, but as she quickly began to replay conversations and details over in her head, unanswered questions began to fall into place like a jigsaw puzzle. As if suddenly greased with Vaseline, Eve's hands became slick and clammy while her heart raced with emotions.

"Holy shit! It can't be!" she gasped.

Eve looked around to see if anyone was watching. She heard Amber and Jai pulling the cart through the side door and with only a split second to make a decision, she lifted her sweatshirt and tucked the braid underneath.

Eve quickly returned the clothing to the box and shoved it back into its original spot. Her hands were shaking as she hurriedly rearranged the items to make space. Quickly, she placed the four boxes into the truck, then slid the last box back into place. She peeked her head around the rear of the truck at the sound of Amber's and Jai's voices.

"You okay back here?" Amber asked, slightly winded.

"I'm fine," Eve said ceremonially dusting her hands off and trying to appear calm. She could tell by the look on Amber's face that she was failing miserably.

"You sure?" Jai asked, double-checking.

"Yeah, one of the boxes was a little heavier than I expected." Eve forced a big grin and pushed the dolly past Amber, entering the garage along the far side of Jai's truck. As she pushed, she gripped the dolly tightly in an effort to keep her hands from shaking, purposely not looking back at Jai and Amber.

"We stacked boxes in the hallway for you," Amber yelled after Eve.

"Okay!" Eve replied over her shoulder. It was the only response she could muster as she made her way back into the house.

Once alone, Eve stood trying to gather her senses, but instead, felt a knot forming in her stomach. She needed to think, but her thoughts were coming so fast she couldn't sort them quickly enough. First the Paula and Jackie scene, and now this! Although, she had known Jackie for a long time, at the moment, she was beginning to wonder if she had ever really known her at all.

Eve felt her shock slowly turn to anger as she rushed to the guest bathroom and closed the door. She pulled the braid from her sweatshirt and examined it at arm's length; it had to be at least two feet long with rubber bands at both ends. She knew the braid belonged to Carmen Garza. *What the fuck do I keep stumbling into?* Eve thought as she leaned back on the sink and closed her eyes.

"Hey! You taking a break already?" Amber asked, knocking on the door.

"Be right out!" Eve said as she reached over and flushed the toilet.

She folded the braid and placed it in the cabinet, then turned and looked at herself in the mirror. While she was a nervous wreck on the inside, she made sure that she looked as normal as possible on the outside. She grabbed a guest towel, dropped it in the sink, and turned on the cold water. Quickly, she dabbed the cold towel on her face and rubbed it across the back of her neck, then tossed it into the hamper. Taking a deep breath, she checked herself in the mirror one more time. "God, please get me through this day," she sighed quietly and opened the bathroom door.

As she exited Eve was startled by Amber who was standing directly outside the bathroom. "Are you *sure* you're all right? You don't look so good."

"I'm fine." Eve dismissed Amber with a wave of the hand. "I guess I just didn't get enough sleep," she said faking a yawn. "I'll be okay. Come on, let's get finished." Eve hurried down the hallway before Amber could protest.

"And where the fuck is Jackie?" Eve yelled over her shoulder.

"I'm right here," Jackie said appearing in the hallway.

"It's about time," Jai snapped.

"Damn, I told you I needed a minute," Jackie snapped back.

"Help us load the cart," Jai said, grabbing a box.

"Are we putting this stuff in my truck?" Jackie asked, lifting a box and placing it on the cart.

"I already put boxes in your truck, but you can probably get a couple more in," Eve said tossing Jackie her keys without making eye contact. "We can start loading mine."

"What's up with you?" Jackie asked, eyeing Eve suspiciously.

"Nothing. Why does everybody keep asking me that?"

"Damn, who pissed in your Cheerios?" Jackie huffed.

"It was hash browns," Jai said trying to lighten the mood. "And why don't you two leave her alone? She said nothing was wrong."

"I was just concerned," Amber said.

"Yea, Eve, what's up?" Jackie continued to pry.

Without responding, Eve shoved the dolly under a stack of boxes, spun it around, and headed for the garage. Before exiting, she stopped and turned to face the trio. "It's nothing. Now let's just focus and get this done, already," she concluded as she rolled the dolly into the garage and out of sight.

Eve lifted the boxes into Chase's truck two at a time. She needed to get Amber moved as quickly as possible. She could hear the ladies mumbling but tried to remain calm. Jackie was a master at reading body language, and right now, she felt like an open book, so she'd have to avoid her at all costs.

Eve stretched and rubbed her shoulders as she slowly walked toward Chase's truck parked in Amber's driveway while Amber, Jackie, and Jai followed a short distance behind. She ached all over from the lifting and pulling, and she had a headache. She could hear the trio behind her expressing the same sentiments.

"What was I thinking?" Jai asked. "I hurt in places I know I shouldn't! Whose big idea was it to have a moving party anyway?" she yelled to make sure Eve could hear.

Eve kept walking, without bothering to turn around and flipped Jai the bird. She could hear them all laughing, but she was too tired to join in. It was nearly eight o'clock in the evening, but the relocation of Amber and Olivia was complete. Amber had insisted that they leave the boxes for her to unpack, but the ladies would hear none of it. Together, the four had unboxed, folded, and placed every bit of clothing, toys, and personal items back in their rightful places.

It had turned out to be more work than Eve had anticipated, but in the end, that turned out to be a good thing. They were all so busy that Eve barely had time to think about what she had found. She had forced it to lie dormant in the back of her mind until now, but once released, the thoughts came rushing back like a tornado.

She climbed into the truck and watched as Amber hugged and thanked Jackie and Jai for the umpteenth time.

"Night!" Eve waved lazily as the two yelled good night in her direction.

Within moments, Jackie's and Jai's cars disappeared into the darkness.

"God, I had no idea this was going to take so long. I promised the girls I would take you all out to dinner after I'm back to a normal routine." Amber stretched. "Damn that feels good!"

"Take your time on that dinner thing. I've spent enough time with the three of you to last me for a while," Eve smiled.

"So are you going to tell me what was up with you today?"

Eve contemplated telling Amber what she had found, but she was saved from making the decision when a vehicle turned into the driveway.

"It's Sean and Olivia," Amber said, shielding her eyes from the bright lights.

"Hey, you go and make nice-nice with the family. I have something I gotta do. We'll talk later."

"Thanks," Amber said, nervously, thrusting her hands into her pockets. "Oh! Guess I won't be needing these," she said, pulling Eve's spare house keys from her pocket and handing them over.

"Let's hope not," Eve smiled as she accepted the keys and squeezed Amber's hand before letting go. "Good luck, boo," she said as they exchanged expressions that needed no words.

Eve started the truck and slowly drove past Sean and Olivia, waving to them through the window. She added a good-bye honk and headed off into the darkness. Eve sighed so heavily that she could feel her breath on her hands as she gripped the steering wheel. She shuttered at the thought of what she would find when she got to the bottom of this latest discovery, trusting that she would, in fact, get to the bottom of it. But in order to get to the bottom, she knew she had to start at the top . . . And now more than ever before, she was sure that the person at the top was definitely Callie Peteers.

the truth about her actions, she'd allowed Callie to take the fall for something Jackie knew Callie didn't do.

"Eve, are you going to tell me what happened or not?" Callie persisted.

Eve took a deep breath, then released twenty minutes' worth of confessions complete with everything from her not actually believing in Callie's innocence to Jackie's bathroom affair with Paula to finally her discovery of Carmen's braid in Jackie's trunk. Eve's body was wet with sweat as she freed herself from the information she'd been holding on to. She circled the room with her eyes until they found their way back to Callie, who sat calmly in the adjacent chair. Eve continued to breathe deeply as she waited for Callie to speak. Yet instead of saying anything, Eve watched as Callie unlocked a nearby desk drawer and pulled out a manila envelope.

"What's this?" Eve asked as Callie handed her the envelope.

"I knew all along," Callie admitted.

"Knew what?" Eve quizzed opening the envelope.

"The truth," Callie answered, taking a seat next to her.

Eve pulled out several photos of Carmen entangled in what appeared to be another sex session. Only instead of the pictures of Carmen and Drew making love, the photos were of Carmen and Jackie.

"I don't understand," Eve declared. "How did you get these? And why didn't you say something?"

"I got the photos awhile back when my private investigator was following Drew and Carmen. While investigating Drew, he also made the discovery about Carmen and Jackie. He didn't consider the information important enough to tell me until he got wind of me being under investigation. He knew I was innocent. The pictures were his way of helping me prove that. But when I saw these, I knew that by exposing Jackie to prove my own innocence, I'd be violating the pact we all agreed to when we joined the association. I couldn't allow all of your hard work to go to waste, nor did I want to put the association in jeopardy of exposure of far greater things." Callie ran her fingers

28

Presumed Innocent

Eve sat motionless while Callie poured the two of them a cup of tea. Although her mind remained numb, her hands were still shaking as she accepted the ginger and pear infusion from Callie's grasp.

"You've got to tell me what happened, Eve. You're shaking like a leaf." Callie gently placed her hand on Eve's back.

Eve took a small sip of her tea as she tried hard to regain her composure. She wasn't sure how she was going to break the news of what she'd discovered in Jackie's trunk to Callie, especially since for weeks she hadn't believed in her innocence. Although Eve had been supportive of Callie and had even managed to finally convince Jackie and Jai to contribute to Callie's legal fund, she hadn't been fully persuaded that Callie hadn't attacked Carmen, until now.

Eve stared at Callie, admiring her ability to try to comfort her when she, in fact, had been the one who had gone through hell for the past few weeks. She wondered about the toll these allegations had taken on her marriage to Drew. The fact that Callie was so concerned about how Carmen's attack would affect her family that she shipped her children off to Brazil to be with her mother angered Eve. Jackie had been guilty all along and instead of trusting the organization with through her hair. "I figured the police didn't and wouldn't have enough information to actually charge me with anything so we'd be safe."

"You did all of this for us?" Eve asked astonished.

"Rule #5, remember?" She paused a moment, recalling how serious Eve had been regarding this point. "I took my commitment to The Wives Association seriously with the assurance that if put in a similar position, you ladies would have done the same for me, right?"

Eve nodded. "I don't know what to say." She stood and gave Callie a hug. "I would've done the same thing for you, Callie."

"I know," she replied with confidence. "Even with the pictures and the braid, we still can't take this to the police, so I'm still in the same position."

"No, you're not. You went above and beyond duty to protect Jackie and the association, so now the association will do everything in its power to protect you. Since technically, Jackie is the one that got you into this mess, I'll see to it that she personally helps to get you out."

"Thank you, Eve. I knew I could trust you."

"You can, Callie," Eve stated. "No matter what, I'll always have your back. Anything you need, just ask."

"There is something," Callie said. "Something I haven't told you or any of the ladies."

"What is it?" Eve asked curiously.

"I have a bit of a past."

"Hell, don't we all?" Eve joked.

"I'm sure not like mine. Let's just say me attacking Carmen wouldn't have been off base. I've done something like that before, which is why Drew accepted a deal to come here to the London I have a record for assault back in Brazil."

"I had no idea. What do you need me to do?" Eve asked.

"Drew thinks I had something to do with this thing with Carmen. He's threatening to leave me and take my boys."

"He's the one who cheated on you, Callie! How can he take your boys away?" Eve protested.

"It's complicated," she said sadly. "And to be honest, I don't have the energy to fight this. I love Drew despite his indiscretions. I'll do anything to keep our family together. That's why I forced myself to get pregnant. I've been seeing a specialist and have been taking fertility pills in an attempt to have another child. Drew has no idea, but I know he'd never leave me if he knew I was having another baby."

"Callie . . . I'm not here to judge you, but do you really think trapping Drew is the answer?"

"It's the only choice I have," Callie stated with desperation. "You've got to help me, Eve."

Eve was stunned by Callie's revelation but knew she had to help her. Regardless of her issues or even her past mistakes, Callie was one of them, and as an association, they protected their own.

"I'll help," Eve whispered. "And don't worry. Your secrets are safe with me."

Eve sat back in her chair and took another long sip of her ginger and pear tea. She couldn't believe the loyalty Callie had displayed with her and the association, especially at the potential cost of her own freedom. In order for her loyalty to be matched, Eve knew that she was going to have to confront Jackie once and for all about the secrets she had been keeping on her behalf.

With Jackie there was no other way to handle her except head-on. She'd have to discuss this face-to-face and woman-to-woman, with hopes that they would see eye-to-eye and agree on what would have to be done in order to help Callie. Eve knew that this meeting of the minds between her and Jackie would not exactly be easy, but in order for the association and Rule #5 to work, it was extremely necessary for everyone involved.

Eve tossed the braid into the trunk, slid into the driver's seat, and flung her bag down. The visit with Callie had been exhausting. She placed her hands on the steering wheel, lowered her head, and sucked in as much air as her lungs could hold.

"Son of a . . ." she whispered as she thought about what Jackie had done. *Jackie has to be stopped,* she thought. It was one thing to have her little tryst with Paula, but what had been done to disrupt the lives of Carmen and Callie was inexcusable.

Finally, she felt she had the ammunition she needed to confront Jackie, and like an automatic weapon that had been locked and loaded, with Jackie O'Connor as her intended target, Eve was more than ready to empty her clip.

Reaching into her bag, she pulled out the picture of Jackie and Carmen and stared at the couple. *Couple,* she thought. That's what had been so confusing. They actually looked like a couple!

Eve tried to imagine what Jackie's reaction would be when she presented her with the photo. Jackie was not easily ruffled, she thought, so it would be confrontational suicide to come at her with some weak shit. What was going on in this photo, however, definitely was not weak shit, Eve thought as she tucked the picture into the crevice of the passenger seat. She and Jackie had history, and she was counting on that history to cushion the fall that their relationship was about to take.

Eve retrieved her phone and slowly dialed Jackie's number.

"O'Connor here, what's up, Eve?"

Eve could barely hear Jackie over her music. Beyoncé's "Party" was playing loudly in the background.

"I need to talk to you," Eve yelled, competing with Jackie's Bose system.

"About what?" Jackie shouted back.

"Can you turn it down?" Eve asked.

"This had better be good," Jackie replied lowering the music.

"Damn, Jackie, how can you concentrate with the music that loud?"

"Well, until you called, my music was my concentration, and right about now, you're disturbing my groove. So, what's up?"

"I need to talk to you."

"So talk," Jackie said sarcastically.

"Not over the phone," Eve said making sure the determination was evident in her voice.

"Eve, I'm on my way home. I've had one too many beers, and I am not in the mood for your usual cloak-and-dagger James Bond shit."

"It's about Carmen Garza and Callie," Eve delivered the words boldly. The silence on the other end of the phone was a clear indication that Eve had Jackie's full attention. "We need to talk face-to-face. I'll come to you."

"I'm in Inglewood. I just dropped my girls over at Mom's in Carlton Square."

"So where can we meet?"

Eve noticed a sudden silence as if Jackie's engine was no longer running.

"I'm in the parking lot of the Forum. I'll give you fifteen minutes, and then I'm going home."

"I'll be there in ten."

Within minutes on the 405, Eve had made the drive from Brentwood to Inglewood. She spotted Jackie's Jaguar in the middle of the parking lot as she turned off Pincay Drive. When she pulled up, she noticed Jackie was already out of her car, leaning against the hood with her park lights still on. Eve parked her Range Rover head-to-head with Jackie's Jag, opting to leave her lights on as well. Grabbing the picture, she exited the car and stood directly in front of Jackie.

"So what's this about Carmen and Callie?" Jackie asked.

"Well, I see you don't want to beat around the bush," Eve said handing Jackie the photograph.

She watched as Jackie, seemingly unfazed, admired the picture, viewing it from different angles.

"Damn, she makes me look good!" Jackie folded her arms. "So what do you think you have here?" she asked.

"Evidence that you had a relationship with Carmen and after

my conversation with Callie, evidence that you had a motive to attack her."

"And if you're right?"

"Not *if,* Jackie. I know I'm right. And because of you, Callie is under suspicion for something she didn't do. You've made her life a living hell, and I'm here to tell you that you are going to fix this or—"

"Or *what,* Eve?"

"Or I'm going to make sure that people know what you've done. You can't play with people's lives and expect there to be no consequences, Jackie!"

"You don't scare me, Eve, and if this picture is all you have as evidence, we could have saved this little meeting. You come at me; you'd better come with more than just a fucking photograph."

"Oh, I have more," Eve replied.

"I don't care if you have a whole fucking photo album, Eve. I'm not worried about you."

"Well, you should be, unless you want me to give a blow-by-blow of what you and Paula Andrews were doing in the bathroom in Baltimore," Eve said matter-of-factly.

"Look at you," Jackie said clapping sarcastically. "Eve done gone and got herself an exclusive! Too bad you won't be able to use it."

"Don't think I won't use this information to take you down, Jackie. You will fix this shit for Callie, or I swear I will bulldoze your little undercover playhouse and expose you for the freaky, two-faced, coldhearted bitch you really are."

Eve waited, bracing herself for the wrath she was sure would follow, but instead, Jackie smiled, locking eyes with Eve's stare.

"You may be smart, Eve, with all your fancy words and legal jargon. And you can call me whatever you like, but at the end of the day when you peel back the layers of your own life, you'll realize that the two of us aren't very different. Yes, you may be the mastermind behind The Wives Association, but this ain't my first time at the rodeo, boo-boo. I know how the game is played. Hell, I even invented some of the rules. I'm going to fix the shit for Callie, but not because of anything you think you have dangling over my head, and in return, you're going to keep your mouth shut," Jackie stated straightforwardly as she folded her arms leaning in closer to Eve.

"The Wives Association is the very reason that you are protecting Callie, and it's also the very reason why you can't touch me. Rule #5, Eve, and I quote, 'All members of the association will be required to sign an agreement that forbids sharing any information regarding the activities of the association and its members with any person or persons outside of the association.' So, you see, Eve, thanks to you and your rules, I'm protected from any recourse. And unless you want to find yourself guilty of breaching that clause and in jeopardy of being voted out of the association, you are bound to secrecy. Now, unless you have something else to discuss, I'm outta here."

"Fix it!" Eve demanded.

"Count on it," Jackie said as she turned to leave. She opened the door to her car and held up the photograph. "Oh, you don't mind if I keep this, do you? It's such a good picture," she said admiring the photo again.

Eve stood silently as Jackie's words resonated in her ears. Once again, Jackie was standing under the umbrella of protection provided by rule #5, and there was nothing she could do about it. *Fucking catch-22*, she thought.

"I'll take your silence as a yes," Jackie said and turned to get into her car.

Eve watched as Jackie started her car and drove away. One thing she knew about Jackie was that she could be trusted to do whatever she said she would do. And although she didn't exactly know how Jackie was going to pull it off, she knew Callie would be exonerated. Still, Eve realized that she had just opened a whole other can of worms, and she needed time to think things through.

As she slowly eased her truck out of the Forum parking lot, Eve couldn't help but think how ironically apropos the location had been. She and Jackie had sparred like verbal gladiators, and while her mission had been accomplished, somehow she didn't feel quite so victorious after all.

29

Now Run Tell That Bitch!

"*. . . and* I told his monkey ass that if he insisted on playing with fire, his ass was eventually going to get burned. But did he listen?" Brandon rattled on. "Hell, no! Instead, he went ahead and fucked ole girl without a condom. And *bam!* Chile, her coochie burned him so bad his dick is still smoking."

Eve found herself laughing at Brandon's morning dose of daily gossip. Since the Leopards had advanced to the National Bowl Championship game, Eve had been working a lot from home, allowing Brandon the opportunity to come over to her house and dish his dirt to her face-to-face rather than having to do it over the phone.

"I've told you about getting in other people's business, Brandon. You better be careful before you talk yourself into some serious trouble. The partners at the firm don't play that meddling nonsense," Eve warned, handing Brandon a stack of finished files.

"I don't go looking for this shit, Mrs. Eve; they bring this bull crap to me. Besides, I have no desire to go and work for one of those stiff-ass partners. I'm perfectly content working for you," Brandon stated.

"I just want you to have options, Brandon. What are you going to do when I'm no longer with the agency?"

"Oh my goodness! Oh my Laaaaawd! Mrs. Eve, *please* tell me you're not thinking of leaving the agency. If you leave, I'ma die." Brandon faked hyperventilating. "I just bought a new condo, and I'm still paying off my damn student loans. And don't even get me started on what I owe on my Neiman's card." Now Brandon started fanning himself.

"Where else am I gonna find a job where I only work thirty hours a week and make over eighty thousand dollars a year?"

"You make over eighty thousand dollars a year—working for me?" Eve quizzed.

Brandon pretended to faint backward on the couch. "Oh, Lawd!"

"Stop being dramatic," Eve demanded. "I'm not leaving tomorrow. I'm just saying."

"What are you saying? Are you saying you're planning on leaving me? When? Why?" he whined.

Eve shook her head, rose from the couch, and walked into the kitchen. She grabbed a bottle of water from the refrigerator, opened it, and took a swig.

"Well, I wasn't going to say anything until we actually officially starting trying, however, I guess now is as good a time as any." Eve took another sip of her water, then continued. "Chase and I have decided to start a family."

"Awwwwwwww, Mrs. Eve!" Brandon squealed. "Oh, girl, that's wonderful! And it's about time too. Hell, I'm surprised you and Chase waited this long to have some babies. Fine as Chase is, I'd be like a freakin' garden. And honey, he could spread his seed *wherever* he wanted."

"All right, now!" Eve said playfully. "Don't be fanaticizing about my man's seed," she laughed. "But seriously, I would never leave you high and dry. I'd make sure you were straight before I'd ever even consider resigning."

"Whew! Thank you, Miss Girl, 'cause you already know . . ." he said, pretending to wipe his forehead.

Eve positioned herself on the couch and flipped on the TV.

"What are you doing?" Brandon quizzed. "We've still got ten files to finish, and I was hoping to get out of here in time to get myself a quick mani and pedi."

"Boy," Eve said playfully, "I'll make sure you get out of here in time, but Jackie's exclusive interview with Carmen Garza is about to come on. I promised her I'd be watching," she said, flipping through the channels until she landed on KTEL.

"I forgot Jackie was your home girl," Brandon said sitting down next to Eve. "I've always wondered how she managed to get all those juicy exclusives. Girl, I heard people have been promising their first-born child in an effort to get an interview with that Tresses model since she was attacked."

"What can I say? Jackie has a way with women," Eve grinned.

"Well, chile, whatever she's doing, she needs to keep it up. Hell, Jackie's the only reason I even bother to watch the news." Brandon focused his attention on the seventy-two inch television screen that nearly covered the wall in Eve's den. "Oh, girl, there she is . . . turn it up!" Brandon shouted.

"We interrupt this program to bring you a KTEL special report with Jackie O'Conner . . ."

"Good evening, I'm Jackie O'Conner, and today, I'm bringing you an exclusive interview with supermodel and Tresses spokeswoman Carmen Garza. If you recall, KTEL was first to break the story of Ms. Garza's savage attack a few months back, and since then, there has been an ongoing investigation and search to find her attacker. Ms. Garza was not only brutally beaten, but her legendary locks were cut off during the attack, leaving her bald and in jeopardy of losing her multimillion-dollar endorsement deal. This bizarre story received both national and international attention and left the world in wonder as to who could have possibly done something so heinous to the young model. While there was a great deal of speculation surrounding the attack, several sources suggested Ms. Garza's assault could have been motivated by revenge. There has been a slew of reports linking Ms. Garza romantically to several Hollywood A-listers, including Bradley Cooper, Idris Elba, George Clooney, A-Rod, and most recently, Los Angeles soccer sensation Drew Peteers."

"Whaaaaat? Girl, did you know Carmen was banging Drew Peteers?" Brandon asked rolling his neck. "Between him and David Beckham, ooooooh, chile, I'd like to be the piece of meat at the center of that soccer sandwich."

"Shhhhhhh!" Eve ordered.

"Oh no, you *didn't*," Brandon said rolling his eyes. "You better be glad I want to hear this."

"It's been speculated that the married soccer star's wife, Callie Peteers has been questioned by the police in conjunction with the attack. It's been alleged that upon finding out about her husband's affair, Mrs. Peteers took matters into her own hands and attacked Carmen as a way of sending her a message about messing with her man."

"I told you!" Brandon shouted out. "I knew that little hussy had pissed off someone's wife. But Mrs. Callie shut a bitch down . . . I see you, boo-boo! I-See-You!"

Eve could hardly contain herself. She looked over at Brandon who was waving his hand in the air but didn't say a word. She didn't want to encourage him.

"Now, my fans know that I pride myself on reporting the good, the bad, and the ugly, and as a fellow athlete's wife,

I understand the frustrations of media speculation and the strain that it can cause on a marriage, which is why I took it upon myself to reach out to Ms. Garza so she could set the record straight once and for all."

Carmen appeared on screen sporting a fierce Halle Berry-inspired hairstyle and wearing a chic mustard-colored wrap atop a black, long sleeve fitted shirt. Her faux leather pants fit like a glove as she sat casually in the chocolate-colored gold-studded chair opposite of Jackie. It was obvious that Carmen had seen a plastic surgeon post-attack because her face was not only scar-free but also foundationally flawless with the perfect amount of rich purple and gold hues accenting her eyes and cheeks.

"Daaaaaaaaamn! Even after a beat down and a buzz cut that bitch still looks good," Brandon praised Carmen's new look. "Hell, I thought she looked hot with long hair, but I don't know . . . she's rocking the hell out of that short hair."

"Ms. Garza's alleged relationship with Drew Peteers hit the wire by storm, and today, she's here to discuss the details of her involvement with Mr. Peteers. Let me be the first to say that I've already spoken to Ms. Garza, and the information she's about to reveal may come as a shock. In her first live interview ever, we welcome Ms. Garza to our KTEL studios. Ms. Garza . . ."

Eve watched as Jackie stood up to greet Carmen. She noticed that their chemistry was awkward yet familiar.

"I can't stand it!" Brandon exclaimed. "I wonder what she has to say."

"Shhhhh!" Eve stated again.

"Okay, Mrs. Eve, shush me again, here!" Brandon said matter-of-factly.

Eve laughed giving Brandon a sympathetic wink. "You know I'm just playing with you," she teased. "But seriously, I need you keep the commentary to a minimum."

"Shhhhh!" Brandon fired back playfully.

Carmen's smile was subtle as she turned to Jackie.

"Thank you for coming, Ms. Garza," Jackie greeted.

"Thank you having me," Carmen said politely.

"Let's just dive right in, shall we? Now, during the pre-interview, you made a startling revelation to me regarding your relationship with soccer sensation Drew Peteers. Explain to our viewers the nature of that relationship."

"I met Drew Peteers during a photo shoot. Drew had just signed on to be the face of the Tresses for Men Hair Care line, and as the company's official spokesperson, it was my job to welcome him to the company and kind of show him the ropes. Throughout the course of us working together, I grew very fond of Mr. Peteers and assumed the feeling was mutual. But I was wrong," Callie admitted.

"So just for clarity, are you saying you made advances toward Mr. Peteers that weren't returned?"

"I'm saying that I allowed myself to read more into something than I should have. I did initiate a sexual relationship with Drew; however, he respectfully declined my offer. However, rather than accept his decision, I took it upon myself to pursue him more aggressively."

"Is it safe to say you became obsessed with Mr. Peteers?" Jackie pressed.

"Yes," Carmen replied shamefully.

"Oh hell, no!" Brandon interrupted. "It never fails. The pretty ones are always the crazies. Look at Halle Berry, Jennifer Lopez, and Denise Richards. All beautiful, and I hear all cuckoo for Cocoa Puffs crazy."

"For years, I've struggled with an addictive personality. I started taking antidepressants when I was fifteen shortly after my father died and formed a habit that I couldn't break. I began mixing medications to numb the pain I was feeling, and before I knew it, I was hooked."

"Did your addiction to pain medication play a part in your attack?"

"It did. I've hidden my addiction for years now. I've been embarrassed to admit that I have a problem."

"Tell us about the night of your attack," Jackie asked sympathetically.

"I forced myself on Drew. Repeatedly he refused me and went home to be with his wife and his kids. I spun out of control, took a handful of pills, shaved my head, and attempted to drive. Apparently, I . . . ummm . . . hit a pole, and when I came to, I realized what I had done, so I panicked and made up the story about being attacked."

"We've obtained photos taken of you leaving the OC Body Repair Shop and after speaking to the shop's owner, he does confirm your story. Why the cover-up?"

Jackie and Carmen studied the photo of Carmen leaving the auto body shop.

"Fear," Carmen acknowledged.

"So you were never attacked?"

"No," Carmen admitted as if she'd been coached to perfection.

"And the affair between you and Drew Peteers never happened?"

"That is correct," she replied.

"So what happens to you now?"

"I've accepted a plea deal with the district attorney's office as it relates to me falsifying information on a police report. Instead of jail time, I've agreed to enter into a drug rehabilitation center, and upon completion, I'll serve six months of probation."

"What about the Peteers family? I know Drew's wife Callie Peteers was questioned by the police as it relates to your attack. What do you have to say to them?"

"Addiction is a tragic, tragic problem. I pray that the Peteers family can find it in their hearts to forgive me for any pain that my actions may have caused their family."

Eve smiled. "Perfect," she stated aloud as she listened to Carmen's apology to Callie.

"Any final words?" Jackie summarized.

"I like to thank all of my fans for their support. I'd especially like to thank the entire staff at Tresses Hair Care for continuing to support me while I get help for my disease."

"You mean this bitch gets to keep her damn job?" Brandon shouted at the TV.

"On behalf of KTEL, I'd like to thank you for coming here today and having the courage to tell the truth about what happened. Our thoughts and prayers will be with you while you enter rehab on your journey to become healthy and whole." Jackie turned from Carmen and looked directly into the camera.

"Thank you for watching, America. This is Jackie O'Conner with another KTEL exclusive."

"Whew, chile! I wasn't ready for all that! Your girl Jackie is amazing."

"She's something," Eve agreed with a grin, wondering how Jackie managed to pull this entire interview off. When she informed Eve that she would handle the situation with Carmen, she never expected this. Even with the threat of personal exposure, Jackie didn't budge. She simply looked Eve in the eye and stood her ground. As much as Eve hated to admit it, Jackie was right; the two of them were more alike than she'd thought. Like Jackie, Eve would do whatever was necessary to protect the things and people she loved. As twisted as it may have seemed, the ladies made a deal. Today's interview with Carmen proved the lengths that Jackie would go to do her part, and Eve knew that the expectation for her to hold up her end of the bargain would now be greater than ever.

30

Home Sweet Home!

"I was so glad to hear that everything worked out for Callie, although I have to admit that the way that Carmen chick said it all went down was pretty bizarre." Amber held the steaming pot over the colander as she strained water from a freshly made pot of pasta.

"I'm glad too," Eve said finishing the last bite of her salad. "That's one more victory for The Wives Association."

"That's right, and by my calculation, the score is Wives' Association two, scandalous bitches zilch," Amber said raising her glass.

Eve glanced around Amber's kitchen taking note of the black custom cabinets with opaque glass, cream and onyx marble countertops, and oversized stainless steel appliances. She admired the long marble rectangular working space in the center of the kitchen and the adjacent breakfast island. It was truly an interesting design, but what was more interesting was the way her friend was moving comfortably around the room.

Eve sat at the island and slowly sipped her wine as she watched Amber scoop a tomato-based sauce of sausage and ground turkey onto two plates of pasta. She wondered what Amber was thinking but fought the urge to pry.

"Not too much for me," Eve warned. "I think I ate too much

salad." She leaned back, rubbed her stomach, and smiled contentedly as she slid her salad plate to the side.

"Sorry," Amber replied. "I forgot I wasn't fixing this for Sean. Should I take some off?"

"No, that's fine. You know I always did love your spaghetti, girl. You can't cook shit else, but your ass could always make some bomb spaghetti," Eve laughed.

"Well, I can proudly say that that is no longer true," Amber replied confidently, swinging her hips and almost singing the words as she carried the two plates to the table and set them down ceremonially.

"What's no longer true?" Eve asked as she shook parmesan cheese onto the pasta.

"That I can't cook worth shit," Amber replied defiantly as she made her way across the kitchen. She slid on an oven mitt and recoiled at the sudden blast of heat as she opened the upper door of her double oven.

Before she could even see it, Eve smelled the aroma of fresh garlic bread wafting toward her. "Damn, girl, you cooked garlic bread too?" she exclaimed as she twirled a huge helping of pasta onto her fork.

"Yes, and it's not store bought either. I made it from scratch," Amber said proudly as she eased the hot tray from the oven.

"Scratch?" Eve stopped with her fork of pasta in midair and squinted at Amber. "Whatchu talkin' bout, Willis?" she laughed.

"Scratch. You know, like make the dough, crush the garlic, grind the basil, and melt the butter . . . scratch!" Amber smiled triumphantly as she grabbed a small wooden carving board from the kitchen counter and placed it on the island in front of Eve. She stood with one hand on her hip still balancing the tray of piping hot bread in the other. "What? You don't want any?" she teased, waving the bread in front of Eve.

Eve surveyed the two loaves of bread on the tray. It certainly looked homemade, she thought. She wasn't sure if Amber was telling the truth or not, but the shit looked good and smelled even better!

"Bitch, don't play with me. You better give me some of that bread," Eve said threateningly. She watched as Amber transferred one of the loaves to the carving board and skillfully sliced it into serving sizes.

"Smells good!" Eve said taking a slice and biting into it immediately. She closed her eyes. "Mmm," she moaned as she slowly opened one eye and looked at Amber suspiciously. "You *really* made this?"

"Yes," Amber beamed proudly as she took her seat.

"Well, I'll be a white man's grandbaby!" Eve exclaimed taking another bite. "This shit is really good, Ams! You been watching the cooking channels or something?" she joked.

"Actually, I have. They're pretty good too. Who knew?"

"Well, if they can get your ass to make homemade garlic bread that tastes like this, they get my vote." Eve finished her slice of bread and grabbed another.

"No, trust me, they are really helpful. I have been making, I mean, cooking, dinner for the past two weeks, and Olivia and Sean have been raving about how good it's been. I discovered that I actually enjoy cooking. I think I have some kind of natural talent or something because once my ass discovered that it wasn't that hard, I started experimenting with different spices and stuff. Don't be surprised if you turn on the TV and find me on my own cooking show whipping up some Amber Ambrosia or some Jackson Jambalaya!" Amber laughed as she grabbed a slice of the bread and bit into it.

"What brought this on?" Eve asked laughing at Amber's TV fantasy.

"Well," Amber said suddenly serious, "I thought about what you said when the whole Sa'Myra thing went down and decided that maybe I should learn to cook." She shrugged her shoulders.

"Girl, I was just kidding. If Sean was going to cheat, it could have been with anybody—the maid, your hairstylist, even Olivia's teacher."

"Damn," Amber said somberly staring at her plate. "That means now I'm going to have to take a domestic class, a cosmetology class, and get my teaching credentials so I can homeschool Livie." She looked up at Eve sadly for a few seconds, and then burst into laughter. "Gotcha!"

Eve grabbed her napkin and tossed it playfully at Amber. "You had me going for a moment," she laughed. Then she twirled her fork into the pasta and contemplated asking Amber how things were really going with her and Sean but decided not to put a damper on the mood.

"Hey, you," Amber said. "I can almost read your mind, and the answer is fine."

"What?" Eve asked innocently.

"Me and Sean. We're fine. In fact, it's better than before. You know the old saying, 'You won't know how strong your relationship is until you have problems.'" Amber scrunched her face and smiled. "Well, that's not exactly how it goes, but hell, you know what I mean," she said waving a forkful of pasta at Eve before shoving it into her mouth. "We're in a good place right now. We . . ." Amber hesitated and glanced at Eve.

"What's the matter?"

"Nothing. I was just going to say we've even talked about adopting a baby."

"Adopting?" Eve asked surprised. "Why adopt?"

"You remember how horrible my pregnancy was. I was sick almost the entire nine months, and I don't care what anybody says, I had the worst labor ever! It was eighteen hours of kicking and screaming and damn near passing out, and that was just Sean! We agreed that neither of us wants to go through that again. I know I don't!"

Eve shrugged. "I've never been in labor, so I can't speak on that. But Sean's really okay with adopting, huh?" She took a sip of wine as she considered her next statement. "You know how they say men always want a son of their own."

"I truly don't believe Sean cares. We haven't made any final decision, but we both agree that adoption is an option."

"Well, whatever you decide, as long as you're both happy, that's all that matters to me."

"Thanks, Eve." Amber extended her glass of wine to Eve, and they touched glasses.

As she took a sip, Eve looked over the rim of her glass and smiled. Amber certainly looked happy, she thought; besides, who was she to question it? She turned her attention to her plate unsuccessfully chasing the last of her fleeting spaghetti around in circles. Frustrated, she grabbed another piece of garlic bread and used it to shovel the last bit of noodles and sauce onto her fork and triumphantly shoved it into her mouth.

She heard Amber laughing and looked up inquisitively. "What?"

"If you wanted another piece of bread, all you had to do was ask!"

"I ain't gone lie," Eve said licking her fingers and laughing. "The shit is good!"

"Want anything else?" Amber asked as she got up from her seat and began clearing the dishes.

"No, I'm good. Need any help with those?"

"No, I'll take care of it. Unfortunately, cleaning up behind yourself is one of the two downsides I've found to cooking."

"What's the other?" Eve asked.

"Tasting everything!" Amber laughed as she patted her ass. "I've put on two pounds in the last week!"

Eve laughed as she stood and stretched. "Well, if you don't need my help, I'd better go because I'm about to catch a serious case of Itis. Besides, it looks like my work here is done. I can cross you off my to-do list because it sounds like you and Sean are doing just fine."

Eve reached out her arms soliciting a hug, and Amber complied. As they rocked back and forth cocooned tightly in each other's grasp, Eve closed her eyes and squeezed her friend even tighter. Finally releasing her hold, Eve held Amber at arm's length and without speaking, they locked eyes, sharing a private moment of kindred spirit and a sense of accomplishment.

"Come on," Amber said swiping at her moist eyes with the back of her hand, "I'll walk you out."

Eve put her arm around Amber's shoulders, and with Amber's arm around her waist, they slowly walked from the kitchen, down the hallway past the now infamous sight of the dreadful birthday party, and to the front door.

Eve gave Amber another squeeze and waited as Amber opened the door for her to leave. "You take it easy," she said.

"I will. I promise," Amber returned smiling.

For a split second Eve thought she detected bit of sadness in Amber's smile, yet it was gone just as quickly as it appeared. She waved good-bye and headed for her car as the tune to "Sweet Home Alabama" popped into her head. She heard the front door close soundly behind her and smiled as she recalled a proverb. *When one door closes another opens.*

Eve slid into her car and started the engine. As she pulled away, she looked back at Amber's front door. She'd thought about the events of the past few months in amazement. With the help of The Wives Association, all five of the ladies had actually managed to come through whatever personal issues that existed in their lives. And although some issues and problems for the ladies were worse than others, she knew as long they stuck together, there was nothing they couldn't overcome.

31

After the Beep . . .

"I still can't believe the Leopards are going to the Champion Bowl," Eve excitedly exclaimed. "See, baby, I knew this was going to be your year. You've worked so hard, and now look at you; you've made it to the championship."

Eve placed a stack of T-shirts in Chase's suitcase, then placed a small pile of socks and underwear in the suitcase as well. He was leaving for New England, host of the Champion Bowl, with the Leopards in the morning, and Eve was doing her wifely duties of making sure he was packed and ready to go for the two-week trip.

"When are you coming up again?" Chase asked as he appeared from the closet carrying several pairs of jeans, a few sweaters, and a pair of sweats.

"I'll be there next Thursday prior to the game," she replied, taking the stack of clothes from his grasp and sorting them neatly into the suitcase. "Also, I've made the flight and hotel reservations for your mom and sisters. Everyone's coming in on Thursday around the same time as me. However, your sister Sylvia called me last night to say she had to work on Friday and needed to come in on Saturday instead."

"Cool. Looks like you've taken care of everything," Chase said, kissing Eve on the forehead. "I love you," he praised.

"I love you too, Chase. And I'm so proud of you, babe," Eve gushed. "It's like all your dreams are finally coming true, and I'm just so excited to be able to witness it."

"You were my biggest dream, Eve," Chase said wrapping his arms around her. "And the moment you agreed to be my wife, all of my dreams had already come true."

Tears formed in Eve's eyes as she leaned her head against Chase's chest. This was too perfect, and for once in her life, she was completely and utterly happy. She wiped away the tears that had managed to escape her eyes, then looked at her man. All those years of negative conversations regarding athletes had proven to be untrue where Chase was concerned, and she was pleasantly surprised. Even though she missed her mother terribly, in her heart she was grateful to know that after all those years of bashing, her mother had been wrong.

"This is getting a little too heavy for me." Eve stepped backing smiling. "I'm the girl! I should be the one creating the Hallmark moment," she teased.

"Oh, you got jokes." Chase swatted Eve on the ass. "Go on! I'll finish packing my bag."

"How about we go to dinner tonight after my association meeting?" Eve started out of the room. "We'll call it a good luck and farewell dinner."

"You act like I'm going away forever," Chase responded playfully.

"Any moment away from you seems like forever to me, babe," Eve laughed, making her way out of the room and down the stairs.

Eve was on cloud nine by the time she made it to the kitchen. She'd never imagined her life could be this good. With all the drama the last few months had brought, Eve was thrilled to know that happily-ever-after actually did exist.

She skimmed through the hundreds of e-mails that awaited her on her iPad, making a mental note of the ones she absolutely had to respond to while deleting the ones that didn't require a response. She'd always enjoyed the quietness of her house in the afternoon, especially on days like today. The stillness and calm gave her a peace that was beyond words, and she enjoyed every minute of it. The past few months had taught her not only about having better balance but also about her need to better prioritize her own life and responsibilities. No longer could she afford to put the needs of others before her own. From now on, she and Chase came first, and everything else would have to get in where it fit in.

The ringing of her BlackBerry startled her, and for a moment, she'd forgotten the sound of her own ringtone. Amber had had her BlackBerry for so long that she wasn't used to having to account for both of them anymore. She laughed to herself, then answered on the second ring.

"Hello," she greeted the anonymous caller.

"Hi, this is Celebrity Cruises inviting you and your family to partake in this year's biggest offer to date—"

"Damn telemarketers," Eve said as she abruptly hung up the phone. It didn't matter how many times she entered her name and number on the Do Not Call list that was supposed to protect people from unsolicited calls, they still managed to get through.

She placed her BlackBerry down on the table before noticing the message icon on her homepage indicating she had four messages. Knowing her mother would never call her on her home phone, she figured that at least two of those messages were from her with the other two being more telemarketers. Rather than wait in suspense, Eve dialed into her voice mail and checked her messages.

MESSAGE #1: EVE, IT'S MAMA. JUST CALLING TO SEE HOW YOU ARE AND TO MAKE SURE YOU'RE OKAY. I'LL TRY YOU ANOTHER TIME. LOVE YOU.

Message deleted.

MESSAGE #2: THIS MESSAGE IS FOR EVE LANDON. THIS IS AT&T CALLING TO INFORM YOU THAT YOU'VE BEEN

PRESELECTED TO RECEIVE A FREE UPGRADED PHONE. TO ACCEPT THIS OFFER, PRESS ONE.

Message deleted.

MESSAGE #3: AMBER, IT'S SEAN. I WANTED TO LET YOU KNOW THAT I JUST LEFT DR. COLEMAN'S OFFICE WITH THE RESULTS FROM THE PATERNITY TEST I TOOK A FEW WEEKS BACK. I KNOW SA'MYRA DECIDED NOT TO KEEP THE BABY AND THE FUNNY THING IS, EVEN IF SHE HAD, IT WOULDN'T HAVE BEEN OUR PROBLEM BECAUSE THE TEST CAME BACK NEGATIVE FOR ME BEING THE FATHER. YOU'D THINK I'D BE RELIEVED, RIGHT? BUT YOU SEE, DR. COLEMAN INFORMED ME THAT I CAN'T HAVE CHILDREN. SOMETHING TO DO WITH A MEDICATION MY MOTHER TOOK WHILE SHE WAS PREGNANT WITH ME. I TOOK EVERY POSSIBLE TEST, AND THEY ALL SAID THE SAME THING. WHICH MEANS, IF I CAN'T FATHER KIDS, THEN WHO IS OLIVIA'S FATHER?

Eve nearly dropped the phone as the message cut off. She gasped for air as she fumbled for the correct phone key in order to save the message. She pressed the save key and quickly moved on to the next. She was hoping the fourth call was Sean calling to finish his message and was relieved to hear his voice again . . .

MESSAGE #4: IT TOOK ME A MINUTE TO THINK ABOUT WHO THE FATHER COULD BE, AND THEN IT HIT ME. AND ALTHOUGH I DON'T KNOW WHETHER TO BELIEVE ANYTHING YOU'VE EVER TOLD ME UP TO THIS POINT, I DO REMEMBER ONE THING. I REMEMBER WHO YOU MESSED AROUND ON ME WITH JUST PRIOR TO YOU GETTING PREGNANT. SO, HERE'S THE DEAL! YOU WILL

BRING YOUR ASS HOME TODAY AND DO EXACTLY WHAT
I SAY, WHEN I SAY IT. OLIVIA IS NEVER TO KNOW THE
TRUTH ABOUT ME NOT BEING HER FATHER. I LOVE HER,
AND SHE DOESN'T DESERVE TO BE HURT IN ANY WAY.
IF YOU HESITATE EVEN A LITTLE BIT WITH ANY OF MY
DEMANDS, I'LL RUIN YOU. IT'S NOT ENOUGH THAT YOUR
GIRL EVE WILL FIND OUT WHAT KIND OF LYING BITCH YOU
ARE, BUT IF ANYONE EVER FOUND OUT THAT OLIVIA IS
REALLY CHASE'S DAUGHTER, IT'LL DESTROY BOTH OF
OUR FAMILIES FOREVER.

Eve sat motionless in her chair as she tried to stop the spinning
in her head. Her chest tightened, and a sharp pain shot down her
back. Grief, anger, and confusion struck her like fists to the face as she
became drunk with emotions. Surely she hadn't heard Sean's message
correctly. Her heart pounded as she replayed the message again . . .
and again.

Exactly six minutes later, Eve had listened to Sean's message
seven times. There was no mistake; she'd heard right—Olivia was
Chase's daughter. Eve replayed over ten years of conversations she'd
had with Amber in her mind, trying to figure out where she'd missed
Amber's confession to sleeping with Chase. For the life of her, she
couldn't recall Amber even mentioning being with anyone else while
she was at USC.

"Oh no!" Eve said aloud as she immediately remembered Amber's
brief encounter with her mystery man. "No wonder Chase and Sean
didn't get along! All these years, their argument had been over Amber."
She shook her head. "Son of a bitch!" Eve said, trying to make sense
of it all.

Eve buried her face in her hands. She didn't know what to feel
first. Rage was the only thing that came to mind. What she couldn't
understand was why neither of them had the decency to tell her the
truth. It wasn't as if Chase had cheated on Eve with Amber. When

they hooked up Eve wasn't even in the picture. Eve racked her brain for a logical excuse but couldn't come up with one. As far as she was concerned, there was no reason for them not tell her. The fact that for eight years the two of them had held on to this lie enraged her. She made a mental list of all the events in their lives that the two of them allowed her go through knowing full on that they had been together and had a child with each other. There was Amber's baby shower, Olivia's christening, as well as her wedding to Chase where Amber served as her maid of honor.

There were seven years of birthdays, anniversaries, Christmases, Thanksgivings, and every possible holiday in between. If you could name it, Eve could promise you that she and Amber had probably done it together. Hot tears burned down her face as she struggled to breathe. If there was one thing that Eve hated the most it was a liar.

All of my dreams came true the moment you agreed to be my wife, Eve recalled Chase saying to her just a few moments earlier. She wished those words still rang true yet after hearing Sean's message on her voice mail. Now she knew the reality of her marriage was no longer anyone's dream come true, but yet, something that was slowly becoming a very real nightmare.

Eve didn't even remember climbing the stairs when she found herself standing on the opposite end of her bedroom door. Her hands shook as she gripped the doorknob. She tried desperately to control the actions that would soon follow.

As if in a trance, Eve snapped and burst through the door with a flurry of obscenities and fists landing blows on Chase.

Her strength was supernatural as she thrust every inch of her body at him in a wild, uncontrollable attack.

Her cries came from the belly of her soul as she interrogated him about why he never told her the truth about him and Amber. Every doubt, every suspicion, every insecurity she'd ever had about dating an athlete smothered her as she begged Chase to tell her that what Sean had revealed in his message was all a lie.

"Eve, say something! Tell us what's wrong!" Jai persisted.

Eve felt her chest as it rose and fell. Each breath was an effort. She felt her head swivel like a gun atop a tank as she surveyed the stunned trio standing before her, but none of them registered as her intended target. She caught a glimpse of herself in the reflection of a picture hanging on the wall and was shaken by what she saw. Her hair was so severely tousled that one could only assess that she had been in a fight. As if on skis, her makeup had ridden down her face on a stream of tears, leaving a trail of mascara that ended at the corners of her mouth.

Eve barely recognized herself or the voice that now came from her mouth.

"Where's Amber?" she growled hoarsely.

"She's in the kitchen. Eve, *what is the matter*?" Jackie persisted.

Over Jackie's shoulder Eve could see Amber making her way into the family room carrying a tray of hors d'oeuvres.

"What's going on?" Amber asked, then immediately saw the disheveled Eve. "Eve, what—"

Eve reacted so suddenly that she would later recall not being aware that she had even moved. She gripped her hand into a fist so tightly that what little nails she had left after her attack on Chase dug into her palm. Without waiting for Amber to complete her sentence, Eve rushed past Jackie and punched Amber solidly in the mouth, causing spit and blood to spew across the room.

Eve ignored the tray of meat, cheese, and crackers that clanged against the wall flying from Amber's hands as she fell backward from the force of the blow.

"Holy shit!"

"What the fuck!"

"Eve!"

Eve heard the combination of dumbfounded and astonished expressions as Jai, Jackie, and Callie reacted in disbelief at what they were seeing, but her assault had only just begun.

When her plea went unanswered, she flung herself to the floor weak from both the beating and mental battle she'd just discharged.

"Eve!" Chase cried out, blood dripping from his mouth, neck, and arms. "I . . ." He struggled to find the right words.

Eve lay on the floor, her face wet from the puddle of tears that rested beneath her. Her sobs were heavy and hard. Through a blur of tears she saw Chase making his way to her. She managed just enough energy to peel herself off the floor. "Don't you *dare* touch me!" she uttered, her screams now a mere hoarse whisper.

Eve rose to her feet not allowing herself to look back at Chase. Her steps were heavy as she walked out the door, down the stairs, and to the kitchen. Although she could hear Chase calling out to her, she ignored him and instead, gathered her purse, keys, and cell phone, then walked into the garage and got into her car. As far as Eve was concerned, there was nothing left to say. Her fairy-tale marriage, just like her twenty-year friendship with Amber, was officially over . . .

Eve drove slowly down the hill from her house with only one destination in mind. She wasn't sure what she was going to say to Amber when she got to her. I mean, how could anyone even begin to explain ending a twenty-year friendship? Although she wasn't sure of the words, she knew a confrontation was necessary. Amber had been a part of her inner circle long before a real circle ever existed. Yet after keeping a secret of this magnitude from her for so long, as of this moment, Eve knew that Amber would be out of her muthafuckin' circle . . . forever!

32

Outta the Mutha' F'N Circle

Eve waited at the bottom of the hill for the light to change. In sheer frustration, she gripped the steering wheel and repeatedly banged her head against the headrest. She realized it wasn't helping the ringing in her ears or the pounding in her head, but try as she might, she couldn't stop herself. Finally, from exhaustion, her body went limp and her head fell forward, resting on the steering wheel. She couldn't breathe, and she fumbled for the window switch, gulping in the sudden flow of air as if returning to the surface after nearly drowning.

Was this really happening? This kind of shit only happened in the movies, she thought. Chase and Amber had slept together! Olivia was Chase's daughter! Her best friend and her very own husband had betrayed her! The thoughts rained down like hail, stoking her fury. As the light changed, Eve floored the gas pedal. She knew she was headed for Amber's house, but she had no clue what she would do once she got there.

Eve drove relentlessly and with reckless abandon. Unfocused and blind with rage, she drove through two red lights as a cacophony of car horns blasted in her wake. She was unfazed. At this moment, she had only one objective, one goal, and that was confronting Amber.

Eve arrived at Amber's house feeling even more enra[g] when she had left her own. Pulling to the curb in an effort t[o] park, she felt her tires and rims scrape the cement, bringing [to] an abrupt stop. She was confused to see Jackie, Jai, and Ca[llie] parked in the driveway and suddenly remembered that the[re was an] association meeting scheduled for today. In the midst of her [confron]tation with Chase, she had completely forgotten!

Undeterred, Eve grabbed her purse and snatched [the keys] from the ignition, tossing them into her purse as she exit[ed] and made her way to the front door. She didn't bother t[o take the] slate walkway, opting to take the shorter distance across [the] lawn. Her hands were shaking uncontrollably as she trie[d to ring] the doorbell. After two unsuccessful attempts, she used [the heel] of her hand and pressed, leaning forward and causing t[he bell to] ring incessantly.

"Okay! Okay!" Jai swung open the door, recoiling a[t the sight] of Eve.

Seeing the shocked look on Jai's face, Eve paused [and realized] that she must look a hot mess, a fact that was immedi[ately con]firmed by Jai.

"What the . . . Eve, what happened? Are you okay?"

Eve stared at Jai but could not make a visual conne[ction. She] looked straight through her. In her mind, Jai held no [more sig]nificance than the furniture Eve could see in the room b[ehind her.] She felt Jai grab her elbow, but Eve pulled away and st[epped past] her and headed for the family room where she knew th[e meeting] would be held. Entering the room, Eve came face-to[-face with] Callie and Jackie. She could tell by the stunned and [shocked] looks on their faces that they shared the same senti[ment] about her appearance.

"Eve, what's the matter?" Jackie exclaimed, hurrying [over.]

"Oh my God!" Callie covered the short distance alm[ost] with Jackie.

Dropping to the floor, Eve straddled Amber and began slapping blindly.

"Eve . . . stop! What . . . is the matter with you?" Preoccupied with warding off the onslaught of blows, Amber could barely get the words out.

"Somebody stop her!" Callie yelled.

"Eve, stop!" Jai screamed wrapping her arms around Eve's waist, but she was no match for the adrenaline-hyped Eve who shook her off like a ragdoll and continued to pummel Amber with a flurry of hate-fueled blows.

Eve felt her arms begin to grow sluggish from the constant barrage of blows, but still bent on destruction, she shoved Amber's arms back pinning them beneath her knees, and managed to get her hands around Amber's throat.

As she squeezed, Eve could hear Amber coughing and gasping for breath, but she continued pressing down with her thumbs so hard that she could feel lumps of air trying to escape from Amber's windpipe. For a fleeting moment, Eve realized that what she was doing could cause death, but she didn't care. She changed position, digging her knee into Amber's stomach and pressing even harder.

Eve felt as if everything was happening in slow motion. It was as if she was not a part of what was going on, but rather looking down, witnessing the whole thing. In the distance, she thought she could hear her name being called. The voice grew closer and louder, and then she felt someone on her back. It was Jackie, attempting to pull her off of Amber.

"Eve, stop!" Jackie, much stronger than Jai, had wrapped her arms around Eve's waist in a desperate bear hug and was pulling with all her might.

Eve could feel herself losing her grip and looked up to see Jai and Callie frantically prying at her fingers.

"Eve, let go! Stop! Eve!" Jackie took a deep breath and gave one last tug. It must have been the combined efforts of Jai and Callie as finally, Jackie and Eve tumbled backward.

With arms and legs flailing, Eve struggled to free herself from Jackie's grasp, but she was exhausted and finally allowed herself to collapse against Jackie's chest.

"Eve, what is the matter? For God's sake, tell us what is wrong," Callie begged as she and Jai managed to get Amber into a sitting position.

"Eve, you damn near killed Amber. Talk to us! What the fuck is going on?" Though loosely, Jackie continued to hold Eve as the five of them sat panting on the floor.

Eve looked at the bruised and battered Amber with disgust. Although Amber's lips were bloody and the entire right side of her face was swollen, Eve felt no remorse, only disdain.

"Why didn't you tell me?" Eve had intended to scream the words, but all she could manage was a pitiful guttural sound.

"Eve, what the fuck is wrong with you?" Amber's eyes were wide with terror as she forced the words past her lips. She could barely speak above a whisper as she tried to massage life back into her throat. "What are you talking about? Tell you what?"

"Why, Amber? Eight years, eight-fucking-years-and-you-never-said-a-word! Not-one-mother-fucking-word!"

"Eight years? Eve, what—" Amber stopped in midsentence as the enormity of Eve's tirade and interrogation registered. She suddenly felt as if she had been punched in the stomach. She had prayed that this day would never come, but if it did, she had hoped that she would be able to find the words that would turn it into nothing more than a shifting of pebbles in the sand. Tears filled her eyes as the realization began to sink in that her wall of deception and lies had just come crashing down like a rockslide.

"Will one of you tell us what the hell is going on?" Jai asked glancing at a bruise on her forearm.

"Eve, I . . ." Amber searched for words that clearly did not exist. "How?"

Realizing that she was still clinging to her purse, Eve riffled through the bag and retrieved the BlackBerry. She hurled it at Amber who ducked, catching the blow on her shoulder. The phone bounced, ricocheting against the wall and shattering into pieces.

"*That's* how! I know everything, Amber. Everything!" Eve spat the words as she shook herself from Jackie's grasp and struggled to her feet. Her legs felt like Jell-O as she adjusted her purse and headed past Amber to leave.

"You're outta the muthafuckin' circle, bitch. Do-you-hear-me? Out!" Eve delivered the words like venom.

"Eve, please." Amber reached out, clutching Eve's leg in an effort to restrain her.

Eve's initial reaction was to shake herself free and leave, but as she looked down at Amber, another wave of rage and anger mushroomed. With her free leg, she drew back as if preparing to punt a football, and delivered a crushing kick to Amber's chin that sent her reeling into a startled Jai and Callie.

Without bothering to assess the damage, Eve turned to exit, nearly colliding with Sean and Olivia who were standing in the doorway in total disbelief. As she locked eyes with Sean, Eve read the expression of hurt and betrayal on his face that mirrored the pain she was feeling inside. For a brief moment, their eyes held a private conversation before Eve lowered her gaze to the frightened and stunned Olivia huddled against her dad. *Not your dad,* Eve thought as she looked into Olivia's eyes and saw Chase's eyes. She wondered why she had never noticed it before.

Eve opened her mouth to speak, but no words came. She lowered her head and quickly brushed past them as they parted and allowed her to pass through the doorway. From behind, she could hear muddled expressions of amazement emanating from the room as she made her way blindly down the hallway. Eve picked up the pace, desperate for fresh air and freedom, and once outside, she sprinted to her car.

Eve fumbled in her purse for her keys and retrieving them,

pushed the button to unlock the car. Once inside, she closed her eyes, took a deep breath, and paused to gather herself. The last five minutes had been surreal, she thought, but as she stared at her chipped and broken nails and the bloodstains on her hands, she knew it had been all too real. Eve was startled by a pounding on her window and looked up to see Jackie standing at her door.

"Where the fuck do you think you're going? Roll the window down, Eve. You're not leaving until you tell me what the hell just happened in there."

The words were muffled by the glass, but Eve heard every word that Jackie was saying. Knowing that she couldn't explain it all right now, even if she wanted to, Eve put the key into the ignition and started the car without responding. Before she could manage to leave, she saw Jackie race to the front of the car and stand squarely in her path. Eve shifted the car into drive and stared at Jackie, who stared back, arms folded defiantly.

"You're not leaving until you talk to me, Eve."

Eve eased the car slightly forward. "Move, Jackie," she yelled at the top of her lungs. Still hoarse, Eve was sure that she could not be heard over the engine, but she knew Jackie had read her lips.

"I'm-not-moving!" Still defiant, Jackie placed both hands on the hood of the car.

Emotionally spent, Eve considered flooring the gas pedal and with that thought, she paused, suddenly realizing that somewhere during this day of revelation, she had crossed over into a mental state that could only be described as temporarily insane.

With a look of dejection and defeat, Eve lowered the window and watched as Jackie triumphantly walked around to her door. When she was sure that Jackie was out of harm's way, Eve slammed her foot onto the gas pedal and sped away with tires peeling rubber. She glanced into the rearview mirror and saw Jackie standing in the middle of street, both hands in the air in dismay.

Eve was relieved that she had escaped. There was not enough

fight left in her to tackle a determined Jackie O'Connor. As she drove, it suddenly dawned on her that she had no idea where she was headed. One thing was for sure: The last place she wanted to go was home.

"Home!" The word resounded in Eve's head as she jerked the steering wheel, executing a perfect U-turn headed in the opposite direction. Love didn't live at her home anymore, and as far as she was concerned, neither did she.

33

Destination Unknown!

Eve moved through the traffic on the 405 Freeway with strategic motions. She knew the sooner she got to LAX, the sooner she would be free from the explanations of Chase and Amber. She reached into her glove compartment and pulled out a handful of napkins in an effort to wipe the smudges of blood from her hands and to clean the tearstained makeup from her face. She knew she'd never get through security looking the way she looked, and the last thing she needed was for anything or anybody causing her further delays.

Her decision to leave town was partly inspired by the day's events, with the other part being her fear of possible criminal charges. Even though she felt justified in her attack on Amber, she knew that after the beating she'd given her, medical treatment would definitely be needed and an explanation with regards to what had happened to her would have to be given. Even if Amber wanted to keep her mouth shut, there'd be no way she could explain herself to a doctor. Unless, the other ladies were to advise her of an excuse, she'd never be able to come up with a good enough excuse on her own.

There's no way Amber would tell Jackie, Callie, and Jai about her and Chase—they'd execute her. Now more than ever she'd need some support, even if it was based on a lie. Beyond her blowup, Eve hadn't taken a second to really figure out her next steps. Although her pain still existed, her tears had long since subsided. Eve prided herself on always being able to persevere under pressure. When other people would fall apart, she'd be the one holding them together and making sure that no matter what, they were able to suck it up and keep it moving. Her mother had raised her to be virtually numb to pain beyond a certain point, which is why Nadia was able to take Hank's indiscretion, tuck it into her chest, and act as if he and it didn't exist.

"It is what it is," she mumbled aloud as she tried to mask her emotions with a plan of action. "I just need to refuel and recharge, then I'll be fine," she said trying to convince herself that that was actually possible.

Eve veered off the freeway when she got to Century Boulevard with her sights on the Departure Exit of LAX, which was less than a quarter of a mile away. As she got closer to the airport, the pounding of her heart returned. Eve knew that running away from her problems wasn't the answer, but until she could sort through some of the questions in her mind, it would have to do for now. The wooziness in her stomach had returned as she tried to focus on where she was even going. In all honesty, she hadn't even thought about it. She just knew she needed to get as far away from L.A. as possible.

As Eve approached the departure terminals her cell phone rang. Before she could press ignore, the call automatically connected through to her car.

"Eve," Chase pleaded, "where are you?" His voice was shaky and uncertain.

"Fuck you," Eve replied quickly.

"Babe, please come back so we can talk about this," he begged.

Eve felt the pain in her chest return while images of him and Amber together flashed through her mind. She was instantly sickened by Amber's account of her sex session with Chase. As she recalled, Amber had said she'd let her mystery man fuck her every way possible. Eve imagined Chase doing to Amber what he'd so generously and lovingly done to her. The thought of Chase pleasing Amber orally repulsed her to her core, yet, she remembered Amber saying that not only did he eat her out for what seemed like hours but that she had sucked him off harder than Karrine Steffans, herself.

"Was she good, Chase?" Eve taunted.

"Eve?"

"Answer the question, muthafucka'! Was she good?"

"Babe."

"You think you're pretty fucking special, don't you? Having been with both of us, huh? And to think all these years I thought that Sean was the smug bastard, when all along, it was your trifling ass."

"Eve, give me a chance to explain."

"Explain?" Eve probed. "How in the hell do you think you can do that now?"

"I can start with the truth," Chase stated.

"The truth?" Eve said sarcastically. "That's rich. Funny, because after eight years of lies, I don't think you know what the truth is." She paused, then continued. "Tell me this, since you want to be so fucking honest . . . Were you *ever* going to tell me the truth?" Eve realized she had made two trips around the airport already. She pulled over near the Delta terminal while waiting for Chase to respond. His silence lingered longer than Eve would allow. "I didn't think so."

Eve felt her tears threaten to return.

"We thought we were doing the right thing by not telling you."

Eve was startled by the tapping of a police officer's hand against her window. "Ma'am, you can't park here," he shouted out.

Eve held up her finger as a gesture for the officer to wait a moment while she finished her conversation with Chase. "If you thought that lying to me for eight years was the *right* thing to do, then you and that bitch Amber were dead wrong."

The officer tapped Eve's window again. "Move your car or get a ticket. It's your choice, lady!"

"Eve, there's got to be something I can do," Chase pleaded.

The officer tapped at Eve's window once more before he began writing her a ticket.

Eve gave him an evil glance, then focused her attention back to Chase's original question.

"Evie ... I'll do anything to make this right. Just tell me what to do."

Eve watched as the officer tore off a ticket and placed it on her windshield.

"Get a lawyer," she replied matter-of-factly, then hung up the phone.

Eve exited the car and stood face-to-face with the officer. Within seconds, she realized she had been spotted because a cluster of people surrounded her car. Her identity had been revealed as someone in the crowd shouted out her name.

"Eve Landon! How do you feel about your husband going to the Champion Bowl?"

A look of embarrassment crossed the officer's face as he looked Eve in her eyes. "Mrs. Landon? I'm sorry, I didn't recognize you."

Eve looked around at the growing crowd. She couldn't imagine what she must've looked like, and the more she thought about it, the more she realized she didn't care. She moved past the officer without saying a word, making her way into the airport.

"Ma'am, you can't leave your car here," the officer shouted.

Eve ignored him and kept walking.

"Mrs. Landon, if you leave your car unattended, we're going to have to tow it," he pleaded.

Eve stopped short of the entrance doors and turned back to the officer who was now standing directly in front of her prized Bentley. She looked down at her keys, then back at him, then down at her keys once more, then back to him. With one swift motion, she tossed the keys in his direction.

"Fuck the car," she shouted, then turned and sauntered away.

Without looking back, Eve made her way into the terminal. It was turning out to be a day of "walk-aways," she thought as she had already walked away from her husband, her best friend, and now a two-hundred-and-fifty-thousand-dollar Bentley.

Eve noticed that a few curious onlookers had followed her into the terminal, and she quickly searched the signs trying to locate the restrooms. Finally spotting the familiar symbol of the stick figure in a dress, Eve lowered her head and headed for the women's restroom.

It was exactly what Eve expected of a ground-level bathroom. It was crowded, and there was a line waiting for the six stalls that were clearly occupied. A woman was changing her baby at the changing table while restraining a toddler between her legs. Two impatient children were darting in and out of the line playing tag. There was a strong stench of stale piss, and as she waited in line, Eve retrieved a scented hand wipe from her purse and held it under her nose.

Finally making it to the front of the line, Eve heard the sound of simultaneous flushing, and three stalls were suddenly free. She quickly made her way to the stall farthest from the door and while still shouldering her purse, eased her pants down and peed.

As she exited the stall and looked into the mirror above the sink, Eve realized more than ever that she would have to clean up if she wanted to make it upstairs without being questioned. She washed her hands and grabbed enough towels to wash her face. She retrieved her brush and brushed her hair vigorously, allowing it to fall about her shoulders. Not satisfied, she gathered her hair and worked it into a tight braid that she let hang down her back. She searched through her purse, frustrated that she had no makeup, and settled for a generous coat of lip gloss. Then Eve slid on her sunglasses, shouldered her bag, and exited the restroom.

Eve glanced at the flight schedule clock which read 6:30 P.M. With not a clue as to where she was going, she checked the departures that were scheduled to leave soon. Brandon was in Hawaii, she thought, Andrew was in London, and she had been dying to go to the Bahamas. She shrugged and with destination still unknown, she headed for the ticket counter.

With ticket finally in hand, she rode the escalator to the second level where she made a phone call. When no one answered she hastily sent a text.

Saddled with only her purse, Eve breezed through the screening process and made her way to the departure gates. Her flight was already boarding as she made her way to the plane. Once inside it, Eve took her seat against the window, turned off her cell phone, and leaned her head back against the headrest. Not interested in the flight attendant-hype or the information regarding the weather she would encounter once she landed, Eve closed her eyes and willed herself to sleep before takeoff.

Eve had slept through the entire flight, awaking only when she felt the sudden jolt of the landing gear touching the ground. It had taken her a few moments to get her bearings and remember where she was, but once her head had cleared, recollection of the day's past events came rushing back like a tsunami. Despite the hours upon hours of sleep she'd managed during the flight, she still had a nauseating ache in the pit of her stomach, and her head hurt like hell.

Nothing she did seemed to alleviate the pain she felt both inside and out. Although what happened between Amber and Chase happened before her and technically couldn't be considered an affair, Olivia was the product of a lie in which Eve wasn't sure she could ever forgive either of them for.

Waiting until the last passenger had exited the plane, Eve rose from her seat. She walked down the aisle and out of the plane, oblivious of the young flight attendant who encouraged her to have a great stay. Inside the terminal, she slowly made her way through the crowd of tourists, past the boarding gates, down the escalator, past baggage claim, and finally out to the arrival curb.

Eve was still wearing her sunglasses, which she adjusted when she noticed a group of women pointing in her direction.

"Nosy bitches . . ." she mumbled under her breath, quickly realizing she didn't have the strength to actually confront anyone else.

Now a celebrity, she had accepted the fact that she was vulnerable to the public attention she had fought so hard to avoid, even though at the moment, she really just wanted to be left the fuck alone.

Eve glanced at her reflection in the terminal window. A BeBe jogging suit, Prada bag, and no makeup, really? In fact, she looked exactly like she did just a few years ago when she was caught fashion slipping in LAX. Right now, however, she didn't give a shit about how she looked or what anyone thought about how she looked. With her heart aching like it was, she knew that if anyone was really paying attention, the only thing they'd truly notice was the pain that covered her entire being—an outfit that was ultimately universal.

Eve rubbed her temples in an effort to distract the pain. She pressed harder, thinking how perfect it would be if she could rub away her thoughts until she eventually erased the memory of the day altogether. She would like to forget that she had attacked her husband and her best friend. And she would definitely like to forget that she had handed the keys to her prized Bentley to a perfect stranger and boarded a plane without so much as packing a pair of underwear. But even more important, she would like to erase every recollection of the fact that her husband and best friend had a seven-year-old daughter together!

"What a fucking nightmare," Eve sighed.

Once outside the terminal she watched nervously as cars pulled up to the curb and left. It suddenly dawned on her that she had no idea what kind of car she should be looking for. Eve turned on her cell phone, and it lit up like a Christmas tree. She had eight missed calls and eight messages. Chase, Jai, Callie, and Jackie were obviously trying to find her. There was no call from Amber, but then again, she hadn't expected one.

Shifting her weight from one foot to the other, Eve peered over her shoulder. She had mixed emotions. Up until now, Eve was notorious for keeping herself guarded and protected from any sort of pain. Her wall of life was as tall and strong as an oak tree, which Amber and Chase managed to just chop down. Although she fought them, her stubborn tears managed a victory she couldn't deny.

Quickly she wiped them away. She didn't want to be standing there looking like a soggy bag lady, but at the same time, she was not looking forward to another confrontation.

In deep thought, Eve didn't notice the white Range Rover when it pulled up to the curb. Nor did she notice the slender well-dressed driver and woman as they exited and made their way around the vehicle. Eve had no idea how long she had been standing there, but her heart skipped a beat as she saw her. Eve was sure that nothing would ever make her happier than the sight of Nadia Inez and the welcoming smile that was on her face. She would soon prove to be wrong, however, as her whole body trembled with joy at the sight of her mother's outstretched, forgiving arms.

Eve walked the short distance to her mother. With each step she remembered every word her mother had ever spoken to her about love and loss. For years, she quested to prove her mother wrong as it related to dating or dealing with an athlete, and, as she thought about it, perhaps what her mother was saying wasn't about athletes at all.

"Love is about divine order. It starts with God, then with you, and opens itself up to others. In order to have true, unconditional love, you've got to follow that order precisely. Anything else with anyone else will never work." Eve's face flushed with tears as she remembered her mother Nadia's words. All this time she'd gotten it wrong!

As she came face-to-face with Nadia, she realized she was at a complete loss. She tried to speak, but for the first time, the tough, self-assured, hard-hitting words didn't come. She was tired, tired of being in charge, tired of being in control, tired of being the rock. Eve had given her heart and soul to her husband and The Wives Association, and she was exhausted, both emotionally and physically. One by one, she had been there for them, but when her world had come crumbling down, she had not been able to trust that they would be there for her. For years, her mother had tried to instill an unshakable strength in her for such a time as this, and instead of embracing it and her, Eve deprived herself of her mother's wisdom as well as her presence.

Eve took a deep breath and closed her eyes tightly, fighting to find an inkling of bravery she prayed existed somewhere inside of herself. When she opened them, she realized that try as she might, deep down and in this moment she did not want to be brave. She did not want to be tough, hard, or any of the words associated with strength. Eve wrapped her arms around her mother, allowed the floodgates to open . . . and cried.

As she clung to her mother, she prayed Psalms 30:5, a prayer she'd learned as a child. "Weeping may endure for a night, but joy cometh in the morning." Eve recited those words over and over again in her head.

There was no making sense of anything. As protected as she prided herself on being, nothing could have prepared her for the level of betrayal she'd just experienced. With the battle lines already established, loyalty had been breached and every line of trust and love, honor and truth had been crossed. She'd lost!

"I promise you, *mija*, you *will* be okay!" Nadia whispered into Eve's ear.

She nodded and wept some more, hoping her mother's words and those from Psalms 30:5 would somehow ring true. If weeping was said to last only for a night, she hoped that joy would fulfill its promise and find its way back to her . . . in the morning.

Epilogue

Sexual Healing!

Eve arched her back to stay in rhythm as her body slowly began to remember the familiar waves of ecstasy she was experiencing. It had been way too long since she had felt this much passion, and she wanted it to last forever. She closed her eyes, still trying to believe that this was happening. Her mother was right, she thought, as her mind drifted to their recent conversation.

"Go back to your husband, Eve," her mother advised.

"You can't be serious," Eve said, staring at her mother as if she were seeing a complete stranger. "After everything that has happened, you want me to go back to him? Mama, I get it; you were right. I should have listened. But telling me to go back to him is ridiculous."

"That's the problem. You listened, but you didn't hear me," Nadia replied slowly. "What I warned you of was that if you dated an athlete, you should be prepared for him to cheat. Nowhere in your story have you told me that Chase cheated. In fact, what did happen, happened before you ever met him. You may not like his methods, but the reality is that all he tried to do was protect you. You can't give up at the first sign of adversity,

mija. You don't stop driving just because you hit a pothole. You owe it to him and yourself to go back and do whatever it takes to make your marriage work. At least talk to him!"

Eve snapped back to reality as the intensity of the stroking increased and she felt her body giving in to the sensation. She writhed seductively in response. She and Chase had always competed to see who could make the other cum first. She usually won, and she wasn't about to be outdone now. She opened her legs wider and squeezed. Chase had never been able to withstand the sensation that this move created, Eve thought, and from the resulting moan of pleasure, she was sure it was working right now. She squeezed even harder, but suddenly felt the stroking subside as he pulled himself from her.

Eve was caught totally by surprise when he lowered himself to her center and began tonguing back her pubic hair, exposing her clitoris. He licked skillfully up and down her pussy with rapid flicks, each one threatening to send her into a lust-filled frenzy.

"Damn, that feels good," she moaned, clasping his head with both knees and forcing him deeper into her center.

"Mmmm," he responded, gently sucking her clitoris as he placed a finger inside her.

Eve opened her eyes. Seeing a man's head buried between her legs had always been a turn-on, and now was no different. Tiny ripples of delight flitted from her stomach down to her pelvis like the crescendo of a classical music piece. She closed her eyes, hoping to avoid the climax that would surely come if she continued to watch.

Chase had an array of tricks he performed with his tongue that made him a master at eating pussy. Eve kept waiting to feel the familiar nibble on her lips, tug at her clit, or slight nuzzle at her asshole. Instead, he gently turned her over onto her stomach and entered her from behind.

Eve opened her legs to allow him easier entry, and her pussy responded with several unforced pulses. By now she was so wet she could hear the smack of their sexual juices with every stroke. He was hitting spots she didn't even know existed, and she found her breath coming in gasps as she struggled to keep up with his intensity. He pushed into her until every inch of him was engulfed, then suddenly, all movement stopped.

"Oh!" The exclamation escaped her lips before she even knew it was coming. She gripped the covers as her body began to tremble.

"Yeah, baby. Damn, your pussy feels good!" He gently pushed in a little more, as if to add punctuation to his statement.

Eve was about to relax and enjoy the sensation when he swiftly pulled himself from her and turned her onto her back. He parted her legs and was inside her before she had a chance to catch her breath. This time he mixed the cadence, using long strokes until only the tip of his dick was inside her, then short pumps until he was completely imbedded again.

Eve bit her lip to prevent the escape of any more unedited exclamations. Her entire body was tingling, and there was a throbbing in her vagina like she had never felt before.

This was not supposed to happen. We were just going to have a drink and talk, Eve reminded herself . . . *and by talking, I did not mean body language!* She giggled at the thought of how quickly she'd given in to the temptation of him.

As their bodies now moved in syncopated tempo, the passion was so hot that every movement nearly sent her over the edge.

So this is what sexual healing feels like, she thought, throwing her head back and totally giving in as he made love to every inch of her body.

Her pussy felt like the pad of a doctor, with his dick being the pen that wrote the prescription for everything her body needed. It felt good, and Eve was enjoying every moment. She could hardly wait to feel that sudden rush of completion, but she was not quite ready to end the intimacy and tenderness she was experiencing.

Gently nudging his shoulder with her palm, she indicated that she wanted him to roll over, and in the shadow of the darkness, she saw the smile on his face as he eagerly acquiesced.

Eve mounted him, slowly lowering herself onto his glistening hard shaft, then reeling him in with adept Kegels. She then began to vaginally write the ABCs, moving her pelvis to draw out each letter . . . *in cursive!* Eve smiled, remembering that Chase rarely made it to the letter N. Her signature dip in the middle of the letter M got him almost every time.

"Damn, girl, you got skills!" he growled huskily as he gripped her waist.

Eve took her time. She could feel his body shudder with the completion of each letter. As she dotted the letter i, she was interrupted by the ringing of her cell phone. She paused, considering her next move. Not answering it would give him the impression that nothing else mattered right now but the two of them and the steamy lovemaking session that had been going on for over an hour. Answering it would be considered tacky. Before Eve could make a decision, he made one for her.

"You need to get that?" he asked, his voice edgy with passion.

Still straddling him, Eve leaned over and retrieved her cell phone from the nightstand. She tried not to react as she read the caller ID. It was Chase! She hesitated, her breath heavy, her mind racing. In an attempt to force any further thoughts from entering into her mind, she pressed the ignore button.

"No," she replied softly as she tossed the phone to the foot of the bed and continued with the letter J . . .

To be continued . . .

Acknowledgments

When I signed on to do *The Basketball Wives*, I never dreamed that that decision would've led me to a place where I'd have the opportunity to do all the things I've been blessed to now do. From showcasing my Florida shoe store Dulce, establishing my Evelyn Lozada online store, to creating my dream cosmetics line E by Evelyn Cosmetics, and lastly being a part of The Wives Association novel series, it has all been truly amazing! From the bits and pieces in my journals where I detailed the experiences of some of us who have dated, were engaged to, or married athletes, this information has given a voice to characters that make up our novel, *Inner Circle*. I say "our" because my coauthor and friend Courtney Parker took all of my personal stories and created a drama-filled series that is as raw and real as the actual situations themselves. Courtney, you were the angel God brought into my life to make this project a reality. I am forever grateful. Thank you!

In giving thanks, I'd like to thank my publishers Baby and Slim of Cash Money Content and the entire CMC staff. Baby and Slim, you all have taken me in, and I am honored to be a part of the YMCMB family. Always one hundred! To Vernon Brown, Marc Gerald, and Molly Derse—I appreciate all of your hard work and promise to do your absolute best in making it successful. To my legal team: Kenny Meselias, Ed Shapiro, and Johnathan Ehrlich—thank you, guys, so much for always having my back. Not only could I not do this without you, I absolutely wouldn't want to . . . To Joe Regal and Markus

Hoffman at Regal Literary—thank you for all of your hard work and for helping to make this the best project ever!

To my VH1, Shed Media & BBW's Family: Shaunie O'Neal, Tami Roman, Suzie Ketchum, Sean Rankine, Angela Castro, Mark Seliga, Stephanie Edmonds—from the bottom of my heart I truly appreciate how you have helped make my life more vivid. Some say you've created a monster; I feel you've created an aspiring mogul.

To my personal "Team Evelyn": Nia Crooks, Danika Berry, Martin Almgren, Sheryl Lawrence, and Sandy Lozano—thank you for your endless support and for always helping me stay true to myself.

To my blood-bound Bronx and New York family—my parents, Sylvia Ferrer and Jose Lozada—thank you for giving me life and loving me in spite of myself. To Anthony, Sylvia, Mia, and Nisa Ochoa— you guys will forever be in my heart. I'm thankful that God paired me with such a loving family. We may not be a perfect family, but together, we make a perfect team. I love you guys!

To my "baby-girl" Shaniece—you are the reason I open my eyes every day. Every part of my journey has been for the love, care, and ability to provide for you. I will continue to work hard so that your life can be everything you've ever dreamed it could be. I love you with all of my heart, I really do.

Mr. Chad "Pepe" "Ochocinco," "The Interesting One," "The Black Guy" Johnson aka Poopie, I honestly don't know what I would do without you. Never in a million years did I think I'd meet my soul mate on Twitter (the gift and the curse). LOL! This has been one hell of a ride, and I'm so happy we're on this journey together. I will forever be grateful to God for our union. Thank you, Poopie.

Finally, to my fans! You guys truly make me who I am. I will forever be grateful for your love and support.

Evelyn

Throughout my fifteen-year career as a writer, I'm always amazed at how emotional I get when I'm nearing the end of a book. It's kinda like being pregnant and giving birth to a child . . . You're excited at the beginning, hopeful in the middle, anxious yet prayerful toward the end . . . and scared senseless upon delivery. The only assurance is that you've done your absolute best and with God's perfect grace and guidance, the blessing that lies before you will be both welcomed and loved by all.

My thank-yous are pretty simple because, honestly, those who know me and have helped me along this journey to cocreate and write *The Wives Association: Inner Circle* know that I don't take their love, trust, encouragement, support, stories, experiences, patience, and most of all, prayers, for granted. You all know who you are! I love and appreciate you so much.

To Vernon Brown, Bryan "Baby" Williams, and Ronald "Slim" Williams—your support of our vision for this book is truly amazing. I don't know anyone in the game who can do what you do and how you do it! I'm beyond thrilled to be working with you and the entire Cash Money Content team!

To my agents, Joe Regal & Markus Hoffman—WOW! pretty much sums it up. Thank you for seeing me through all of my crazy ideas and for helping me turn each one of them into something amazing. Special thanks to Tracy Christian, Jaimie Roberts, Kenny Meselias, Ed Shapiro, Johnathan Ehrlich, Molly Derse, Marc Gerald, La Shawn Thomas, and my manager/friend Kristel Crews. To my aunt Yolanda McCarty-Taylor: I really couldn't have finished this book without you. Thank you for every chapter and page that you helped me with. I can't wait to share center stage with you. To my immediate family—Leonia, Tony, Walter, Camille, and Jay—thank you for always keeping me covered with your love, support, and prayers. To my daughter Caley—everything I am and everything I do is for you. I love you so much, Toot! To the Young Family (Eric, Marlo, Allura,

Erin & Sweets)—thank you for taking such great care of my little one while I'm away.

Lastly, what started as business clearly turned into something very personal, and I am honored to call you my friend, Evelyn. We often joke about becoming our own versions of Oprah and Gayle, and I'm excited to say that I think we're off to a great start. Thank you for trusting me with the truth of your words and the loyalty of your friendship . . . You are an absolute blessing and definitely a major F'N factor . . . in my life! (LOL)

Courtney

1 Corinthians 15:10

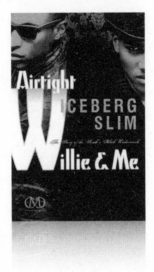
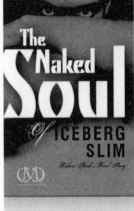

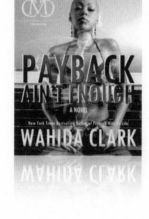

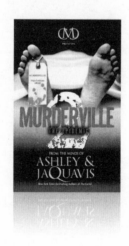
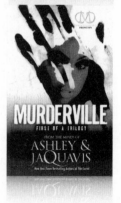